DAUGHTERS
OF
STEEL

Also by Naomi Cyprus

Sisters of Glass

NAOMI CYPRUS

DAUGHTERS OF STEEL

HARPER
An Imprint of HarperCollinsPublishers

With special thanks to Rosie Best

ISBN 978-0-06-245850-6

18 19 20 21 22   CG/LSCH   10 9 8 7 6 5 4 3 2 1

First Edition

To every little girl who dreams of a better world

Don't wait for a hero

Be one

Chapter One

Sisters

When all the fires go out, the dust will rise:
A cloud of hate and bleeding lies.
The choice is left to balance, love and trust:
A parasite or sister? Door or dust?

> From The Rubaiyat of the Sands, *attributed to the*
> *prophet Cyrus and said to foretell the future*

Cobalt, the glass falcon, spun and glittered in the air above the royal palace of the Magi Kingdom. He spread his wings, his feathers chiming against each other as he soared on the hot currents that rose from the sunbaked bricks of the Magi City and the endless Sand Sea.

As he circled, he could see the haze-shrouded deserts around the city, the far-off patches of green around the Delta Lake, and the cold black peaks of the Talon Mountains looming in the distance.

Below him, peals of laughter echoed between the high walls of the palace, and Cobalt tipped his wings and swung down toward them. On a terrace high above the city, among the peach trees and tall trellises covered with flowering peonies, two almost identical figures were sitting in the speckled shadow of a cypress tree, their heads and feet bare and their shoulders shaking with stifled laughter. They were playing a game they'd grown to love over the past few weeks, a very special kind of guessing game. They'd realized, after they met, that they had the ability to communicate through their thoughts, a benefit of their special bond. They'd quickly gotten used to using it, sending each other messages even when they were in the same room. Now, Halan was concentrating on sending Nalah an image of Lord Helavi in his yellow robes, transforming into a cheeping little chick, pecking at the ground.

Nalah must have received it, because she was consumed in a fit of giggles.

"Oh, poor Lord Helavi," snorted Queen Halan Ali, Ruler of the Magi Kingdom. "I gave him enough trouble when he was trying to teach just me, and now there are two of us!"

"It's a promotion, at least," said Nalah Bardak, Halan's twin and the Queen's Sword, cupping her chin in her hands. "Not many Thauma lords get to go from royal tutor to chief vizier in the space of a day."

"No, but in some ways I think he was happier as a teacher," Halan said. "He could hide up in the tower with his books for days without being bothered. But now—" She broke off with a yelp as something smooth and solid landed on her foot, its tiny jaws closing gently on one of her toes.

"Oh, it's just you, Chestnut!" Halan said, and reached down to scoop up the little wooden kitten. "I thought you were a scorpion or something." He was warm from lying in the sun, and he immediately pressed himself against her throat and began to purr in his strange, creaking way.

"Someone's happy to be out of storage!" Nalah said, reaching over to stroke the top of the kitten's head.

Halan put Chestnut down in her lap, and he trod the purple silks down with his paws before curling up in the folds of her dress. She'd received him as a gift at one of the great showing-off banquets where the Thauma lords used to present their best work to her mother and father—

She stopped herself and put a steadying hand on Chestnut's small, polished body.

Actually, the Thauma had brought their goods to Asa Tam, the last king—the man she had *thought* was her father.

That banquet seemed so long ago now. A lifetime away. So much had changed in only two months.

Now I know there's a whole other world, just on the other side of the mirror.

Asa has been banished, I'm the queen, and I have a sister. . . .

She scooped Chestnut from her own lap and put him down in Nalah's. The girl wasn't *really* her sister—she was her tawam, her mirror-self. While Halan had been raised a princess in the Magi Kingdom, in the world on the other side of the mirror, Nalah had been a pauper. Halan lived in a land of powerful magic, but didn't have a magic bone in her body; meanwhile, the extent of Nalah's amazing powers had yet to be seen. After traveling to the Magi Kingdom, Nalah had discovered that she was a Fifth Clan Thauma, the kind of wonder worker who came around only once in a generation.

They were opposites, and yet they were exactly the same. Both of them had had everything and nothing. And now they had each other. In the weeks since Halan had taken the throne, she and Nalah had been almost inseparable. Whenever Halan wasn't dealing with the trappings of being a queen, she and Nalah would steal away to explore the palace, visit Ester in the laundry to gossip, and occasionally take a couple of horses down to the market to check out the newest Thauma items the vendors had to offer. The more time they spent together, the closer they became—they were fascinated by their differences and delighted by their similarities. It was strange and wonderful, and Halan could no longer imagine a world without Nalah in it.

Nalah cradled the kitten to her chest and grinned with delight. "How was he made?" she asked. "Was he carved all in one piece? Or did his maker put him together out of parts? How did they bring him to life?" She held Chestnut up in front of her and examined his belly. He stuck out a dark wooden tongue at her and blinked.

Halan stared up at the branches of the cypress tree, watching a bird flit between the leaves. "I remember the lesson," she said, frowning. "It was something about blood. *The blood of the maker can infuse a craft with life.*"

"Blood . . . ," Nalah said, and looked up into the sky, where the glass falcon was still swooping and circling, like an indecisive shooting star. Then she looked down at her hands. Halan noticed that Nalah's hands weren't quite like her own: they were the same brown color and shape, but they were lightly scarred and callused from handling molten glass. Halan's hands were unmistakably those of royalty: clean and soft and smelling faintly of sandalwood and jasmine.

"When I made Cobalt, back in New Hadar, he wasn't alive," Nalah said slowly. "But he did crack in my hands. The cracked glass must have cut me, and he was infused with my blood then."

Halan nodded. "Lord Helavi said that as long as the maker lives, it'll draw power from them. I remember a story about an ancient Thauma who carved a whole wooden menagerie, but it made her so weak she could never work again."

Nalah shot her a shrewd grin. "I thought you said you never listened to any of Lord Helavi's lessons."

Halan elbowed her, but gently. "Perhaps I listened more than I let on. Anyway, it's good that I did. I'm not just the princess anymore, I'm the queen. If I can't make any Thauma crafts myself, I at least need to understand how my subjects do it."

She tweaked one of the ropes of gold and amethyst that hung around her neck. Chestnut leaped out of Nalah's hands and pounced onto a trailing golden tassel.

"Woodworking's still a bit of a mystery to me." Nalah sighed.

"Well, that's why we're here, isn't it?" Halan said, getting to her feet and stretching. Chestnut danced around her feet, chasing the tassel as it dangled just out of his reach.

"Is it?" Nalah said. "I thought you were hiding from Lord Helavi and his accounts book."

"How dare you?" Halan said, planting her hands on her hips and faking shock. "A queen would *never* try to get out of a lecture about cumulative interest loans. And anyway, don't change the subject. We came out here to practice your woodwork. Come on." She reached out and pulled Nalah to her feet.

Nalah got up and turned to look at the huge cypress tree, her shoulders drooping.

"You were the one who said you wanted to try it," Halan reminded her again, stepping back. "You can do it—I'm sure you can!"

"I'll do something," Nalah muttered. "I'm just not sure what."

"All the more reason to try it out while we're alone—and

on wood that's still planted in the ground. What's the worst that can happen?"

Nalah didn't reply, and Halan wished she hadn't said that.

The truth was, being a powerful Fifth Clan Thauma was . . . complicated. Halan had spent many nights as a child dreaming of what it would be like to be a Thauma. Any clan would do—wood, glass, metal, fabric—as long as she had the power to create *something*. When she first found out about Nalah's ability to create with all four elements, she envied her so deeply that it hurt. But after seeing how unpredictable those powers were, and how they brought her such suffering, Halan felt only the desire to help her sister.

Halan sat down on the low wall that encircled the garden, her back to the steep drop down into the city, a light breeze stirring her long black hair.

"Go on," she urged. "Don't be afraid."

Nalah stepped up to the cypress tree and gingerly put her hands up to touch it. The trunk was as wide as four adults, and in the shade of its far-reaching branches she almost felt cold, despite the beating sun just a few steps away.

She glanced back at her tawam and immediately felt steadied. Having Halan there was almost like having an external brain: someone who would always listen, even if they couldn't really understand. It was nice not to feel alone. And as the only living Fifth Clan Thauma, she felt alone a lot. Especially since the battle with Tam in the courtyard on that beautiful, terrible day two months ago.

As soon as she had picked up the Sword of the Fifth Clan, in the midst of that chaos, everything had gone quiet. In that moment, she'd felt a deep, strange connection to the whole world, and she knew, without a doubt, what she was meant to do. She spoke with the voice of the earth and commanded the very winds to banish Tam and his cronies from the kingdom.

And it felt *awesome*.

But it was as if a dam within her had been opened that day, and now there was no way to close it. And the ensuing flood—of power and strength and emotion—threatened daily to consume her.

When she lived in New Hadar, her power sometimes exploded out of her when she was frightened or upset, but most of the time she was just an ordinary Thauma. Now steering her power was harder than ever, and she felt more and more like a tiny boat, tossed and beaten on a stormy sea of her own making.

I wish Papa were here. The thought came out of habit, but every time it did, it still took her breath away. *Not now,* she told herself. *You have to concentrate.* If she let those feelings overwhelm her, grief and magic would tangle up with each other and come out as a painful mess that did nobody any good.

While she was in the palace, she had to be the Queen's Sword. For two months, she'd been learning to swordfight with Soren and getting daily history and thaumaturgy lessons from Lord Helavi's assistant, Lady Nadia. She'd participated in a handful of formal ceremonies, standing next to Halan's throne while she made pronouncements to the people of the kingdom. Most of the time, she felt excited and proud of what she was doing. But then there were moments, when she was alone in her chambers, when she was filled with doubt.

In those moments, in the darkest part of her mind, she began to wonder if Tam had been right. If all this power had been given to the wrong girl. Because if she were truly the hero that Fifth Clan Thaumas were supposed to be, why couldn't she control her powers? Why did everything always go wrong?

When those thoughts filled her mind, Nalah longed for her father. He always knew the right thing to say to make her feel better. She missed him terribly, but she tried to put on a good face for Halan. Her sister already carried the burden of knowing that Tam—the father she'd defended until he betrayed her—was the one who killed Nalah's papa. Nalah didn't want to be a constant reminder of that pain. She didn't hide much from her tawam, but she hid that.

Maybe later on, she could go down to the Astodan, the tombs where Amir Bardak's bones had been interred with the greatest honors and ceremonies the Magi Kingdom had to offer. Then, and only then, surrounded by nothing and no one except stones and the dead, she might allow herself to cry.

For now, she needed to continue to work at controlling her power. Taking a deep breath, she concentrated on the cypress tree. She felt the rough bark on her fingertips and, beyond that, the sap of life pulsing through it. She sensed the way it moved all the time, growing and swaying in the changing winds. She smelled its spicy, velvety scent and allowed the whole of its being to fill her until she felt as if she and the tree were one.

Nalah hadn't been trained to work with wood—like her father, she was a glassworker. She'd learned to use tools and magical materials to create glass Thauma objects. But as a Fifth Clan Thauma, she could create those things just with her touch. And not just glass, but wood, fabric, metal—all four of the elements. But just because she could do it didn't mean she could do it well. Too often, her attempts blew up in her face. That's why she had to practice. She had something in mind for the cypress tree, something she'd been wondering ever since she'd first held a piece of wood in this world and felt the life of the tree pulsing through it. She'd made little things out of pieces of wood, but she hadn't heard of anyone manipulating wood that was still alive. What would happen? she wondered, a little thrill passing through her body.

She was about to find out.

Her heart was beating strong and steady. Nalah closed her eyes and visualized the garden she was standing in— its beautifully symmetrical paths and shady trellises, and the water that was constantly pulled from a deep well to trickle between the flowerbeds. She held the image in her mind, and then she changed it. Instead of the cypress tree in the center, there was a beautiful wooden gazebo. It was eight-sided, with elegant supports crisscrossing as they rose toward a roof of deep green leaves.

Trunk and stem, she whispered, and her voice sounded like the creaking of ancient branches in the deep forest, *shelter and shadow, open for me.*

A burst of exhilaration made Nalah dizzy, but she managed to control herself, focusing only on the flow of magic through her palms. Her hands moved apart as the trunk of the tree split, unwinding and spreading out around her. It felt almost as if the tree had wanted this all along—that it had been growing here all these years because it knew that one day Nalah would come along and help it transform into something more than a tree.

Soon she was standing with her hands out to her sides, still touching the bark that had been in front of her. She opened her eyes slowly and found herself staring into a green space, floored with twisting roots, with a leafy canopy above. Eight open archways faced the sunshine, perfectly framing a magnificent view of the palace's towers rising into the sky.

"Nalah," Halan breathed behind her. "It's amazing!"

Nalah allowed herself a moment of triumph, a moment of pure joy, and then—there was movement on the path between one of the arches, and a voice:

"Your Majesty! Where are you?"

Nalah twitched. *Someone's coming!* She sent the thought out through the air to Halan, who received it immediately and met Nalah's eyes.

It's all right, Halan thought back. *I'll deal with it—just focus on the tree!*

But Nalah was already shaken, wondering what the newcomer might think, worried that she would lose control and ruin everything. Her pulse quickened, and the tree trembled as if it were an extension of Nalah herself. The archways twisted. A shower of leaves fell around her, and Nalah tore her palms away from the trunks and stumbled back, staring up at the cypress tree. Instead of a graceful conical roof over the gazebo, its upper branches were standing out stiff and straight, like the prickles of a frightened hedgehog.

"Oh," said Halan softly.

"Queen Halan, there you are. I have been looking for you— Good gracious! Nalah, what on *earth* have you done?"

The voice belonged, of course, to Lord Helavi. He came striding down the path, his faded yellow robe fluttering around his ankles. He blinked at Halan and Nalah, and then up at the tree, trying to understand exactly what he was seeing. There was another man with him—the head gardener, Nalah realized with a sinking feeling—and he was standing with his hands clasped over his head, as if he were afraid it might fall off.

"My *lady*," the gardener gasped. "That tree was hundreds of years old! It survived the Year of Storms! Now it's a—a—" He stammered, at a loss for words.

Nalah wrapped her arms around herself and clasped her elbows. Power quivered through her, cut off suddenly with nowhere to go. It was just as she'd feared it would be.

She opened her mouth to apologize to the gardener, but Halan stepped up to her side and linked her arm through Nalah's.

"Master Rumiya, you will not speak to the Queen's Sword so rudely," she said in her most stern and regal voice. Softening, she added, "The tree is still very much alive. In fact, you now have *eight* of the oldest trees in the Kingdom, where you used to have only one. As well as a lovely sitting area for visitors. Many things have changed around here lately—all for the better, I should think—so just consider this tree another one of our recent improvements."

Nalah saw the man's jaw working. Then he swallowed, as if he had eaten the words he'd wanted to say.

"Yes, Your Majesty," he said, forcing a smile.

Halan squeezed Nalah's arm, and Nalah nodded. The

knot in her stomach loosened just a little. She was grateful for the way her tawam stood up for her, and for the confidence Halan had in her, and for everything the queen's parents had done to make Nalah feel at home. But would any of that matter if everyone in the kingdom feared her? Would it be any different than it had been in New Hadar?

Papa, what can I do? she thought, gazing up at the spiky cypress branches. *You said I was destined for great things, but how can I do* anything *if I ruin everything I touch?*

The thought reminded her of the time she had shattered a month's worth of glasswork on that terrible morning when she had first met Asa Tam in disguise at the market— the event that had set the whole adventure in motion. This was worse. She was supposed to be a legend to these people, a hero. But if she didn't get control over herself, she would only ever be a *problem.*

"I actually like it this way," Halan said, following Nalah's gaze up to the splayed branches. Nalah glanced at her face. *Really?* she asked with her mind.

Really, Halan thought back.

If the queen was lying, she was very good at it. Halan turned and gave Nalah a wink. "Maybe we'll start a fashion. Rebellious trees. Soon all the Thauma Lords will be trying to train their trees to grow like this."

This time Nalah smiled for real.

What would I do without Halan? she wondered.

"Your Majesty," said Lord Helavi again. "Not to interrupt

your . . . leisure time, but your subjects are becoming restless. You are aware that today's supplicants have been waiting in the throne room for nearly fifteen minutes?"

Halan dropped Nalah's arm and smacked her palm against her forehead. "Oh, I'm so sorry! I completely lost track of time."

"It is the queen's prerogative to arrive whenever she chooses," said Lord Helavi smoothly, one thin gray eyebrow raising. "But if you are sorry, then it is not to me you must apologize."

Halan winced. "Of course."

Halan was still very much getting used to the heavy burden of the crown. When she was the princess, not only did she have no responsibilities, but Tam went out of his way to keep her sheltered and ignorant of what he was really doing behind closed doors. Halan had to become a ruler basically overnight—a very young one at that—and she could sense that the nobility, as well as the people themselves, were holding their breath to see what kind of ruler she'd be. Would she be too weak to mend the pieces of her broken kingdom? Would she make foolish, naive decisions that would only make things worse? Would time and struggle reveal that she was no different from the tyrant she drove away? Halan saw those searching questions in the eyes of every person she met.

Halan wanted to be a good queen more than anything, and the worry was like a small animal living inside her chest, constantly mewling for attention and reassurance. Several nights in a row Halan had found herself staring out at the glittering stars through her chamber window, wondering what she would do if she didn't have her mother and Lord Helavi to help her.

I want to know. But I'm afraid to find out.

The last time she had been truly independent, making her own decisions, she had escaped the palace and gotten herself kidnapped.

And I eventually returned to help the rebels who drove Tam out, she reminded herself. It wasn't all bad.

It wasn't all good, either, the little voice in her head added, reminding her of the terrible choices she'd made, the betrayals, the deaths . . . all for loyalty to the man she'd thought was her father.

Where is Tam now? she wondered. She'd sent her guards out into the city in an attempt to root out any Tam loyalists left within its walls, but they'd returned empty-handed. No one had any information about Tam's whereabouts, nor of the Thauma lords who had conspired with him to murder Thaumas in New Hadar to absorb their powers. It was as if they had vanished like smoke. It gnawed at Halan, and she worried about what the scorned king might be planning.

She shook the thought away. No time for that now; she had work to do.

"I should go too," said Nalah. "I'm meeting Soren at the Storm Quarter to help with the rebuilding."

Halan nodded. "Duty waits for no one." She squeezed Nalah's hand. *When you get back, maybe we can go raid the kitchen for pastries,* she thought to her sister.

Nalah chuckled. *It's a date,* she sent back.

Then the two girls parted, Halan following Lord Helavi's sweeping yellow robe toward the palace, Nalah taking another path down to the lower courtyards and out into the Magi City.

Chapter Two

Halan

WHAT DO WE KNOW about our YOUNG QUEEN?

Queen HALAN ALI has NO POWERS, yet her tawam is of the FIFTH CLAN.

The QUEEN addresses audiences DAILY, yet we have CONCERNS about her leadership.

The TRAITOR ASA TAM has not been seen. We applaud the end of his CRUEL REIGN.

The YOUNG REBEL LORD Soren Ferro pledges his ALLEGIANCE to the queen.

Could the YOUNG QUEEN bring PEACE and PROSPERITY to the Magi Kingdom?

Or will she only RUIN those not already ruined by her SO-CALLED Father?

Pamphlet distributed on the streets of the Magi City

The woman knelt in front of the royal dais, her head bowed before her queen. One hand was wrapped in bandages and held tightly in her lap, and the other reached up and adjusted her head scarf, which was faded and speckled with sand. She was doing her best to hide a huge and vivid scar that marred the top half of her face.

Halan had immediately recognized the mark of the Dust, a metalwork weapon King Tam had allowed his guards to use on any citizen who made even the slightest trouble. Only a few months ago, Halan had never seen a Dust scar—nobody with one would ever have been permitted to enter the palace, let alone the great hall. Now she'd seen dozens of them, on men, women—even children. On the very first day of her reign, she'd stopped Dust production and forbidden its use. She hoped that no one would ever be hurt by it again. Still . . . for people like this woman, the damage was already done. And Halan couldn't help but feel partly responsible.

On a whim, Halan stood and walked to the woman, kneeling in front of her. The young queen put a hand on the woman's shoulder. The woman looked up and met Halan's eyes, full of surprise at the unexpected closeness. "I am so sorry for your suffering," Halan said sincerely.

The woman nodded, grateful. "Thank you, Your Majesty," she murmured.

It's slow, but things are changing. Halan felt a flush of pride as she looked up and saw the line of people snaking through the hall, waiting to speak to their queen. The powerless, the powerful, and everybody in between were all mixed together now, the Thauma nobility in their jewel-colored robes standing beside paupers in rags and tradespeople in their hardy work clothes. She stood up and returned to her seat on the dias.

"The problem is," the woman continued, "without the use of my hands I cannot work, but if I don't work, the supervisor says she'll hire someone else—how am I to feed my family?"

Halan shifted on the pile of golden cushions where she reclined to address her subjects. She glanced over to the smaller and less brightly colored pile where Queen Mother Rani, Captain Bardak, and Lord Helavi all sat upright and attentive, carefully staying silent unless she asked their opinion.

"I will write to the workshop myself," Halan said, and out of the corner of her eye she saw Lord Helavi's shoulders sag slightly as he wrote this down at the end of the long, long list of things she had already promised to do today. "You were hurt at the loom, and I won't allow your employer to punish you for his carelessness. When your hand heals, they will take you back or answer to me."

"Oh! Thank you, Your Majesty!" the woman cried, clapping her hands to her face in joy and disbelief.

But for now, the supervisor will hire someone else to do your job, Halan thought, almost hearing the words in Lord Helavi's voice inside her head. *And what happens to them when you need it back? Will they come to me to complain about being fired? And what if the supervisor decides not to heed my orders? I am not King Asa. I will not hurt those who disobey me. What then?*

Halan closed her eyes, willing the clamoring voices in her head to be quiet.

Listening to people's problems was one thing, but solving them was quite another. Frustration bubbled away underneath her worry. There was so much to do, and so much of it stemmed from King Asa's cruel reign. She knew all too well that she couldn't just improve her people's lives one at a time, little by little—the big things needed to change too.

The woman rose and was ushered out of the way by Steward Osaya, bowing as she went.

The man behind her in the line didn't wait to be introduced. He strode forward, deep green robes flowing around his feet, and swept a low and elegant bow to Halan.

Halan's heart sank as she watched him. They had met once before, soon after she'd become queen. Somehow, the nobles who bowed the lowest always seemed to be the least trustworthy.

"Lord Esmailian, Your Majesty," Steward Osaya announced.

"My queen, what an honor it is to be in your royal presence once more," said Esmailian smoothly. "I only wish I could come to you with happier news."

"Tell me what you came to say, Lord Esmailian," Halan said pleasantly, but what she really meant was *Stop wasting my time and get on with it.* It was a trick of Queen Mother Rani's that Halan was determined to perfect.

"Your Majesty may recall that my family's mines provide the best and purest quality metal ores to metalworkers all over the kingdom," Esmailian began. "Black iron from the Lower Talons, gold from the Alwafira Mines . . . "

He's listing his mines, Halan thought distantly. She glanced behind him at the queue of petitioners—how many of them would she be turning away today, their problems unheard while Esmailian droned on?

"I'm waiting for your bad news, Lord Esmailian," she said, cutting him off in midflow.

The Thauma lord gaped at her for a moment before sweeping another bow so low the tassels around his neck brushed the flagstones.

"My queen," he continued, his face a mask of virtue, "I cannot supply the city with these valuable resources if my workers refuse to work!"

Halan quirked an eyebrow. "And why, my lord, aren't they working?"

Esmailian cleared his throat. "They have all gone on strike, claiming I don't pay them a living wage. It's ridiculous, Your Majesty! I run a competitive business, not a charity. I seek your permission to have the ringleaders imprisoned—they are the malcontents inciting all this. We need to make them see sense!"

The clamoring voices piped up inside Halan's head once more. On one hand, the ores from those mines were essential to the kingdom's welfare—without them, the metalworkers would have no materials, and the vendors would have no wares. The improvement projects Halan had launched would stall. But on the other hand . . . the miners were her people too.

King Asa would have given Esmailian permission to imprison whichever workers he liked and probably sent guards to help him do it. The king had valued order above everything, even his people's lives.

What would Queen Halan do?

"Lord Helavi," she called out as regally as she could manage without looking back at the vizier, "please instruct one of the clerks to travel to Lord Esmailian's mines and find out just how much he is paying his workers—and how much he keeps for himself. They will then help to negotiate wages that are fair for all concerned."

"Your Majesty!" the Thauma lord protested, but Halan held up her hand—fingers stiff and straight, no hesitation.

"Thank you, my lord." In a moment of inspiration, she placed her hand over her heart and inclined her head slightly. "Your contribution is noted and deeply appreciated. We are all very thankful for your excellent work, and I am sure you will give my clerks everything they need to assist you in rectifying this situation, for the better of the kingdom. Now you may go."

Esmailian's face turned from a sickly green to red and back again. He bowed, muttering angrily under his breath. Steward Osaya had to practically manhandle him upright before she could escort him away from the dais.

Halan glanced back at the cushions where her mother and father sat with Lord Helavi. Rani gave her the tiniest of nods, and Halan let out a sigh of relief, carefully, so that the people waiting wouldn't see.

It was a victory—but a small one. Halan couldn't help but feel that all these little successes only served to highlight the enormity of what she needed to accomplish.

The whole kingdom was struggling—everyone but the Thauma lords who had enjoyed the king's favor. She wanted to promise her people that she would solve all their problems, would fix everything that the former king had broken, but she knew she couldn't. Not by herself, and not in a matter of months. It would take time, and she would need help. A lot of it.

Because it wasn't only the Dust that Tam had kept from her. There was a bigger secret, one that took her breath away when she'd uncovered it during the first weeks of her reign.

There wasn't enough food or water. The resources that the Magi people had been depending on since the Year of Storms ended were running dangerously low, and it was only a matter of time before they ran out altogether. Unless they found more resources, her kingdom would starve.

It was a hard truth to learn after thirteen years of living in the palace surrounded by plenty and believing that everyone else at least had *enough*. The wells that had been sunk during the Year of Storms had been keeping people alive for a hundred years, but who controlled them? The Thauma lords. There were farms out by the Delta Lake, where there was water to grow crops and rear animals—but the Thauma lords who owned the farms refused to sell at a price the poor could afford.

All this time, the Thauma lords had been living with reckless abandon, accelerating the kingdom's path to ruin. There had to be a solution, Halan thought. If they made big changes, if they finally got people to work together toward a common good, maybe they could find a way to save the kingdom. But how?

"Your Majesty," whispered Rani, interrupting Halan's thoughts. "Perhaps this audience has gone on long enough?"

"One more," Halan replied. She could see that the woman at the front of the line was Lady Khora, the metalworker. She was one of the Thauma ladies who had taken on the reconstruction projects with genuine enthusiasm. She was probably here to ask for more money for materials or something equally straightforward.

"Welcome, Lady Khora," Halan called out to her. "What have you come to ask me?"

Lady Khora stepped forward and bowed smartly, her worn and practical leather jerkin creaking.

"Your Majesty, I come with a request. It's the Queen's Sword—your tawam."

"I believe Lady Nalah is down in the Storm Quarter right now," Halan said, smiling. "I'm sure she'd be willing to help with any task."

Lady Khora suddenly looked very ill at ease. She took a deep breath before continuing. "That's rather the problem, Your Majesty. I'm afraid Nalah is *not* helping—quite the contrary actually."

Halan blinked. "What do you mean, Lady Khora?" she said, her mouth suddenly feeling very dry.

"I know that your tawam means very well, Your Majesty," said the Thauma noble, clasping her gloved hands in front of her, "but as you know, her powers are still unstable. Whenever she tries to use them, something goes wrong. Just yesterday one of the foremen asked her to help fit glass into a window, and it shattered at her touch—as did all the other windows on the street! It was a wonder nobody was hurt. I'm sorry to say it, but Nalah is dangerous, Your Majesty."

"Dangerous?" Halan gasped. Her face was heating up, and she was painfully aware of the crowd watching her again. How could Lady Khora say such things in front of all these people? Now every one of them would leave with this gossip on their lips! "How dare you, Lady Khora!" she snapped.

Lady Khora paled and fell into another bow. "I mean no offense, my queen, but please, you must see—"

"I *must*?" Halan snarled, sitting bolt upright. The

Thauma lady shrank back from Halan as if she was expecting to be physically attacked. Halan stared at her, and a creeping sensation started up on the back of her neck.

Tam casts a long shadow, she thought. *Even over me. I have to prove to them that none of his blood flows through my veins.*

"I . . . I apologize, Lady Khora, for my outburst," Halan said, and several of the people in the crowd gasped or muttered to their companions. "Thank you for bringing this information to me—I'm sorry if any damage was done. But I promise you, the Queen's Sword is working hard to make sure such things do not happen again."

That's why she wanted to practice out in the garden, Halan thought. *Away from people. Nalah's worried about this too. So worried she didn't tell me about the broken windows.*

"If the crown can help you replace the glass," Halan went on aloud, "or if there is anything else you need, we will do our best to compensate you for the loss. Please speak to Lord Helavi after the audience is concluded."

Halan looked over at Helavi and at her mother.

Rani gave another small nod, but her forehead was creased with worry.

Lady Khora, who looked immensely relieved, thanked Halan and stepped aside. Steward Osaya pronounced the audience at an end. As the remaining crowd was escorted out of the palace by guards who reassured them they could try again tomorrow, Halan rose from her pile of cushions and left the hall through the huge back doors, which swung open by magic as she approached.

Finally, out of the glare of the public eye, Halan found herself chewing on her thumb.

This wasn't the first time Nalah's powers had gone awry. There was the incident with the wine jugs and the spare suit of armor that had . . . well . . . gone a bit rogue after Nalah had tried to practice her metalwork on it. And there was the cypress tree. As charming as its bizarre new look was, Nalah had still lost control.

But how can I help her?

"Halan, please don't let that kitten walk all over the table," said Rani, spearing the last slice of curried lamb on her fork just as Chestnut crouched to pounce on it, his wooden tail clacking on the table as it swished.

"Chestnut, come here," Halan called, and clicked her tongue at the little wooden kitten who had turned and was making a big show of sniffing Omar's empty bowl. "You don't even eat food—come on."

They were lunching together in the Sun Garden at a small table positioned in a patch of shade between the crisscrossing beams of light. Though the garden was in a courtyard at the center of the palace, polished mirrors reflected the sunlight from the roof down into the space so it was warm and bright. They twisted gently throughout the day, sensing when the garden needed light or shade.

The kitten, not caring that Halan was the queen, ignored her orders, and Captain Bardak scooped him up and glared at him fake seriously before handing him back to Halan. He met her eyes and, a little hesitantly, bent close to give her a peck on the cheek. Halan smiled at him awkwardly before lowering her gaze to the kitten. Things had been a little strained between them since Halan had discovered that the captain—not the king—was her real father. It had been shocking enough to find out that her mother had been secretly in love with Omar Bardak all these years, but to find out that this stranger was her father was a shock she found herself still recovering from. As was the kingdom. Rani had decided that it was best to tell the public the truth about Halan's parentage—better to be the daughter of a loyal captain than an evil tyrant. It had been a good decision, but not everyone took it well. Some of the Thauma lords felt that Halan's place on the throne was in question, and many of the other guards hardly knew how to speak to Omar, now that he was the queen mother's consort. Like everything else since Halan had become queen, it was complicated.

Omar hesitated by Halan's side, opening and closing his mouth as if he wanted to say something but couldn't decide what. Finally he sighed and returned to his seat. Halan watched him exchange a glance with Rani, who gave him a look of loving reassurance that said, *Don't worry, my love. She'll come around.* Halan knew that the captain was trying to forge a relationship with her, wanted to start making up for all those years that he'd lost, watching her grow up from a distance. But Halan just wasn't ready for that. Not yet.

The servants began to clear the empty trays and bowls from the table. "Thank you," Omar said to one of them, who gave a hurried and slightly embarrassed-looking curtsey. Halan smiled. She had grown up with servants to do everything, and while she often thanked them, if you did it all the time you would be thanking people all day. Captain Bardak had grown up as a commoner and come into the palace as a lowly armsman. He wasn't used to this, and it was sweet, but it was awkward too.

I don't think I ever saw the king address a servant directly except to tell them off, Halan thought. She shook the thought away. Memories of Asa Tam haunted her like ghosts, bringing gloom into every moment that reminded her of him.

Halan's mother was gazing at Omar with a kind of soppy smile Halan had never seen her wear until Asa Tam was banished. There was an open, unguarded joy in her mother's face that made it hard for Halan to believe that this was the same woman she'd known all those years. The same woman who had been cold and hard and stiff was now like a flower blooming in the light of her freedom from the king and her love for Omar Bardak.

"Halan," Rani said, finally tearing her eyes away from

the captain, "I've told Lilah to bring parchment to your chambers later, so you can write those letters. Lady Amalia will help you—I know you don't like her, dear, but she's an expert at writing letters that get things done, and you can learn a lot from her. It's all very noble, promising to intercede on the people's behalf, but you *must* take responsibility for your promises. Do you understand?"

"Oh—yes, of course," Halan said quickly. She couldn't believe she had forgotten. Lady Khora's words about Nalah had driven everything else from her head.

"You'll be at the Treasury again this afternoon," Rani went on. "But don't forget you have a meeting with the delegation from the Delta, and Master Gilani wants to talk to you about the plans for the Eastern Road, and before dinner Lord Helavi will have more documents for you to read and sign."

Halan sighed. Her mother was certainly different now, but some things never changed.

"I know, Mother," Halan said, rubbing her forehead. "We talked about it this morning."

The list of things she had to do piled up inside Halan's mind and she suddenly felt breathless, as if she were drowning in them. The immsense responsibilities she faced made her feel as if she had aged twenty years in the last few weeks.

It was strange. Her life was so different than it had been when she'd been the princess—back then, all she wanted to do was escape from the prison of the palace. To get out into the world and away from the suffocating protection of her parents. Now that she was queen, she had the freedom to do whatever she pleased. If she wanted to go out into the city, she could. If she wanted to outlaw figs because she did not like them, she could. And yet, with the weight of the kingdom placed squarely on her shoulders, with every person under her rule counting on her, she felt as trapped as she ever had.

"I'd better go," she said, standing up abruptly. Chestnut clambered up the folds of her purple robes and onto her shoulder. "There's so much to do in the Treasury; we're barely through the first room."

"Be careful," her mother said, frowning and reaching for Omar's hand. "I'm still not sure Lord Helavi should let you handle it yourself; who knows what Tam was hoarding in there. . . ."

She shrugged. "Well, Papa went in there all the time, and—" She broke off, her face suddenly hot. "Um. I mean Tam. The king."

Halan glanced at Omar, her *real* father. His gaze focused on the table in front of him for a long second before he looked up and gave Halan a smile.

"It's all right," he said. "I guess we're all still . . . getting used to things."

Halan gave a small nod and then turned and hurried away. She wished she could say something to make it better, but what could she say? He was her father, but he wasn't her *papa*.

The Treasury was in a secret part of the palace Halan had never set foot in before she was crowned, another one of the king's many secrets. To find it, you had to open a Thauma door with a secret knock, walk down a dark, tightly spiraling staircase, and then find your way through a mazelike set of empty passages that smelled of dust and magic.

By the time Halan arrived, the Treasury was already full of people—a few torches burned in the sconces, and guards and clerks bustled between the rooms.

Still perched on her shoulder, Chestnut pressed himself into Halan's hair and made a creaking, yowling sound.

"It's all right," Halan said, reaching up to stroke between his tiny ears. "I'm not going to put you back in the box."

The kitten stopped yowling, but Halan could feel his little thornlike claws hook tightly into the fabric of her robe. Halan hated the thought of Chestnut trapped in a box down here all that time before she'd discovered him and let him out. Tam had had him tossed down here with all the other Thauma gifts they'd received, with no regard for the little creature. But why would he have treated a Thauma animal with any compassion when he couldn't even muster it for his own people? Halan felt the heat of rage rise within her, as it did from time to time. Without an outlet, it simply burned in her stomach like an ember.

"Her Majesty, Queen Halan," announced a guard as she walked into the treasure room. It was dim, even though more light had been brought down since yesterday. The murky corners of the room were full of shadowy stacks of rolled-up fabrics, trunks and boxes, shelves laden with multicolored glass, and weapons. Hundreds of weapons.

There were three clerks in the room, each holding a board with a sheaf of papers and a bright glass candle hooked onto the end. They all turned to bow as Halan came in, and Halan smiled and nodded back, her rage cooling under their respectful gaze.

"Please, carry on," she said. Lord Helavi emerged from behind a teetering tower of wooden chests, brushing grit from his yellow robe. "What have you found today?" she asked him.

"Another two boxes of Dust, Your Majesty," said the vizier. "More Robes of Restriction, and a few other crafts that are very, ah . . . inventive. Your Majesty does not, if you'll pardon my presumption, need to examine some of these things too closely. They will soon be disposed of safely."

Halan swallowed and nodded, thinking of the silver circlet she had seen cause unbearable pain to the wearer and the obsidian glass dagger that could cut through anything. "Whatever you think is best," she said. She was curious, but decided that she didn't really want to know just how *inventive* her papa had been. Some things should be left in the dark, where they belonged.

"My lord," said one of the clerks, approaching with a very long piece of smoke-colored silk draped over her arm. "I'm fairly certain this is a piece of the Ashen Mantle! It was stolen from the Androzani family vault twenty years ago!"

Despite the clerk's excitement, Lord Helavi simply sighed and made a note on his sheaf of paper. "Put it with the other stolen goods," he said.

"I wish it surprised me that so much of this treasure was stolen," Halan murmured. "Make sure it's all returned to its rightful owners."

"A good decision, Your Majesty," said Lord Helavi. "Some of the more recalcitrant Thauma lords will look more favorably on your reign if you return their family treasures."

Halan nodded solemnly, hoping her vizier couldn't tell she hadn't even thought of that.

"Your gloves, Your Majesty," said another clerk, holding out a spare board of paper and a pair of soft leather gloves. Halan pulled them on with a grateful smile. She never would have thought that sitting in a dim room and cataloguing items would be so pleasing. When she would daydream of what she would do when she was queen, she'd imagined herself riding out to the Delta and the mountains, walking among her people, being . . . well, more *queenly*. Those things still appealed to her, but there was something special about being in the Treasury. Sometimes she would find wonders, like Chestnut, who had been stuck in a small box on a lonely shelf, or a Pauper's Lute that could play itself, or a set of Greensteel Keys that would open any door. No one watched her or judged her here, and the quiet simplicity of the task made her feel more relaxed than she'd been all day.

She settled down on the floor beside one of the shelves and began to look through the objects, taking careful notes. Chestnut leaped off her shoulder and began playing with the swirling motes of dust on the floor while she worked. There was a circlet of gold that gave off an aura of such sadness she couldn't hold it for long. And then there was a silver mirror that reflected a face she mistook for her mother's before she realized it was moving along with her own.

It's me, she thought. *But older.* There were wrinkles around her eyes and mouth from smiling, and her jet-black hair was peppered with white. She had a wise look about her, and Halan wished that she could get a little more of that wisdom right now, instead of having to wait for it to come with time. *How many mistakes will I make before I become the woman in that mirror?* she wondered.

She moved on to the next piece, and the next.

At the bottom of a huge pile of trunks, Halan found a moldering wooden box. By the look of it, Halan couldn't imagine that anything particularly valuable would be inside, but for some reason she felt drawn to it. Curious, she lifted the lid to find a glass orb. Gingerly, she picked it up. It was heavy, about the size of a coconut, and perfectly clear. Seeing nothing special about it, Halan shrugged and was about to replace it in the box when through her gloves she could feel something happening. The glass grew warm and began to hum, a not unpleasant *wumwumwumwum* sound, like the thrumming of a heartbeat. She looked around, but no one seemed able to hear it except her.

The orb filled with swirling colored smoke, blue and green flecked through with sparks of gold and silver. Halan held it a little farther away from her body—she remembered the smoke bombs she had used to cover the rebels' attack, and her heart juddered inside her chest. Was this some kind of weapon?

She was about to call out to Lord Helavi when out of the colored smoke there rose a shape. A sword, floating in the swirling air. But although it was small inside the orb, she couldn't escape the feeling it was really a large sword coming from a long way away. It floated closer, and she realized she knew this blade—it was the Sword of the Fifth Clan. She'd recognize its silk-wrapped wooden handle and iron blade with the pane of inlaid glass anywhere.

Nalah's ancestral weapon.

As if responding to Halan's thoughts, the smoke swirled over the blade and then away to reveal Nalah's face. Halan knew it was her tawam and not herself—her skin was a little darker, with the odd small scar, and she had cut her hair a little shorter to make it easier to tell them apart. She was wearing the shoulder pieces from the armor that Soren had made for her. Her expression held determination—and fear.

What does this mean? Halan wondered, as Nalah turned away and the smoke began to dissipate, leaving the orb clear once more. *Is this another vision of the future?*

Halan held the orb in her lap for a moment, then scribbled a note on her sheaf of paper and stood up. The Treasury could wait. So could the Delta delegation and Master Gilani. Nalah needed help, and Halan couldn't shake the feeling that she was holding it in her hands right now.

Chapter Three

Nalah

My Lady,

*We humbly beg you to go to the queen. We all know she
means well, but the Queen's Sword has cost us time, money,
and materials. It's only a wonder she hasn't cost anybody
a limb yet. She may be of the Fifth Clan, but she's also an
untrained child. You must get her off our site.*

Signed,
Your Concerned Workers
—A note slipped into Lady Khora's pocket

The afternoon sun beat down on the Storm Quarter, glistening on the sweat-streaked brows of the workers and on the new gold-colored bricks that they were rolling and heaving along the edge of the city. Nalah stood on the wooden scaffold that rose up the side of one of the buildings and gazed along the line of crumbling houses that faced the Sand Sea, still hardly able to believe that this place was the mirror New Hadar, the city she had come from all those weeks ago.

Generations ago, New Hadar and the Magi Kingdom had been one and the same world, a world consumed with war. The Thauma War was long and bloody—and when it seemed like it would end only when the last soldier died, a weapon was forged to put an end to the war once and for all. The weapon was meant to rid the world of magic altogether, but instead, it split the world in two. One world, Nalah's world, was left with little magic, while the other experienced such a rush of it that it caused endless sandstorms that dried up the oceans and turned the city to ruins. The survivors of the Year of Storms built the kingdom Nalah saw now, ruled by Thauma lords—while in New Hadar, technology replaced magic, and where Thaumas were once revered, they became hated and feared.

But though they lost the magic, New Hadar still had the sea. Where Nalah was used to seeing a calm blue ocean with ships steaming in and out of port, here in the Magi Kingdom there was only an endless desert. This was the poorest quarter of the city, wracked by sandstorms and farthest from the wells that provided the city's water.

But now things were changing. She watched as the workers tugged on their pulleys, lifting the bricks into place. They were building a wall to break up the force of the storms and protect the homes here from the wind. All along the edge of the city, buildings were being rebuilt, stronger than they had ever been before. When they were done, the houses closest to the Sand Sea would be as safe as any others in the kingdom.

We did this, Halan and I. We made this happen.

Even though the workers stared at her with distrust, and she was banished to a distant, out-of-the-way perch, she was proud of that.

Nalah sat down, her legs swinging from the wooden platform, and pulled the box of metal shavings toward her. She scooped out a handful and shut her eyes. Then she turned her face toward the sun, channeling the heat of it through her skin and into the palms of her hands.

"A *nail*," she said simply. The metal in her voice sounded like cutlery scraping together. She felt the shavings in her hand melt and re-form, knowing the molten metal would have burned a scar into anyone else's skin. She opened her hand and looked down at the simple iron nail there— nothing more than a short metal spike with a flattened end and a pointy end. There was no magic in it at all, except the traces she'd left in making it.

She dropped it into the bucket of water on her other side with a small sigh, and it sent up a barrage of bubbles and a little puff of steam before settling on the bottom with all the others.

I'm helping, she told herself. *I can make nails out of scrap a lot faster than any forge, and nothing goes to waste. I'm practicing. It's good.*

She tried to stop there, but the little nagging voice went on.

But I could do so much more. If only I could control my powers. . . .

She took another handful of shavings and forced herself to concentrate. Pointy at one end, flat at the other.

"How are you getting on?" asked a voice from behind her. Nalah jumped, and so did the half-formed nail in her hand. It slipped between her fingers, a twisted lump of red-hot metal making a bid for freedom. Nalah yelped and reached out to catch it.

She tossed the still-steaming twist of iron back in the box of shavings. Then she turned to glare at Soren Ferro. "I was getting on fine before you startled me!"

The handsome young noble stood on the end of the scaffold, the sun gleaming off the copper highlights in his wavy black hair. Instead of the fine costumes of the court, Soren wore a pair of black boots over leggings and a loose white cotton tunic. At the moment, he looked more like his alter ego, the rebel leader Ironside, than the dashing bachelor everyone at the palace knew him as.

Soren chuckled and handed Nalah a flask of water. "Here, drink this. The heat is making you cranky."

Nalah continued to glare for a moment before accepting the flask and taking a long swig. She hadn't realized how thirsty she'd been until the cool water hit her throat. She felt instantly better. "Thanks," she said a little begrudgingly.

"You're welcome," he replied with a wink. Soren was

almost impossible to stay angry at—not only was he possibly the most good-looking boy she'd ever met, he always
managed to get his way. She'd ended up working as his spy
in the palace, when he'd been waging his rebellion against
the king, even though he'd been holding Halan captive.
His young followers seemed to think he could bring down
Tam by sheer force of personality, and in some ways she
guessed they weren't wrong.

Soren wiped the sweat from his face and shaded his
eyes, staring out into the Sand Sea. "Do you see that, on
the horizon?" he asked. "That dark thing sticking up from
the sand?"

Nalah squinted and could sort of make out something
black against the endless pale sea. "What is it?" she asked.

"A ghost ship," Soren said. "There are a handful of them
out there. They must have been on the water when the
king activated the weapon and split the worlds." He sighed
deeply. "A whole ocean . . . I can't imagine it. Tell me
again, what's across the sea in your world?"

Ah, Nalah thought. *That's why you've come to see me.*
Ever since the rebellion ended with the battle in the palace
courtyard, Soren hadn't been quite the same. At first, he
was full of the glory of victory, hailed as a hero by crowds
of people overjoyed to be liberated from Tam's tyranny. But
once the fanfare subsided, and the real work of rebuilding
the city began, Nalah noticed that Soren's fierce brightness began to fade. Sure, he wanted to help as much as the

next person, but she couldn't help but notice that he just wasn't quite the same fiery boy who she'd first met down in the tunnels of his secret hideout. He'd begun to come to Nalah, asking her questions about her world, fascinated by her stories. Nalah found that while he listened to her, a little of that fire seemed to return to his eyes.

"Across the sea, huh?" she said, thinking. "Well, the rest of the world, really. There's Ikhtiyan—we trade them glass and metal for spices and fabrics. Apparently, they have the most amazing food—though very spicy. They have elephants there too! Over the mountains, if you go far enough, you get to the Moon Peaks. There, monks live at the tops of mountains and tend to herds of goats, never coming down except once a year. And in the east, there's the Provinces, where it rains for half the year and the grass grows as tall as this building. At least, that's what I was told. I've never been to any of those places myself. Why are you so interested, Soren?"

Soren had a faraway look on his face as she spoke, and when he realized she'd asked him a question, he snapped out of his reverie and said, "It's . . . a whole other world. So many places unexplored, adventures to be had. Who wouldn't be interested?"

Nalah sighed, feeling homesick. "Well, maybe one day you can take a trip there and see for yourself. Marcus could show you around. . . . "

Nalah paused, feeling a sharp stab of heartache as she

said his name. What was her best friend in New Hadar doing now? she wondered. He'd gone back through the mirror, to her world. It was where he belonged, with his friends and family. But New Hadar held its own dangers. She shivered thinking about the Hokmet and their Enforcers, always cracking down on the Thauma, giving them less and less freedom. . . . Nalah had been so busy with her new life here in the kingdom, she hadn't given Marcus much thought over the past few weeks. But now that she did, she realized how much she missed him.

"Marcus's family is from Svalberg," she went on. "It snows all year round there, and it's dark most of the time. Anyway, what's over the Sand Sea? Or behind the Talons? Are there magical versions of Ikhtiyan and Svalberg out there somewhere?"

"Nobody knows," said Soren. "After the Year of Storms, we were completely cut off. We struggled enough to reconnect with the Delta and the Talons. No one's really tried to cross the Sand Sea, so there's no telling what's beyond it."

Nalah was about to ask why no one had considered exploring more of the world when she saw the distant frown on Soren's face.

Nalah could hardly believe that this was the same boy who had helped overthrow a king only weeks before. What was wrong with him? After weeks of dancing around Soren's black moods, she decided to just ask him. "Soren," she said, keeping her voice soft, "are you okay?"

Soren looked at her in surprise at the directness of the question. An expression of casual indifference passed over his face. "Yes, of course I'm okay, why . . . ?" His words trailed off when he saw Nalah cross her arms and give him a stern look. He deflated. "I just . . . it's just that . . . I don't know . . ." He opened and closed his mouth like a fish gasping for air. After a moment he gave up and sighed, staring off into the Sand Sea once more. "Getting rid of Tam was my whole life, Nalah," he finally said. "Ever since my father was killed, it's been all I've thought about. And when we got rid of the king, and my father was avenged, I thought that staying here in the kingdom and helping rebuild would be the life for me. I thought that I'd be happy. And for a while, I was. But lately—and I know this sounds terrible—but part of me misses the adventure of the rebellion. The feeling that I was doing something dangerous—but important."

"You're still important, Soren," Nalah protested.

Soren looked down. "Perhaps, but any lord can do what I'm doing now. It's not the same as doing something that no one else will do. I know, it sounds stupid and selfish— the city is free—isn't that what I wanted?"

"No, I get it," Nalah said. "When you have an ability that no one else has, you feel incomplete if you aren't using it to do something good."

Soren lifted his eyes to meet Nalah's and nodded.

"Hey!" yelled a voice from below. Nalah looked down and felt her face flush as she looked into the angry, sweaty face of the foreman, Master Garai. He folded his arms over his thick leather apron. "Get down from there before you drop those nails on someone's head!"

Nalah forced out an apology and got to her feet.

I wasn't going to drop them, she thought, bitterly. *Not unless I was startled by people yelling at me. I'm only trying to help!*

Master Garai shook his head and hurried off, muttering something under his breath that Nalah was glad she couldn't hear.

"That's no way to address the Queen's Sword," Soren growled. "I should go down there and challenge him to a duel for insulting you like that."

The old Soren probably would have, Nalah thought, worrying that the young lord's swagger might be gone for good.

She handed Soren the box of metal shavings and hooked the bucket over her arm. It was quite heavy, about half iron nails and half water, but she could manage it as long as she took the ladder slowly, making sure she had a good grip on each rung before she moved—

There was a scream. Nalah, startled, started to slip with a shriek before wrapping herself around the ladder, hugging it with her whole body. The water in the bucket slopped over the sides, drenching Nalah down one leg.

There were more screams and the sound of splintering and crashing wood. Clinging on to the ladder for dear life,

Nalah yelled up to Soren on the platform, "What happened?"

"One of the beams fell—I think there's a man trapped underneath!" Soren called down.

Nalah's heart gave a lurch, and she felt the wooden ladder under her hands twist slightly.

No no no. I want to get down, but not that quickly!

She checked below her to make sure no one was around and dropped the bucket. It hit the ground with a hideous *clang*, water and iron nails spraying across the sandy street. But Nalah didn't care. She flew down the ladder as fast as she could and hit the ground running. Her loose copper-colored robes billowed around her as she dashed toward the noise, dodging the workers who stood around, gaping in horror at the scene.

There was a large crowd of people gathering, most of them yelling at the others to stand back while they themselves crowded in closer. Nalah squeezed between them, forcing her way to the front. *I can help, I know I can, if only they'll let me.* She could feel power coursing through her, looking for a way out. It made the skin on her palms tingle almost painfully.

"One, two, three, *lift!*" Master Garai commanded. Nalah finally broke through the crowd and saw ten of the strongest workers kneeling beside a beam as long as a medium-sized tree, trying to hoist it off the ground. A man's lower legs were poking out from underneath it, a trickle of blood pooling around his knees.

"Let me through!" Nalah commanded. If the workers were worried about having her around, it didn't show now—a path to the man opened up in front of her.

She ran forward and laid her hands on the beam. The sensation of the wood on her skin was like the jolt she'd once gotten from a faulty electrical light back in New Hadar, a feeling like a circuit connecting. The wood was still trembling from the force of the break and the sudden crash to the ground. It was weak, dry, vulnerable. Feeling for the splinters in the wood's core, she concentrated on them and willed them to open like a wound.

The beam split apart under her hands, and the strong workers took up the strain and pulled the two ends apart. The man trapped underneath let out a pained gasp as the beam was dragged off his lower torso. Blood was flowing freely from the legs of his trousers, where a jagged spur of bone was poking through his skin. Nalah didn't want to look—she staggered backward, exhilaration and nausea mingling in her blood. More people swooped in, examining the man, using their hands to put pressure on the wound.

The crowd jostled her from side to side, and she became aware that many of them were staring at her. She dimly heard voices calling out:

"My lady, are you all right?"

"The Queen's Sword saved him!"

But she couldn't seem to focus on the faces of the people. She had to sit down, but she couldn't get out of the crowd.

I can't breathe.

She leaned against the fallen beam next to her, gasping. Her hands shuddered against the wood as she struggled to regain control, and she felt it vibrating underneath her palms. The intensity of the moment, the wild beating of her heart, it made the power whirl within her like a sandstorm—ferocious and uncontrollable.

She smelled smoke. The wood under her hands was burning.

Soon the smoke was everywhere, stinging her eyes and filling her mouth with its choking stench. And suddenly, the world seemed to fall away, there was no Magi City, no Sand Sea, no palace—there was only the little house on Paakesh Street back in New Hadar, where one night, when she was a child, her world had burned. The night that her mother had saved Nalah's life with powerful Thauma magic and lost her own in the process. Suddenly she was the little girl once more, clutching her blankets over her head, seeing her father's soot-stained face as the fire raged, calling out for her mother over and over into the flickering flames—

"Get away from there!" someone yelled, and then she was falling back onto hard sandy bricks, the noise and chaos of the Storm Quarter flooding back in a deafening roar.

"Start a bucket chain! Get all the wood Thaumas!" Master Garai was shouting. "And someone get Ravarian out of the way!"

Nalah sat up, rubbing her eyes. The beam in front of her was rippling with fire.

Smoke billowed from the scaffold beside her as the flames began to lick up the side of the house. Nalah managed to stagger away, her hands over her face. She couldn't take it all in. Her shoulders were shaking, her breath coming in tight gasps that stuck in her throat. The smoke smelled of magic, tingly and sickly sweet. Thauma smoke. The kind that had filled her house and killed her mother, and now it was happening again. . . .

She was trying to help, Nalah thought. *Just like I was. . . .*

One of the wooden beams cracked and the workers around it leaped back as it fell in a pile of smoldering ash.

I have to do something! Nalah thought desperately.

She started to walk toward the flaming scaffold. Already there was a bucket chain forming from the houses to the edge of the Sand Sea. Veins stood out on the workers' arms as they passed pails of sand up toward the fire to smother it. But they would be too slow. Nalah had to act *now*.

She held up her hands, palms out, and walked toward the flames.

Fire couldn't hurt her, or that was how it seemed when she'd melted metal or glass in her bare hands, but this was different—the heat seared across her face and she felt her hair curl, sweat dribbling down the back of her neck. Still she pressed forward, her hands out in front of her. If she could just get a grip on the burning wood and metal of the scaffolding—

"Nalah, no!"

Soren gripped her shoulders and dragged her away, and Nalah let out a frustrated sob even as she felt the relief of the cooler air on her face.

"Let me go, Soren! I have to stop this!"

"Not that way, you don't. Here, take one of these!"

She blinked away the sweat and saw Soren holding out a long metal pole. A group of people were running up behind him, all holding similar poles they had grabbed from another part of the site. Soren pressed one into her hands and she saw what he meant to do—the group started trying to pry the scaffold away from the house it clung to.

With the metal in her hands, Nalah finally knew how she could help. She thrust the end into the flames and commanded it in a voice like metal tearing in half, "*Grow!*"

The pole lengthened until she could get it right between the scaffold and the nails that held it in place. She pushed and pulled, prying and levering at the beam, until something came free.

"It's coming down!" Soren yelled. The workers backed

up as fast as they could as the whole structure started to topple. It crashed to the ground in a shower of sparks, and there was a scream as part of it flew off and caught a young woman square in the chest. She dropped and rolled, and people ran to help her.

Others took up the bucket chain again, throwing more sand onto the smoking heap. Flames licked from the windows of the building.

It's spreading—we were too late. . . .

Nalah dropped the pole, afraid that her pounding heart would overtake her and the metal in her hands would melt from her touch. She backed away, gasping for breath.

"Farah!" a man's voice called out. He was standing beside the stricken woman, tears streaking down his face. "What happened?" He looked up and found Nalah's eyes among the crowd of faces.

Soren grabbed Nalah's elbow. "You need to leave," he muttered. "*Now.*"

"I was trying to help," Nalah tried to say, but it came out as a sob. "What about the houses? What was I supposed to do? I couldn't stand by and let that man be crushed, I couldn't—"

She was rambling, but she couldn't seem to stop. Soren grabbed her into a hug and then took hold of her shoulders and firmly led her away. "There are already people who wish you harm, remember?" he said darkly. "Let's get back to the palace before they decide this is the perfect excuse!"

Nalah just shook her head as he helped her down the street and up onto the back of his horse.

Why would they bother? she thought. *If Tam wants to undermine Halan, he doesn't need to get rid of me. He can just leave me loose to keep causing chaos.*

She thought back to the other market traders in New Hadar, the way they'd shield their crafts when she walked by, calling her "No-Luck Bardak."

She was in another world, living another life. But still, somehow, she couldn't escape her past.

Chapter Four

Sisters

While a few Fifth Clan legends tell of whole lives lived, battles fought, families raised, and romances and political schemes played out, there are others that speak only of great or terrible deeds. These Fifth Clan Thauma are often not even named by their ancient storytellers, or else their names have been lost to history. From the terrifying Lady Slice, whose villainous inventions have haunted the imaginations of many a young magi child, to the popular tale of the unfortunate Lord Hirbod's bottomless rice bowl, only their heroics or hubris remain.

From Tales of the Fifth Clan *by Lady N. Bagheri*

Halan was halfway to her tawam's rooms, the crystal orb tucked into a pocket of her gown, when a voice spoke in her mind as clearly as if Nalah had been standing in the corridor beside her:

It's getting worse.

"Nalah?" Halan gasped. *Hold on, I'm coming,* she tried to project back, but she wasn't quite sure if Nalah heard her. When they were close together, they could often hold entire conversations without speaking aloud, but if Nalah heard her now, she didn't reply.

Something was very wrong.

Halan turned on her heel, almost running into the guards who shadowed her steps.

"The front courtyard, now," she commanded as she strode past, not waiting for them to keep up. She took the first set of stairs two at a time, swinging down with her hand on the wooden rail like she hadn't done since she was six years old and she was trying to escape Lady Amalia's needlework lessons.

She burst out into the searing sunshine of the courtyard, startling several servants who were bringing in deliveries from the city, just as Soren's horse galloped in through the gate with Nalah clinging on behind him, her face pale and covered in ash.

"What happened?" Halan asked, helping Nalah down. Her tawam leaned heavily on her shoulder.

"There was a fire." Nalah paused, and she seemed to sigh with her entire body. Her eyes were red rimmed as if she'd been crying. "It was my fault. Someone was hurt. I was just trying to help—but it doesn't matter."

Halan's stomach turned over. She looked up at Soren, wide-eyed. He nodded.

"We did our best, but the fire spread to some of the

new houses, and . . ." He shook his head, looking almost as exhausted as Nalah.

"Come inside," she told them. She turned to the guards, who were standing a polite distance away, looking nervous. "Armsman Sabri, take some men down to the Storm Quarter and make sure everything's . . ." Halan trailed off. Everything was obviously not all right. "Do what you can if the fire's still burning, then see what the damage is and report back to me."

"Yes, Your Majesty." The guard snapped a smart salute and gestured for a group of the other guards to join him. Together they left the courtyard at a quick march.

"Was anyone inside the houses when they caught fire?"

Soren shook his head.

Halan gripped her tawam's trembling shoulders and waited until Nalah met her eyes. "Listen to me," she said. "They are just houses. Not people. What's fallen can always be rebuilt—that's the Magi Kingdom way. We've suffered a lot worse."

Nalah nodded, but Halan could see her words were not enough to stanch the wound that this incident had dealt. Her tawam's face was twisted up with despair—reminding Halan of the way she had looked when Tam murdered her father down in the dungeons. She had hoped that she'd never see Nalah look so hopeless again, and yet already it was happening once more. She pulled Nalah into a hug and didn't let go even when the other girl stiffened and tried to pull away.

I don't want to hurt you. Nalah's words floated up into Halan's mind in a whisper.

You won't, Halan thought back. "Come inside," Halan said out loud. "Come up to the East Tower, and we'll talk. You don't have to see anyone else yet."

To her intense relief, Nalah nodded.

Nalah's legs ached by the time she had climbed to the top of the East Tower, but it felt good to have something to focus on besides the churning guilt that filled her stomach. She waited for Halan on the landing at the top, catching her breath and looking out through the high, glassless window over the city. She almost cried with relief as she realized there was no more smoke rising from the roofs, and the whole Storm Quarter did not seem to have been reduced to ash.

The East Tower was one of the most secluded places in the palace, far away from the everyday bustle of servants and guards and nobles jostling for position. Lord Helavi had adopted it as his vizier's office, and Nalah was beginning to understand why: all those steps would surely make people think twice before coming to bother him with anything remotely trivial.

Halan reached the top of the stairs, then crossed the landing and opened the door to the office without knocking.

Lord Helavi was there, studying one of a pile of scrolls on his desk. He looked up and one of his gray eyebrows rose. Nalah found herself shrinking back under his gaze.

"Ah," he said. "Speak of the devil, and he will appear, hm?"

"What is that supposed to mean?" Halan demanded, crossing her arms and glaring at him.

"Only that I've just been reading some of the most ancient texts we have about Fifth Clan Thaumas," said Lord Helavi with a conciliatory bow toward Halan. "As you might remember, Your Majesty, like most reputable scholars, I truly did think that they were a myth. A comforting story cooked up by desperate people in desperate times. Your Majesty's Sword has rather ruined that theory with her . . . existence." He looked at Nalah, his eyes curious, the way she thought someone might look at a very rare insect.

"And now that you know you were wrong," Halan said pointedly, "what have you found out? Do the old texts say anything useful about how Nalah can better control her powers?"

"Cantrips and prophecies . . . *door or dust* . . . doom and undoings," Lord Helavi muttered, staring down at the scroll again. Then he shook his head. "I am sorry, Your Majesty, but I'm afraid the mystery of it still confounds me. My records—though exhaustive—are incomplete. There seem to be certain books and scrolls missing from my collection that may have included more information about this subject. I find that suspicious. It is possible that the king or his loyalists spirited them away as they plotted the murders of their tawams in the other world. But that's merely guesswork." The vizier sighed in frustration. "However, I have found . . . *something*. I can't speculate on what it means. Not yet. It seems to be a lost prophecy from Cyrus, the blind seer, but I can't be sure. At any rate, it is merely one of a dozen such scrolls that I'm currently trying to decipher—each one more cryptic than the next."

Nalah let out a heavy sigh. Lord Helavi rolled up his scroll and slipped it into a silk carrier at his waist.

"I do apologize, my lady, that I cannot provide more illumination. But I am sure that I can decipher it, given time. I must go to my library. There are texts there that might shed light on all this. I will leave you now, unless there was something else, Your Majesty?"

Halan fingered the smooth surface of the glass orb in the pocket of her gown. She considered showing it to Helavi but decided against it. *I want Nalah to see it first*, she thought. "No, you may go," said Halan. "Thank you, Lord Helavi."

Lord Helavi bowed and left the room. Nalah stared after him. It was still slightly weird to her, the way everyone deferred to Halan. Of course, she was their queen, but it was a strange feeling to see someone her age, with her face, dismissing an old man like Lord Helavi this way.

"Halan," Nalah said, "I'm sorry—I'm sorry about the fire, and the tree. I know things are hard enough for you without me being here, making it harder." She hung her head. "Everything I touch just seems to fall apart," she whispered.

Halan sat on the edge of Lord Helavi's desk and swung her legs, making the golden tassles on her robe jingle against each other. "Nonsense," she said, hoping she sounded more confident than she felt. "It's all just still so new. We'll find a way to help you. Maybe you can train more, and not just swordfighting, but your powers. I'll summon the most powerful Thauma lords, and—"

"It won't help," Nalah said, cutting her off. She threw her hands into the air and slumped down on a pile of cushions in a corner of the room. "I mean, I'd love to learn the crafts and the spells—but normal Thauma craft isn't what I do, it's something *else*. And there's no other Fifth Clan Thauma to teach me. If there was, I'm sure Tam would have known about it. He wouldn't have been keeping the sword locked up in his treasury."

"Speaking of the treasury," Halan began, "I found something there that I thought you should see. I wanted to wait until we were alone to show you." She hopped off the desk and knelt on the floor beside Nalah, pulling the glass orb from her pocket. "I know it's clear now, but when I first held it, it filled up with smoke and then showed me the sword, your sword—and then an image of you!"

Nalah reached up to take it, then hesitated. Her palms prickled with electricity. As her hand got closer to the glass, a strange sound began ringing out, a low, musical tone like the vibration of a gong after it had been struck. She pulled her hand back, trembling.

"I don't want to break it," she murmured.

"You won't," said Halan. "I think it's meant for you."

Still, Nalah hesitated. She could still feel the heat of the fire on her palms, the buzz of terror in her heart. She felt as if anything that came close to her at that moment would shatter at her touch.

Don't be afraid, Halan thought to her, her voice cutting through the fear. *Trust me.*

Nalah let out a long breath and, finally, opened her hands. Halan placed the orb in them.

The orb was heavy and cool to the touch. Nalah tried to keep her breath deep and regular as she gazed into its depths. For a moment nothing happened, except the musical note getting louder and louder. Then, from the absolute center of the orb, a pinprick of light.

"What is that?" she murmured, and then the light flashed, and the world changed.

The walls of the East Tower fell down around her and she was flung out into the air, soaring like Cobalt, surfing on the thermals around the palace. She was so high up she could see the whole city and the barren and sandy expanse around it.

Below her feet, a light flared, brighter than any flame. It snaked away into the desolate land, a trail of fire leading her toward the Talons. The black mountains rose in front of her, and the white light picked out a path that wound up into the craggy cliffs.

She saw a shrine.

Figures carved from obsidian, set into the surface of the mountain rock, and pillars of white marble that framed an opening into darkness.

And above the pillars, a great eye floated in a swirling cloud of blue smoke. The white of it was like glass, and the iris had a blue Thauma flame burning at the center.

The eye focused on Nalah, and she felt as if in one glance it had seen her whole life, every moment she'd lived and every moment still to come.

You are lost, Child of the Clan, *said a deafening voice that seemed to come from the mountains themselves.* Take the journey and be found.

Nalah felt herself falling, and then—

Her back hit the pile of cushions and she gasped as if she'd fallen hundreds of feet. The orb slipped from her hands, and she heard Halan yelp as she lunged, managing to catch it before it smashed on the stone floor.

"Nalah, are you okay?" Halan said. "What happened? Your eyes . . ."

"All white, with blue fire in the middle?" Nalah said, not moving from where she lay on the cushions, staring at the exposed beams in the ceiling of the tower.

"Yes . . . ," Halan said slowly. Suddenly, Halan remembered her lessons about glasswork, and how great objects of glass had the ability to alter perception and increase sight, to reflect aspects of life unseen by the naked eye. "The orb—did it give you a vision?" Halan demanded. "What did you see?"

Nalah got up. She went to the window and looked out. The Talons were there on the horizon, barely a black smudge in the rising haze of afternoon heat.

"I saw a path. A path leading to a shrine in the mountains." She turned back to Halan, who was staring at her with a wary expression. "I think the orb wants me to go there," she whispered.

"Go?" Halan mouthed the word as if it were in a foreign language. The idea of Nalah going away from her had been struck from her mind ever since her tawam had decided to stay in the Magi Kingdom instead of going back to New Hadar. Before Nalah came into her life, Halan's deepest wish was to have a friend, a real friend who truly understood her. And with her sister, Halan got that and more. The idea of losing her, even for a little while, and going back to that old loneliness, made Halan feel ill. An ache of fear settled into her chest like a small, cold stone.

"Yes, into the mountains," Nalah said, her mind whirling. She turned to Lord Helavi's desk and cast around for a piece of paper and a charcoal pencil. She could still picture the path the white fire had taken through the desert, and the location of the strange shrine, but the details were already fading. She talked breathlessly as she worked. "I saw a giant eye, with a blue flame at the center, and it told me to follow this path. I've been looking for a way to find out more about my powers, about my destiny. This is the sign I've been waiting for, I'm sure of it. This is where I need to go."

She pointed at her rough drawing of the shrine and the eye, and Halan came over to peer down at it.

"There was a voice, too. It said I was lost," Nalah said.

Halan pushed her own worries aside and concentrated on what Nalah was saying. *She needs me,* Halan told herself. She concentrated on the drawing. "I think I've seen something like this before," she said after a moment. "The blue flame . . . I think that's the mark of Cyrus, the Prophet of the Sands. He was a seer during the Great War, before the Year of Storms. Before the worlds were split."

"Cyrus?" Nalah turned to Halan. "I remember that name. He was in the stories, the ones Papa used to read to me." She frowned, her racing pulse giving a little jump at the thought of her father's gentle voice, telling her all about the blind prophet who had tried to stop the war, his strange pronouncements going unheeded until it was too late.

"Perhaps this is a message from him," Halan said. "Placed into the orb and left behind until the right person came along." She looked meaningfully up at Nalah, who was staring out the window, the drawing gripped in her hand.

"Are you sure about this?" Halan asked her. It took all of Halan's will not to project her innermost thoughts to her sister, which at the moment were crying out, *Please don't go. Please, Nalah. Don't go.*

Nalah felt a thrumming in her stomach, as if a dozen butterflies were taking flight in her belly. "I'm not sure about anything," she admitted. "But it's all I've got." She turned away from the window to look back at Halan, who was nervously tugging at the tassels of her dress. The idea of going out into the desert on this mad quest, leaving her beloved sister behind, filled her with dread. But behind that fear, there was a tiny seed of hope. "I've been wondering what my purpose is in this world," she finally said. "I thought things would be better after Tam was gone and everything calmed down. But nothing has gotten better, Halan. I'm still like a bomb, waiting to go off at any moment." Halan met her eyes, opened her mouth to protest, but then chose to stay silent. "If there's even a small chance that I can get some answers at this shrine—" Nalah continued.

"I know," Halan said, cutting her off. "You have to go." Nalah nodded.

"I wish I could go with you," Halan said quietly.

"The kingdom needs you here," Nalah replied.

Halan nodded.

They were silent for a moment before Halan reached out to grip Nalah's hand tightly. She took a deep breath, pushed away all the worries and sorrow, and smiled.

Go find your destiny, Sister, she thought to Nalah. *Even when we are apart, I'll be with you.*

Nalah returned the smile and sent her own thoughts back through the air between them.

I know.

"Leaving?" Rani clutched Omar's hand, looking from Nalah to Halan and back again. "You can't just go swanning off into the desert—many have tried, never to return! I know things have been hard for you, Nalah, but this is madness!"

Nalah could feel all the eyes in the great hall on her, and a hot blush crept up her neck. Halan had brought her here, in front of the court of nobles and the royal family, to announce her journey. It seemed like a good idea, but now Nalah realized that perhaps they should have broken the news to Halan's parents in private first.

What if they're right? This is all happening so fast. What if the vision was wrong? What if it's a trap?

She took a deep breath and pushed the doubts away. *It doesn't matter,* she told herself. *I need to find out. I need to try.*

Nalah stood up straight and tried to look like a grown-up warrior who could follow her fate wherever she liked. It was hard to look at Rani and Omar—her parents, but not her parents, the tawams of her own dead mother and father—and feel like anything but a child.

Their faces were the same, but the people were not.

"I understand your concern, Mother," said Halan, drawing herself up regally and steaming on. "But Nalah has been called away on secret Fifth Clan business, and so we are sending her on her quest with all our goodwill and blessings." She turned to Nalah, working to keep her voice level and free of emotion.

Rani seemed to be doing everything in her power not to contradict the queen in front of the assembly. She looked at Nalah, then at Halan, then back at Nalah again. She sighed, and Halan saw a little of that old pain, that old worry that had filled her back when Tam still walked these halls, come back into her mother's dark eyes. "As you wish, Nalah," she finally said.

Halan bowed her head and took Nalah's hands in hers. "Go speedily, Sister," she said. "And come back to us safely." Improvising, Nalah knelt down. There was a surprised, gossipy murmuring from the assembled nobles. Nalah thought she could sense some approval in it too. She glanced at the crowd and saw that not all of them were waiting attentively on their queen—a few slipped out quietly through the doors at the back of the hall.

Probably off to spread the good news, Nalah thought, trying not to feel bitter. *The liability is leaving the city. She won't be burning anything else down for a while.*

But she couldn't blame them. She swallowed and stood up, setting her shoulders resolutely. She was hoping as much as anyone that the shrine in the mountains held the secret to not setting things on fire, as well as the grand secrets of her fate.

"You must follow your heart," Omar said, and Nalah's breath caught in her throat. He wasn't her papa, but she knew that if Amir had been here, he would have approved of her quest too. With a gentle bow of his head, Omar made her feel as if she could conquer any mountain, cross any desert. "But," Omar added, "I cannot in good conscience allow you to go on this journey alone. Even the most experienced explorer would have a difficult time navigating the dangers of the Sand Sea. You'll need someone at your side."

"She won't need to go alone," said a familiar voice, and Nalah turned around, a smile already creeping onto her face. Soren pushed to the front of the crowd and stepped up to the royal dais. Cobalt was perched on his shoulder, and both of them were preening in a haughty kind of way. Soren swept down to one knee, his pale gray robe billowing behind him in a dramatic fashion. "I would be honored to accompany the Queen's Sword on her quest," he said, flashing a charming smile at the crowd. Nalah heard a couple of the young ladies behind her swoon.

Nalah chuckled. *That's more like the old Soren Ferro,* she thought. *I guess you found your adventure, didn't you?* "There's nobody in this world," Nalah said, "save the queen herself, who I would rather have with me." She gave Soren her best sweeping curtsey, and he winked.

It was true. There was only one person she might have preferred, and he was in another world.

I'm going on a quest, Marcus, she thought. *Wish me luck!*

Halan's heart was full to overflowing. She held on tight to Nalah's hand as they walked down the dim tunnel that led from the palace toward the edge of the city, hope and excitement and pride and fear all mingling inside her in a muddle of emotion.

Queen Mother Rani and Omar were with them, and so was Soren, but they had left the guards and nobles behind. They were using the secret passages to speed Nalah and Soren on their way—and besides, Halan didn't want anyone but family to see them off.

Nalah walked next to her, Cobalt perched on her shoulder, dressed in loose cream-colored traveling robes under the breastplate and shoulders of her shimmering black armor. She looked like a real adventurer, ready for the long journey across the desert, with her pack and the Sword of the Fifth Clan strapped to her back.

She was going to explore the kingdom, find her destiny—who knew what incredible adventures she might have in the black mountains? What would she find there? How soon would she come back? "I've changed my mind," Halan muttered, her voice sounding slightly choked in the echoey space. "I forbid you to go." She grinned at Nalah, hoping it was clear that she was joking.

Nalah smiled back. "Maybe I should stay; I'm sure Lady Khora would be delighted." She squeezed Halan's hand and sent her a reassuring thought. *We'll be all right. I've got Soren and my sword.*

I know we haven't tried communicating when we're very far apart yet, Halan thought back. *But please try. Let me know that you're all right. I'll listen for you. Even if it's just a whisper.*

Nalah nodded.

"You have all the food that was packed for you? And your scarves? And the Aqua Needle?" Omar was asking. Nalah was fascinated when she first saw the hollow wooden stake, its end sharpened to a point. Apparently all you needed to do was follow its magnetic pull to a point in the desert and push it into the sand. Within moments, water hidden deep within the earth would begin flowing from its mouth.

"We have everything we need," Soren reassured him. "I checked twice."

"And you'll be careful of strangers?" Rani added darkly. "It's been months and we still don't know where Asa is, or who is working for him. He'll be biding his time—but you still can't trust everybody you meet."

"Don't worry," Nalah said. "I doubt we'll meet many people in the middle of the Sand Sea anyway. We'll have to worry more about scorpions than anything else."

They reached the end of the tunnel, a small open doorway out into the blazing sunshine, and Halan pulled Nalah into a hug, as tight as you could hug someone who was wearing part of a suit of armor. Her eyes filled up with tears, but she didn't let them spill over.

Be careful, she said in her mind. *And come back safe.*

Nalah nodded and squeezed Halan back. She wrapped her cream-colored scarf around her head, ready for the punishing brightness of the desert. She smiled at the royal family, her own eyes watery, and then Halan watched her and Soren step out through the doorway and into the sunlight. The magical armor cast scattered, splintered rainbow reflections back into the dim tunnel for a moment, and then Nalah was gone.

Halan walked back through the tunnels with Rani and Omar, all three of them silent. She held out hope like a torch in her heart, but with every step that led her farther and farther away from her sister, she felt an ill wind blow. She shuddered, hoping it was merely the chill of the tunnel, but inside she felt certain that something was coming. Something big.

Chapter Five

Halan

There can be no doubt that, at least in New Hadar, magic is an outdated and dangerous pursuit. But are those who have magic in their blood truly less trustworthy or hardworking than normal Hadari citizens? The Hokmet's recent tightening of Thaumaturgic restrictions clearly implies that many of our ministers think so. Minister Dejagah was unusually evasive on Friday when questioned about the Hokmet's treatment of the Thauma living within New Hadar.

"The Hokmet's attitude has not changed," he told a gaggle of reporters. "The Thauma are potentially very dangerous and must be regulated properly for their own safety as well as ours." That answer did not satisfy this paper's Thauma source, who declined to speak on the record but described cases of Enforcers assaulting and harassing Thauma, and even of Thauma of all ages going missing.

From an article in the New Hadar Herald

By the time Halan walked into the library later that day, she felt as if she were carrying the world on her shoulders.

She had been very late to her meetings with the delegation from the Delta Lake and Master Gilani. They would have been frustrating even if she hadn't kept finding her gaze drawn to the windows, in case she could catch a rainbow glint from the distant Sand Sea that would tell her where Nalah was now.

They brought her tales of sabotage, problems with supplies, wild theories about what could be done if only they had this material or that Thauma talent. Master Gilani even told of brief explosions of violence. The desperate impatience of the workers who had been told things would be better under the new queen clashed against the insecure fury of the Thauma lords who were afraid she might appear and confiscate all their familes' wealth on a whim. Her kingdom was scrambling to find its footing under Halan's reign, and she felt herself scrambling along with it.

Something must be done, she thought. *But it's too hard to be fair when there isn't enough for everybody to begin with. How can I make the cattle fatter and the water flow faster?*

Halan cast her mind back to the days when she was still a princess. When she would spend her days bored, living in blissful ignorance of the problems facing her kingdom and the terrible wrongs being commited, all while she ate candied fruits and practiced her needlework. She would never wish to go back to those days, but during times like this, times that threatened to crush her under the weight of the crown, she wished for a little of that ignorance once again.

But that wasn't an option anymore, not for Halan. The kingdom needed solutions—now—before things got any worse. And she knew just the place to start looking for them.

"Lord Helavi?" Halan called as she walked into the library. She remembered Lord Helavi droning on in her lessons about previous rulers, about the kinds of things they'd done for—and to—their people. There were histories here, books about farming, about economics and magic. She hadn't seen her vizier since she'd left the East Tower, and she was hoping he was still here—perhaps he could help her find what she was looking for. But the library was empty and silent. It was the kind of crowded silence you only got in a room surrounded by books, as if thousands of voices were holding their breath.

Oh well, she thought. *If you want something done, might as well do it yourself.* Halan rolled up her sleeves and began pulling books off of the shelves. She might not be a Thauma, but she had other kinds of powers at her disposal. Maybe by the time Nalah returned, Halan would have a plan to fix everything once and for all. Maybe Nalah's powers would stabilize and together they could truly make a difference.

As she scanned the shelves, she couldn't help but glance into the swirling sheen of the Transcendent Mirror. It was still in the same place as it had been before—in the hustle and bustle following Tam's basnishment, Halan hadn't thought to move it. The king had used it to travel into Nalah's world and kill his own tawam, the act that had set all the events that followed into motion. What if Nalah ran into him on her journey? What else was he capable of, especially now?

She remembered reading somewhere, during her lessons on courtly politics and matters of war, that there was nothing more dangerous than a man with nothing to lose.

Halan tried to put the thought out of her mind. She had enough real troubles to focus on without jumping at shadows. If she allowed the ghost of Tam to haunt her thoughts like this, she would never be truly free of him. After gathering as many books as she could carry, she plopped them into a tottering pile on the large desk under the window, settled into a chair, and began to read.

Hours passed; the sun was beginning its long descent toward the horizon on the far side of the Sand Sea, and the patterns of light from the windows shifted and changed around Halan as she pored over the books and took notes on long coils of scroll. Finally, she laid down her quill and leaned back in her chair, her back aching from bending over all those pages. The history books had given her ideas, some of them good, some of them a little bit crazy, but none of them felt big enough to solve her problems. There were simply not enough resources in the kingdom to sustain her people for more than a year or two. No amount of Thauma magic could create something out of nothing. Her parents, as well as Lord Helavi, knew that things were dire—but Halan, after her many meetings with farmers and nobles around the kingdom—had only recently realized just how bad they really were. And here she was with no solution in sight. What was she going to do? It seemed like the answer to her problem simply didn't exist anywhere in the kingdom.

Feeling the threat of panic rising up from her stomach, she put down the book she'd been reading and walked to the window, opening it up and breathing in a little of the kingdom's spice-scented air.

Outside, the streets of the Magi City steamed as they cooled, more and more of them falling into shadow or being lit by blue Thauma flames. In the library, with its insulating layer of books and its Thauma lights and rugs on the stone floor, it was still warm. But she knew that the cloudless desert nights were as cold as the days were hot. Her thoughts strayed to Nalah, starting out into the desert. She wondered how far her sister would get before she had to make camp and what it would feel like to be out in the endless desert with darkness as far as the eye could see.

A shimmering rainbow light caught Halan's eye, reflected on the glass of the window. Her pulse quickened— was Nalah back already?

But when she turned around, it wasn't Nalah's armor giving off the glow.

It was the Transcendent Mirror.

Before Halan could react, a breeze blew into the room— a breeze that smelled of salt and flowers, and a bittersweet odor that was a little bit like Thauma smoke but at the same time completely different. Golden light spilled out from the mirror, flickering and dancing on the library rugs.

The mirror—it's coming to life! she realized with horror. Few people in New Hadar knew how to use the mirror— and most of those who did she wouldn't want to face alone. *So who is doing this?*

Halan's hand went to the small pouch sewn into the folds of her robe where she kept a tiny bottle of sleepsand in case of emergencies. If anything she didn't like came through—

But she didn't even get to pull the bottle from its pouch before a figure burst out of the mirror at high speed. It looked like he had taken a running jump from the other side. He crashed onto the stone floor at Halan's feet with a grunt: a small, pale figure with hair the color of straw falling over his eyes.

"Marcus!" Halan gasped. She reached down to help him up, and Marcus scrambled to his feet and backed away from the mirror. "What are you doing here? Why—"

Before she could finish, another figure clambered through the mirror. He was more hesitant than Marcus, stepping through one leg at a time. He sized up the library with a suspicious expression.

Halan stared at him, openmouthed. She had never seen such a strange-looking man. He was wearing a tightly tailored suit of stiff dark blue fabric and gold braid. There was so *much* of the suit—it went all the way down to his ankles and along his arms to his wrists, and the coat was buttoned up to a high collar that encircled his whole neck. He had a full beard, but the hair on his head was cut so short, it was almost all hidden underneath a box-shaped blue hat with a stiff peak and more gold braid.

Once the man got his bearings, he focused on Marcus and grinned wolfishly, brandishing a polished wooden stick at him and Halan.

"I've got you now, Thauma scum!" he snarled. "Your filthy magic isn't going to help you anymore."

"How dare you!" Halan shot back, shoving Marcus behind her. "You are in the presence of royalty, sir! I demand you leave this place at once!"

The man looked at her and chuckled. "I don't know who you think you are, missy—but if I were you I'd get out of the way before I got hurt." The man spat a thin brown stream of spittle onto the library rug, and Halan fought a wave of nausea. "I'll have you this time, Cutter, and your little girlfriend too."

Halan barely had time to let out a growl of outrage before the man lunged, swinging his heavy stick, and Halan had to push Marcus aside as she dived out of the way. Marcus toppled to the ground, quickly scooting away until his back rammed up against a bookshelf. Halan went for the pouch, clumsy with adrenaline, and fumbled the small glass bottle out into her hand. The man was still stalking toward Marcus, swinging his weapon. Marcus tore a book off the shelf and threw it at him, but it didn't slow him down.

Her heart in her throat, Halan uncorked the bottle and charged, getting herself in between the man and Marcus, grabbing onto the stiff blue coat and throwing the contents of the bottle into his face. A cloud of delicate golden sand hit him right in the nose and he recoiled, staggering, and then crashed to the floor. Halan felt some satisfaction seeing that he landed facedown in his own spittle. She held her breath until she heard the man start to snore. Then she straightened up, brushed herself down, and turned to Marcus.

"Well!" she said. "What a thoroughly unpleasant man!"

Marcus looked up at her, his eyes goggling. "What—what did you do to him?"

"Just a little sleepsand. I carry it with me in case of kidnappers."

"Well," he said, a grin starting to cross his freckled face. "Thanks very much, Your Queenness. I owe you one."

Halan felt a matching smile spread across her own face. "Not at all. Consider this repayment for that unfortunate whack on the head back at the rebels' hideout." Halan bent to help Marcus to his feet. "I welcome you back to the Magi Kingdom, Marcus—but I have to ask, why are you here? And why have you led this . . ." She nudged the prone man with the toe of her gold slipper. He snorted and turned over in his sleep. She cleared her throat. ". . . this *gentleman* into my domain?"

"I'm sorry, Halan," Marcus said. "I didn't know where else to go. Things in New Hadar are bad. And getting worse. Where's Nalah? She needs to hear about this. I need her help."

Halan's smile fell. "Ah. . . . Well, that could be tricky. One moment, please." She went to the door and looked down the corridor. There was a guard standing a few feet away, looking toward her anxiously.

"My queen, is everything all right?" the guard said. "I heard a bit of a commotion in there, but you said you were not to be disturbed. . . ."

"Everything is fine, armswoman," Halan replied. "But I need you to do something for me."

"Yes, Your Majesty!"

"Find my parents and Lord Helavi, please, and send them to me. Oh, and bring more guards. Half a dozen will do. I may need them." She could see the woman's face contort with the effort of not speaking out of turn—she must be wondering what on earth was going on in the library—but in the end, she simply nodded and hurried away down the stairs.

Rani and Omar seemed more wary than pleased to see Marcus standing in the library. They had both met him, briefly, before he'd returned to his own world, but everything had been pretty chaotic. Rani was staring at his clothes—the strangely muted New Hadari colors, the white linen shirt tucked into rough canvas trousers. Omar was more preoccupied with the sleeping Enforcer on the rug. His hand didn't leave the sword at his belt—he was still the captain of the guard, after all. Lord Helavi simply seemed fascinated by the entire situation, his eyes darting from Marcus to the Enforcer and back again, and Halan could almost see him committing every detail to memory so he could scribble it all into his records later on.

"First things first," Halan said. "Marcus, I'm sorry, but Nalah's not here."

The blood drained from Marcus's face and his whole posture sagged with disappointment. "But . . . where is she?"

"She had a vision," Halan explained, putting it as plainly as she could. "Something about her destiny as a Fifth Clan Thauma. It showed her the path to a shrine in the mountains. She thought she might learn how to control her powers there, so she had to go."

Marcus let out a shaky breath. "But I need her," he said simply. Halan could tell he wasn't prepared for this. He folded and unfolded his arms and trod a nervous circle around the room. "I don't know what to do. . . . She was my last hope." He looked up at Halan. "The situation for Thaumas in New Hadar has gotten worse—much worse.

The Thauma market was broken up for good a few weeks ago—now we can't even sell nonmagical wares. They started raiding homes and workshops in the night. And a week ago, they just started . . . taking people. And not just a few. A lot."

Halan bit her lip in sympathy.

"Monsters," Omar growled, still watching the Enforcer like a desert hawk. "They sound as bad as Tam."

Halan tried not to flinch at the way he spat the sentence out, as if merely speaking Tam's name disgusted him. *Why should it not? Tam was a terrible king. He did cruel, awful things. It's even worse that he did it all behind the mask of a loving father.*

"My family tried to lie low," said Marcus. "We had contacts at the Hokmet, so Mother said we would be all right, that they would leave us alone if we just kept our heads down. But then a few days ago, my brother, Kadir, went missing. He was taken, just like that. We're all powerless to do a thing about it. I thought if I could just bring Nalah back with me, she could use her powers to find him and stop the Hokmet. They would never have seen anything like her." He fell silent, his normally cheerful face drawn with worry. Halan knew what he was thinking: without Nalah, he would never find his brother, and the people of New Hadar would go on suffering under the Hokmet's cruel regime.

Halan thought about Nalah's journey to the Magi

Kingdom and how by stepping outside her own world she was able to begin to find herself, began to find the answers to the questions that haunted her—and saved a kingdom in the process.

What if, Halan asked herself, *Nalah's absence was meant to be? What if I'm meant to help save her world, as she saved mine? Can I truly leave New Hadar to ruin after everything Nalah did for my own world?*

Not while I still have breath.

"Marcus," she said, laying a hand on his shoulder, "I promise you, we won't leave your family to suffer. You helped to save the Magi Kingdom once, and we haven't forgotten it." She drew herself up as tall as she could. "In the place of your friend, would you be satisfied with the help of a queen?"

The impact of her offer hit the room like a Thauma smoke bomb. Everyone gasped as one.

"Halan, what are you saying?" Rani demanded, the alarm clear in her voice. "You can't be thinking of going through this mirror yourself?"

"That's exactly what I'm thinking," Halan said. Rani, Omar, and Lord Helavi all began to protest at once, but Halan cut them off. "Marcus and I will go through the mirror first. I'll assess the situation and then return through to speak with the guard about formulating a strategy. Prepare a phalanx of the royal guard and brief them, the best people we've got—Lord Helavi, you'll make sure they're armed and armored with the finest Thuama metalworks we have. We'll infiltrate this Hokmet of yours and free the prisoners."

Marcus was openmouthed in shock. "You'd really do that for me? But if you came into New Hadar—I mean, who would be queen?"

Halan turned to Rani. "I think my mother is perfectly capable of such a task."

Rani shook her head, her hands upturned and pleading. "Halan, please, think about this."

"There is nothing more to consider," Halan said. She swallowed, feeling light and a little bit dizzy, as if she was floating just off the ground. "If Nalah had not traveled to our world, we would still be suffering under the reign of Tam. Her actions led to our liberation, and I will not stand here and allow her own people to fall prey to a similar evil. I realize that there are still problems in my own world to contend with, but perhaps . . . " And at this, Halan came to the heart of why she wanted to go through the mirror.

Everything that Nalah had told her about New Hadar came rushing back into her mind. The amazing machines they used, since they didn't have much Thuama magic. The forests and beaches, the great Hadar Sea. Halan couldn't find the answers to her problems here in the kingdom, but maybe—just maybe—she could find them there.

"Perhaps by helping others," she finally said, "we will help ourselves."

"But what you're suggesting is war, Your Majesty," said Lord Helavi. "War with an unknown enemy. From what I have gleaned from young Nalah, this other world may not have Thauma magic, but they have weapons unlike anything we've seen. How do you fight what you do not understand? You're no general, and no Fifth Clan Thauma, either."

"I am quite aware of that," Halan replied. "But remember, Nalah and the rebels didn't take down Tam alone. I'm not afraid to fight, in my own way. Our enemies here are powerful, but these people hate Thaumas, and they can reach our world as long as the mirror exists." She looked down at the unconscious Enforcer. "Who knows what damage they might do? I need to see it, and I need to know I can face danger without hiding behind the ones I love."

She stopped and caught her breath. Certainty burned in her like the setting sun. She needed to do this. To be away from the palace, from her parents, to make her own decisions and test herself against an enemy she could actually fight, instead of the specter of thirst and economic unrest.

And there was Marcus. He was Nalah's best friend. How could she leave the safety of his family to even her most trusted guards?

"You all underestimated me once," Halan said, looking each adult square in the eye. "I am asking you not to do it again."

To her surprise, Rani's expression softened. She put a

hand on Halan's shoulder. "My dear, I have fought to keep you out of trouble your whole life," she said. "But you must be the queen you were born to be, and if that means going through that mirror, then I will defend your kingdom for you to the best of my ability."

Halan's heart swelled, and she fought back some very unregal tears. Her mother's demeanor and behavior had changed as soon as Tam was gone and her relationship with Omar was out in the open, but Halan had never expected her to freely give her permission, even her blessing, to something like this.

But Omar was shaking his head. "No," he said, his eyes squeezed shut.

"Omar . . . Father—" Halan began.

"No, you listen to me," Omar said, the pain laid bare in his voice. He ran his hands through his long, curly hair. "I've had to watch you grow up from the shadows all these years, and I don't doubt that you want to help this young man, but I can't—I can't lose you now, don't you understand that? Rani, why would you give her your blessing to launch herself into danger?"

Rani looked from Omar to Halan, her mouth open, for the first time caught between the two people in the world she loved the most. Halan hated putting her mother in this position, but there was no other way. "Mother knows I can handle it!" Halan replied, color rising in her cheeks. "You can't stop me from doing this."

"Halan, I am your father!" Omar shouted.

"And I am your queen!" Halan shot back, raising her voice. "You may have watched me grow up, but you weren't *there*. You never said a word. You are my father, but don't you dare try and tell me how to rule my kingdom."

There was a horrible pause. Halan's heart was hammering in her chest, and she turned her back on Omar. Marcus was looking paler than usual, staring at the bookshelves and the ceiling—anywhere but at the royal squabble going on in front of him.

"Marcus, is the mirror safe?" Halan said, walking over to it. "On the other side?"

"Er," Marcus said, "Well, it's hidden in Nalah's basement—"

"Good. Then Marcus and I shall go through at once. Armsman, throw this unconscious miscreant through after us—it wouldn't do for him to awake in our world. Lord Helavi, ready the soldiers. I'll be back with my report as soon as I can."

"Y-yes, my queen," stammered Lord Helavi, bowing out of the room.

Halan couldn't bring herself to look back at Omar. Was he angry with her? Was he upset? She couldn't allow it to affect her. This was her decision, and hers alone. "Are you ready, Marcus?" Halan asked him.

He nodded. "Ready as I'll ever be." He took a step toward the mirror and looked back at her. "By the way, thanks for doing this, Halan. I know you didn't have to."

"Don't thank me yet," Halan replied with a grin, and watched the boy disappear into the golden light. Taking a deep breath, she walked toward the glowing mirror and stepped through to another world.

Chapter Six

Nalah

I, Queen Halan Ali, first of my name, ruler of the Magi Kingdom, do declare that the glassworker Lady Lang, the fabricworker Lord Malek, and the woodworker Lady Kayyali are all traitors to the Crown. They are guilty of conspiring with Asa Tam to prolong his cruel and despotic reign over the Magi Kingdom.

From now on, all three individuals should be treated as dangerous criminals. Their properties shall be seized and their wealth redistributed. If they are sighted within the city limits after this date, their lives shall be forfeit.

A proclamation signed by Queen Halan, nailed to buildings all across the Magi City

Nalah was glad to have Cobalt and Soren by her side as she walked through the very edges of the Magi City. They were in the Thauma royal workshop district now, passing through canyons of shadow cast by the tall buildings. Nalah shivered. It was going to be cold in the desert at night. They had brought what they could to keep themselves warm, but she wasn't looking forward to it.

Nalah could sense the magic here, all around her—with a smell that tingled right at the back of her nose. The dust underfoot glinted with strange colors, and the walls of the workshops themselves seemed to move when she wasn't looking at them. So much magic had soaked into these places over hundreds of years that they weren't quite of this world anymore. Nalah wondered what it must be like to work in such a place, making magical crafts day after day.

"Through here," Soren said, pointing to an archway. "This leads out through the city wall, toward the Eastern Road. We can borrow horses from the stable there and then strike out north before we lose the light."

Nalah nodded, grateful to have someone with her who knew his way around. "Have you ever been to the Talons?" she asked him.

Soren shook his head. "Few people have, aside from the most ambitious miners. My father used to visit the mines in the Lower Talons, but it's a dangerous road. People don't travel that far unless they absolutely have to. Some don't come back. And I've never heard of anyone actually trying to *climb* the Talons." Nalah looked up at him nervously and saw that he was grinning.

They passed through the archway and found themselves in another tunnel. It was wide and quite dim, lit by flickering Thauma lamps in blue and green. Cobalt took off from Nalah's shoulder and hopped from lamp to lamp, keeping a little way ahead of them. In the colored light, he looked more like a ghost than a bird.

"It'd be great to have a motorcar about now," Nalah said, thinking out loud. "We could probably get to the Talons in a couple of hours."

"What's a motorcar?" asked Soren.

"It's like a wagon that drives itself—very fast, some of them—but not by magic. It's one of the things people in my world invented. I guess that because my world was left without much Thauma magic, we were forced to figure out other ways of doing things. With machinery."

"But if there's no magic, then how does it work?" Soren turned to give her a perplexed frown.

"Well, it's . . . science," Nalah said. Soren gave her a blank stare. "Um. Well, you put gasoline into this metal engine—flammable stuff, like oil. But more . . . oily. And then you turn a key, and you . . . burn the oil, and . . ." She made some flapping hand motions. "That makes it go."

Soren's eyebrow twitched skeptically, and Nalah sighed. A mechanical genius from New Hadar could have made a lot of improvements in the Magi Kingdom. But she was not that genius.

"It's like Wild Thauma," she said with a shrug. "You don't need to understand how it works to know how to use it."

"I'd like to visit your world one day," Soren said dreamily.

Nalah was about to reply when she hesitated, listening. She could hear a strange humming sound. She opened her mouth to ask Soren if he could hear it too.

Then all the lights went out.

Darkness swallowed Nalah, as complete as if someone had thrown a thick hood over her head. She gasped and turned on the spot. Behind her she could faintly see the archway, outlined in the red rays of the setting sun, but that was all she could see.

"Soren!" she called out. "What happened? Are you all right?"

Nalah's blood ran cold as the only answer was a scuffling of footsteps and a heavy thump. She drew her sword and held it in front of her, but her hands were shaking.

Cobalt began to screech.

"Soren, answer me!"

There was the faintest hint of a sound that could have been "I—" and then a gasp, and silence.

Nalah swallowed, suddenly afraid to breathe. *We are not alone.*

Suddenly there was a glint in front of her. Two circles of glass flashing in the darkness.

And then the lights flared back into life.

A dozen men and women stood in a circle all around her, armed with knives and wearing round-eyed goggles of green glass. Those must have let them see in the dark.

Ahead of her, Soren was on his knees, his arms twisted behind his back by one of the men, and a knife held to his throat by another.

Nalah shifted her grip on the sword. Could she take on twelve armed adults—some of them possibly wielding Thauma weapons? If she could summon up the full power of the Fifth Clan, like she had that day in the palace courtyard, maybe she could.

But even then, there was no guarantee that Soren wouldn't get hurt.

Cobalt took off from a lamp and tried to attack one of the guards, but the woman batted him away with a slash of her knife, and the man holding Soren pressed his blade harder against the skin.

A thin, bald man in a dark green robe stepped forward, removing the goggles from his face. "Call off your bird," he said. "Or the young traitor won't see another dawn."

Nalah's knuckles went white as she gripped her sword tighter. She knew that face. That reedy voice.

"*Malek*," she spat. He was the fabricworker, a loyalist to the king—one of the nobles Tam had empowered when he'd traveled to New Hadar and murdered their tawams.

Nalah hadn't known the other Malek well—he was just another fabricworker who she sometimes saw at the market—but Marcus had. He was a kind, quiet man— nothing like his monstrous twin. Nalah's blood boiled in her veins, and she fought to calm her nerves before her powers exploded out of her like a firework.

"The bird," Malek repeated. *"Now."*

Nalah swallowed. She looked into Soren's eyes. They were wide and dark and full of fear. Though whether it was for himself or for Nalah, she couldn't be sure.

"Go, Cobalt," Nalah said, not taking her eyes from Soren's. "Fly away."

From his perch on the top of the lamp, Cobalt tilted his head at her. Then Soren made a swallowed sound of pain, and Nalah saw a tiny dribble of blood coating the edge of the noble's blade.

"Go!" she shouted. Cobalt took flight at once, skimming over the heads of Malek's followers with an angry *skeeee!* and vanishing through the archway.

"Now," said Malek, in a cool and pleasant voice, as if he was asking her to tea. "Toss your sword over there, and put these over your hands."

He drew something from his pocket and threw it at Nalah's feet. She held on tight to the sword and prodded it with her toe. It was a pair of small black sacks with drawstring openings. They were presumably made of woven fabric, but they were so black they looked like holes in the ground.

"If you try anything, girl, I *will* kill him," Malek reminded her. He glanced at Soren and tsk-tsked. "You wouldn't want us to ruin such a pretty face, now would you?"

Soren's face was shiny with sweat, and he had closed his

eyes, readying himself for whatever was coming next, his throat bobbing against the bloodied surface of the knife.

Halan! Help me! She tried to send her thoughts out into the ether, searching for a response from her sister. But there was nothing, not even a ripple in the air. Why wasn't her sister responding? She tried again, concentrating even harder this time. *Halan, if you can hear this—Malek's back. He's got us. I don't know what he's going to do. . . .*

It was no use. It felt as if Halan was a long, long way away. But how? Where could she possibly have gone?

Nalah's shoulders sagged. She had no choice but to obey.

It was hard to throw the sword away—the fabric wrapped around its hilt almost seemed to stick to her palm like a magnet, clinging on until she threw it from her with some force. It fell to the earth with a horrible, echoing *clang*.

"Now, the gloves," Malek commanded.

She bent down and picked up the bags. They were heavier than they looked. She ran her fingers over the material, hoping there was something she could do, something they weren't expecting, but Soren gasped again, and Nalah shook her head and slipped them on. The fabric closed around her wrists on their own, and she felt that the inside was a wholly different texture from the outside— smooth and almost hard.

"They're lined with leather, in case you were wondering," said Malek, approaching Nalah and picking up the sword. "No Thauma can transmute skin—not even you."

Nalah felt a sob rise in her throat.

Wear your gloves for now, darling.

The last time Nalah had worn leather gloves, she'd been a world away, back home in New Hadar. Papa had made her wear them to minimize the chaos her raw power could cause to anything she touched. These were just crude, twisted versions of the gloves her father had given her— those had been thin and light, made with love, and she had left them behind on her bedside table in New Hadar when she'd stumbled through the Transcendent Mirror. But at the end of the day, they were still gloves, still barriers between her and the world. She'd thought that after she came to the Magi Kingdom, she'd be done with those barriers forever.

Staring down at her hands hidden in the dark shackles of these bags, she saw she'd been wrong about that.

Nalah gathered herself and looked up into Malek's black eyes, forcing herself not to flinch under the glare of his smug little smile. "So, what now?" she demanded. "Are you going to take us to Tam? Is he planning to kill me, after all? You should know if he does, all my power will just go to Halan. Do you really want that?"

Malek shook his head and chuckled. "No, Nalah. King Tam is . . . otherwise engaged at present. I have much more creative plans for you." He turned away. "Seize her."

Two of the nobles grabbed her elbows and dragged her

back toward the darkening streets of the workshop district. They pressed her into a stumbling walk, and she heard Soren being dragged along behind her.

They emerged from the tunnel and immediately turned into a narrow alleyway that ran between two workshops. Nalah looked up and saw empty windows set into the walls high above them.

"If you cry out, nobody will hear you," muttered one of the nobles holding her elbows, "and Malek will kill Ironside."

Nalah swallowed her scream. Her palms began to prickle, then heat up, then burn—but there was nowhere for the power to escape to. The thick leather hide couldn't be unwoven, melted, or burned.

Nalah kicked herself for being so naive—so impulsive. Everyone had warned her about the dangers of this quest, but she was so focused on herself, on her own *spiritual journey*, that she had put her own needs above theirs. What havoc would Malek bring upon the kingdom if he had Nalah's powers at his disposal? Whatever it was, it was probably intended to hurt Halan. *No*, Nalah thought, *I won't let that happen. I won't!*

They turned into another alleyway, and then another, stepping around empty crates and piles of trash, ignoring the squeaking of rats as they passed a can full of shredded scraps of fabric. One of them raised its head to watch Nalah pass, its eyes glowing green in the murk.

Up ahead, Malek opened a heavy metal door with a key and led the way inside. Nalah's hands were shaking violently as she was forced in after him.

The workshop was deserted and dim, lit only by the last light of the sun that filtered through a high window. All around her, Nalah saw the silhouettes of looms and spinning wheels, vats and racks. Their jutting angles and sharp spindles made Nalah shudder, and their crisscrossing threads hung loose and wavering, reminding her of the abandoned webs of long-dead spiders.

Malek and his followers took lamps from beside the door and held them up high as they marched Nalah and Soren to the center of the huge room. Their lights didn't illuminate much—they just made the shadows shift and flicker, as if something huge and shapeless was moving alongside them, keeping pace.

"It was so *petty* of the little queen to seize our property." Malek sighed. "This workshop used to make the most beautiful fabrics in all the kingdom, and it has been lying empty for weeks. It's a travesty, really." He pouted in a mocking way, but only for a moment. "Luckily for me," he added, turning on Nalah with a terrible smile, "that means we won't be disturbed."

"What are you going to do?" Nalah asked.

"Something *wonderful*," Malek whispered.

He gestured to his followers. The ones holding Soren began to drag him away.

"Don't give up, Nalah! We'll find a way out of here—" he yelled before one of the men punched him hard in the stomach and he doubled over, gasping for breath as he was pulled through another door, which slammed with a clang.

Nalah had not given up, but she was helpless to stop them from dragging her over to a wide wooden table in the center of the workshop. They thrust her against it hard enough that it pushed all the air from her lungs. She tried to wriggle out of their grip, but before she could, one of the women had leaned over and seized her wrist, pulling it across the table to rest palm up across a shallow metal bowl. The woman snapped a shackle over her arm and another over her other wrist, so that she was pinned down, the edge of the table digging into her stomach. Nalah tried not to panic, but her heart felt as if it was going to burst out of her throat.

She didn't like the look of that shallow bowl underneath her wrist. Not at *all*.

"I've been reading some very interesting texts," Malek said. He moved around the table to where Nalah could see him. "Some ancient scrolls that my king . . . appropriated from the palace for me in the final days of his reign. He was particularly interested in Fifth Clan Thaumas. It is said that the blood of one of these Thaumas, when joined with certain other materials, can make a substance so powerful, it becomes like an extension of the Thauma themselves. It draws power from the Thauma and imbues that power into whoever is wearing it—Fifth Clan or not. Is that not . . . *thrilling?*"

Malek leaned in closer to Nalah, grimacing as if he were being forced to smell something foul.

"You're too young, too *stupid* to have these powers, you see? They should never have come to you—they're *wasted* on you. You're not even from this world! You're a street rat, a guttersnipe—more likely to burn this city to the ground than to use your powers for the betterment of Thauma-kind."

"I won't let you use me to hurt these people," Nalah growled.

Malek tsk-tsked again. "Selfish child. But no matter— when I have finished my beautiful new cloak, you—the grand, cosmic *accident* that you are—will grow weaker with every moment that I wear it. I will absorb your powers, and you will be left as what you've always been: a stupid, ordinary little girl."

Nalah's mind went blank save for one singular thought.

I will destroy you, Malek. If not today, then someday. I'll find a way out of this, and I'll make you pay.

But even inside her own head, her words felt empty. She had no idea how to get herself out of this mess. Her friends were gone, and she was alone and helpless.

Malek reached out a hand, and one of his followers placed a knife in it. Nalah tensed, gasping, her hands clenching and unclenching within their leather cages.

She knew it was useless, but she found herself trying to pull back, her feet scrabbling on the floor, the metal of the shackles pressing painfully into the flesh on her arms. She wanted to cry out in fear and pain, but she bit it back—she didn't want to give him the satisfaction.

Malek admired the blade and then looked at Nalah hungrily. He smiled.

"I've always liked the color of blood."

Chapter Seven

Halan

Uniquely among glassworks, Transcendent Glass allows the user to see beyond reality. A mirror or bowl of Transcendent Glass is a powerful, dangerous thing that must be kept safe from those who would use it unwisely. I fear that looking too long or too often into what lies beyond our world may damage the fabric of reality.

Xerxes Bardak, Technical and Magical Aspects of
Thauma Glasswork

Halan's first impression of New Hadar was that it was dark, damp, and smelled like old socks.

When she opened her eyes after stepping through the mirror, she found herself in a cellar lit by a single lamp that burned a smoky orange color. She stood aside quickly as Marcus followed close behind her, dragging the Enforcer along.

"I hid the mirror here at Nalah's house," he said. "I didn't want anyone to find it, so I borrowed a Chameleon Rug and disguised the trapdoor as a part of the floor—*oof,*" he grunted, dropping the Enforcer's arms and brushing himself down.

Halan walked over to the sloping ladder that led out of the cellar and looked up at the trapdoor. She hesitated, her hand resting on one of the flat metal rungs.

Nalah's house.

Many things had gone through her mind when she'd decided to come through the mirror, but this hadn't been one of them. *I'm going to get to see Nalah's old life,* she thought. *The place she lived with her father, before he was taken by Tam. The place where her mother lived and died. A whole other world—just like mine, but different.*

Suddenly, she wasn't sure she was ready for this. But Nalah hadn't had the luxury of being ready to face another world when she had followed her father through the mirror. She would have to be brave like her sister.

She looked over her shoulder at the mirror, already feeling a little homesick, a little afraid, and then—

"Marcus, look out!" she cried. While they weren't looking, the Enforcer had staggered to his feet, grabbed the edge of the mirror to steady himself, and—

"No!"

As the mirror toppled forward, time seemed to slow down. In the eternity of moments that followed, Halan noticed so many details about the mirror. Nalah's mirror. The frame was plain, but the glass itself was a wonder to behold. It held sparkling, opalescent depths within it. Her sister had made it with her own hands. And now it was falling.

Halan heard herself scream, distantly. She threw herself through the air toward the mirror in an attempt to place her body between it and the hard stone floor.

But she was too late.

The mirror hit the ground a few feet away from her with a sound like a thousand panes of glass shattering at exactly the same moment.

Halan knew she would hear that sound in her nightmares.

A burst of wind blew out from the impact, showering Halan, Marcus, and the Enforcer with a million glittering shards. The golden light that had been streaming through the mirror faded and was gone, leaving only darkness in its wake.

Halan lay on the ground, her cheek pressed against the coolness of the stone. Her whole body was shaking and her mind was blank. The path was broken. With one clumsy act, this man had closed the door between this world and her kingdom.

Her home.

She struggled to her knees and watched Marcus drag the frame upright. Watched a waterfall of glass cascade out of it onto the floor. She reached down and picked up a single shard of glass, the only piece still large enough to hold. It was long and jagged, and about the length of her hand.

It glittered like an opal, broken but still alive with magic. She gripped it tightly, and the pain as its edge bit into her flesh centered her mind. She turned to see the Enforcer saying something and staggering toward her. Halan felt her pulse quicken—for the first time in her life, she truly felt like hurting someone.

She never got the chance.

"Halan, get down!" Marcus shouted. Halan ducked, and something flew past her head. She blinked, coming back to herself a little, and realized Marcus had lobbed an old kettle across the room, striking the Enforcer on the shoulder. The man tripped over a box and landed on his back on the floor, cursing with words she'd never heard before. "Get out, now! Upstairs!"

Halan scrambled to her feet. The Enforcer was back up too, his face murderous. Marcus gave her a short, desperate shove, and Halan snapped into action, spinning on her heel and leaping for the ladder. The shard was still in her hand, and she felt it dig into her finger, drawing blood, but she didn't stop climbing. She put her shoulder against the trapdoor and heaved, clambered out, and cast around the room to see where she was.

It was small, cozy, dusty. There was a heavy wooden bench at one end, and a furnace set into the wall.

Mr. Bardak's glass workshop.

There was a cooling cupboard. And a soft-looking

brown armchair beside a small bookshelf, a few books haphazardly stacked on it.

And there was a long metal pole standing in a bucket of stagnant water.

Halan dropped the shard on the bench, seized the pole, and spun around. Marcus emerged from the cellar, saw what she was holding and hit the floor, rolling out of the way. The Enforcer burst out from the trapdoor, and by the time he saw the pole coming toward him it was too late. Powered by panic, the blow hit home, and the man dropped like a stone and sprawled there, unconscious once more.

Halan dropped the pole and bent over, leaning her hands on her knees, trying to catch her breath. Her vision swam. She thought she might throw up or faint. Or both.

"Marcus," she whispered, "how am I going to get back home?"

She sank to her knees, clutching at her robes, trying not to cry.

Marcus swore, another word Halan didn't know, but the vehemence with which he said it made its meaning perfectly clear.

She took a deep breath, steadied herself, and looked up at him with dry eyes. "We'll find a way, right?" she said.

Marcus must have seen the determination on her face, because he mirrored it on his own, nodding. "We'll find a way." Halan watched as he hesitantly fussed with the trapdoor, closing it over the secret cellar and laying down a rug that wavered and changed to match the texture of the floor around it. Then he stood back, his fingers hooking into the pale strands of his hair, looking from the hidden trapdoor to Halan to the Enforcer and then back again.

"We can't stay here," he warned. "He won't stay down long."

Halan felt as if she was standing on a wobbly flagstone, tilting this way and that, dizzy and uncertain.

What do I do now?

Slowly, leaning on the glasswork bench, she got to her feet.

Forward. There is no other way.

She began looking around the workshop, taking in every detail with curiosity. This place was different than the Magi Kingdom, that was clear in even the smallest of things. The neat, patterned curtains over the windows, each one so identical to the next that they could not have been made by hand. The strange rumbling noises filtering in from outside. The smell in the air, that same bittersweet, oily smell.

She wandered about the room for a minute, reaching out to touch the things that Nalah used to touch. A chipped mug, an old newspaper, a bowl of multicolored glass pebbles. A tattered, blue-covered book, left open on top of the bookshelf, made her heart leap into her mouth when she read the title, picked out in gold leaf. *Tales of the Magi*. From the look of it, it must have been read hundreds of times.

"Nalah's family was happy here. I can feel it," she murmured. But all that life was gone now, forgotten by everybody in this world except for Marcus. A pang of guilt struck her deep in the stomach when she realized it was gone because of the sins of Tam. In his terrible quest to take Nalah's powers for Halan, he had destroyed the life Nalah and her father had shared in this world.

Halan could never give Nalah back the happiness that Tam had stolen from her. But if she ever got back to her own world and they were together again, Halan vowed to spend her life trying.

The next room was just as small, just as dusty. There were more chairs, and a table with some fruit rotting in a bowl, and thick porcelain cups with handles lying beside a metal sink, as if they'd just been washed and left to dry. There were shoes by the front door and a head scarf draped carelessly over the stair banister.

As if in a dream, Halan walked over to the sink and twisted the handle on the tap. Water flowed out, thick and clear and fast. She held out her hands and let it stream over them.

"We need to get out of here," Marcus said again. "Let's go up to Nalah's room. You can change into some of her clothes. We'll figure this out," he added, and Halan finally turned off the tap and faced him. "Okay?"

She put her hands together and held them very tight, so that they wouldn't shake too much. "Okay."

Halan knew that Nalah and her father were poor—Nalah had said so. And Halan had seen terrible poverty in the Magi City, poverty that made Halan's heart hurt. Homes in the Storm Quarter where people slept five to a room on piles of filthy cushions. But the cozy bareness of Nalah's bedroom made Halan feel even worse. Because it was personal.

It was barely the size of a closet in the palace—Halan could stand in the middle with her arms outstretched and touch both walls. There was one dust-covered window, a small bed, and a tiny rack of clothing. On the table beside the bed there was a pair of beautiful tan-colored leather gloves and a picture. Halan's heart lurched as she picked it up. The subject was Rani—or rather, Rina, Nalah's mother and her own mother's tawam—sitting in front of a vast body of blue water, her hair blowing in the wind.

Halan's lips twisted with emotion as her own mother's face swam across her imagination—the panic she'd feel, the tears she'd shed, when she realized that the way through the mirror was shut. That her precious, vulnerable daughter was stranded in another world.

What's more, the picture itself stunned Halan. It was too flat to be a painting, but it was *perfectly* lifelike, better than if the woman had sat for a master illustrator for hours and hours. How could it have been done, if not by magic?

"Here," said Marcus, picking out a few items of clothing from the sparse rack. They were all shades of brown—a long mud-brown skirt, a sand-brown tunic with a collar that looked green next to the other colors but was actually also brown, and a pale cream head scarf.

They were not pretty clothes, but they were soft, and they smelled like Nalah. Halan hugged them to herself, thinking of her sister and wishing she were there.

Nalah, can you hear me? she thought, casting her message out into the ether. *I'm in New Hadar—I'm stuck but I'm alive. I'm going to make it back to you. Nalah? Can you hear me? If you can, please answer me.*

But aside from her own racing thoughts, Halan's mind was silent. Halan blew out a long breath and leaned against the wall to steady herself. She'd hoped that somehow even across the worlds, Nalah would get her message.

Halan started to remove the top layer of her dress when she looked up at Marcus, who was standing there, somewhat stupefied, it seemed, to be in a girl's bedroom. "Are you planning on standing there while I change?" she asked him. The way his face changed color was truly amazing, from milky pale to blotchy red in less than two seconds.

"No!" he exclaimed, holding his hands up and backing out of the room. "No, no . . . no," he went on, from outside in the corridor.

Halan removed the circlet of gold and the dangling

chains that ran through her hair, peeled off the purple silk robe, then removed the loose and flowing sleeves that attached separately around the back of her neck, the carefully wound strip of material that formed the bodice, the tunic, then finally the loose trousers. When it was piled up on the bed beside Nalah's simple garments, it looked like a mountain of silk and gold, and yet Nalah's clothes *felt* heavier and harder to move in. Halan wrapped the head scarf around her hair and went out into the corridor.

"Will it do?" she asked Marcus.

Marcus stared at her. "Wow, you look exactly like Nalah," he said. "I mean, I know I shouldn't be surprised. You *are* her! Sort of. It's just . . . you look different without all the—" He waved his hands around his face and wiggled his fingers. Halan guessed he meant the gold and silver and the jewels.

Halan was glad there was no mirror here for her to look into. She already felt uncomfortably like a hermit crab, like she'd crawled into Nalah's house and into her clothes, and now she was going to walk out wearing her history, her family, as if it were her own.

"Nalah," Marcus breathed suddenly, and Halan glanced at him, her own cheeks heating up. "She's in your world, and I'm here. When am I going to see her again? I don't know where we're going to find a glassworker talented enough to fix that mirror," Marcus finished, running a hand through his hair.

"Maybe in the Hokmet's prisons," Halan suggested, and she was gratified to see Marcus's eyebrows shoot up and a faint smile form on his lips.

"Yeah!" he said, leading the way back down the stairs. "That's right. We'll free Kadir and the others, and one of them will fix the mirror." He went to the kitchen window and peered out onto the street, while Halan picked up a heavy leather bag from the floor. She wrapped the shard and put it inside, and then on a sudden impulse she ran back upstairs and picked up the picture of Rina and the thin leather gloves. When she saw Nalah again, she wanted to give them to her.

"Halan!" Marcus hissed, and Halan's heart gave a sick little jump. "Come here! Quick!"

Halan ran back down the stairs and Marcus gestured for her to join him at the window.

The street outside was strange. The sun had gone down, but the area was lit with the same kind of smoky yellow light as there had been down in the cellar. The road was paved with thick, perfectly square bricks, and there was hardly any sand in the cracks. A few people passed them by, all of them wearing the same strange Hadari fashion— trousers on the men, skirts on the women, and pale shirts or tunics on everybody.

"What am I looking at?" Halan asked.

"The people. There!" Marcus nodded toward an older woman who had paused opposite the house to fix her head scarf. "We're being watched. One old lady stopping to look at the house is nothing, but I've seen four or five people *just happen* to pause outside this door."

Halan drew away from the window, her skin crawling. "Why would they be watching an empty house?"

"Enforcers." Marcus shook his head, backing away to join her. "All of them. Undercover. They've probably worked out that our friend back there in the workshop was last seen going in here, and now they're staking the place out."

"So what do we do?" Halan frowned. "Is there a back door?"

Marcus nodded. "We should—" he began.

There was an almighty crash as the kitchen window shattered. Marcus and Halan both shrieked and leaped backward as a heavy metal object sailed into the room and struck the ground, spewing blue smoke.

"Smoke bomb!" Marcus gasped, and threw his arm up over his face. "They're coming in!"

Halan tugged the corner of her head scarf over her mouth and nose and backed away. The smoke tasted foul and bitter, and it snaked into her lungs and began to choke her. Trying to clear the burning tears from her vision, she turned and ran for the workshop door. Marcus barreled through it after her in a cloud of blue smoke, and she slammed it behind them. The horrible stuff was streaming through the gaps around the door, but it bought them enough time to get to the back door and sprint blindly into the alleyway behind the house. Halan sucked in a breath of clean air, then felt Marcus grab her hand.

"Can't stop," he croaked. "Come on."

They ran, and Halan was happy to just hold on to Marcus's hand and let him steer, focusing all her attention on simple things like breathing and not tripping over the uneven flagstones or tangling her legs in Nalah's skirt.

Suddenly they emerged from the alleyway into a bright space, as large and square as the Magi City markets, but much brighter. Halan looked up and her jaw dropped. There were lights everywhere, strings of them hanging from tall poles that had been set into the ground. These were no flames trapped in glass bottles, either—she didn't know what they were made of, but they glowed with a light so bright it hurt to look at them directly. Marcus squeezed her hand as something huge and fast and loud passed by only inches in front of their noses. It had four big black wheels, but it wasn't a cart, not even a Thauma one—it was a closed metal box with glass windows, and it chugged and spat as it rolled down the road.

It wasn't the only one. The box-carts were everywhere, big ones with words painted on the side, small ones with one or two passengers sitting in them, and ones with leather tops that had been folded back to let the air in. They were all moving around the square in an orderly fashion, seeming not to bother the citizens of New Hadar in the least, who swarmed around Halan and Marcus obliviously, often crossing the roads just in time to avoid being hit by one of the chugging behemoths.

The more she looked, the more strange things Halan noticed—there was writing everywhere, and most of it was too neat, the sweeps and swirls and dots identical across entire buildings. Everything was glass and metal, and shops were open even though the sun had set, with people sitting inside the brightly lit rooms behind large windows, eating and drinking and talking. And the smell . . .

"That smell that's coming from the carts, what *is* that?" Halan asked Marcus.

"Gasoline," he replied. "Those are motorcars, and gas is the fuel that makes them go."

Halan shook her head. "This place, it's so . . . bright! And there are so many people. Won't someone see us here?"

"Not if we act like we're supposed to be here," Marcus said cheerily, and he took her hand again and swung it as he walked along the side of the road. "If anyone asks, we're just taking the scenic route back to my house. That's basically what we *are* doing," he added. "Look out for the crack."

Halan looked down just in time to not trip over a deep crack in the stones. She followed the jagged path of it with her eyes until it vanished underneath—no, *through*—one of the buildings.

"You had the Year of Storms, we had the Great Quake," Marcus said. "Some of the cracks are still here."

They headed downhill, and the streets became darker and less busy. Then they turned onto a wide boulevard with tall and beautiful houses along one side, and on the other, nothing but darkness. A cold, salty breeze blew across Halan's face, and she stopped in her tracks. She let go of Marcus's hand and crossed the road, breaking into a run, leaning over a wet metal railing and looking down.

The Hadar Sea. The one Nalah had told her about. Halan had imagined what it would be like to see this much water, all in one place, but it paled in comparison to the actual experience.

Under the light of the moon, the sea glittered like a jewel. She watched the waves move rhythmically with the wind, making a dozen tiny boats bob and dance with the current, the lights from their cabin windows casting bright reflections on the water. The sound of it lapping up against the land below—a hushing, burbling sound—was as calming as a mother's whisper in the night.

"It's *beautiful*," she said. "I don't understand how there can be *this much water!*" *Maybe*, she thought, *when all this is over, the people of this world could help my kingdom with our own water problem. Maybe my answer is here after all.*

"I think I took it for granted," Marcus said. "Before I saw the Sand Sea. My great-grandparents came from a land a long, long, long way over there," he added, pointing out into the darkness. "I used to come here with Kadir when we were younger. He'd tell me stories Grandpa had told him about Svalberg, and the floating ice cities, and . . ."

He trailed off. Halan clutched the cold railing, staring out at the sea.

"It's all my fault," Marcus said. Halan looked at him sharply.

"What do you mean?"

"You being stuck here. I should never have come to your world. Now you're here, and Nalah's there, and I might never—" He broke off, as if he couldn't bring himself to say the words aloud.

"Marcus, look at me," Halan said, turning away from the incredible emptiness of the ocean and fixing Marcus with her haughtiest, most imperious stare. Marcus looked up at her from under his pale eyebrows, wariness in his blue eyes.

"You certainly *should* have come, and we certainly *will* see Nalah again. Nalah came through the mirror with nobody but you by her side, and she saved my world. I plan to return the favor. I will find a way home," she said. "But this world is amazing too—it belongs to Nalah, and to you, and I won't abandon it just because I'm afraid. Even here, I'm still a queen, and you still have my word: we'll find your brother first, and then we'll find a way back to the Magi Kingdom."

Marcus let out a shaky breath. "Thank you, Your Majesty." Then he nudged Halan with his shoulder. "Come on, let's go home. We can come back here." He smiled. "You think this is amazing? Just wait till the sun comes up."

Chapter Eight

Nalah

Nobility is a privilege and a duty. Being born with a home, a fortune, a talent—whatever it is that sets you apart—that's a challenge, to care for others and do no harm with what you've been given. We are Thauma lords. That hasn't always been a byword for honor and responsibility, but I hope one day it will be.

From a letter David Ferro wrote to his son, Soren

There was pain, and then there was numbness, and then there was pain again. Nalah's arms throbbed and her vision swam. Her knees gave out, but the manacles held her in place, still stretched over the table. Her shoulders and her calves ached from the strain. It had been an eternity since the last time she could feel her fingers.

Her mind tried to wander, far away from that place of suffering, to her old bedroom in New Hadar and to the shrine on the slopes of the Talons, but the stinging agony of the cut on her wrist always brought her back.

There was so much blood.

It ran into the bowl underneath her arm, hot and dark. Apparently it ran out through some unseen channel, because she heard it dripping, first with a clang against the bottom of something metal, and then with a splash.

I have to get out of here, she thought, over and over, but the harder she worked to try to summon up her powers or to wriggle out of the shackles, the faster her blood flowed and the weaker she became.

The world in front of her started to look strange, as if things weren't quite where they should be. The end of the table was a distant land, shrouded in fog, but the jutting shapes of the looms around her were too close, jabbing at her, threatening to draw her into their web.

The blood-spattered bowl gleamed. It was white now, not silver, and the blood running from her wrists was turning to blue flame.

Nalah blinked, trying to clear her vision. She knew she must be hallucinating, but she couldn't make it stop. Reality was slipping through her fingers like water.

A door opened, and Nalah looked up, blinking. Malek was walking toward her, but he was different now. He had three eyes, two beady black ones and one huge, unblinking white eye where his mouth should be.

"How are we?" he asked, but his mouth-eye didn't move. As he came closer, he seemed to dance along, moving to his own smug little tune. Was that real? Was anything?

All the buttons on his robe were eyes, white with a blue flame at the center.

"Are you still with us, girl?" he asked, tilting his head. It turned almost all the way upside down, like an owl.

"You . . . will fail, Malek," Nalah moaned, her voice slurring.

Malek made a *hm!* noise and his head slowly turned back the right way up. The button eyes blinked as he bent down and reached underneath the table. When he stood up again, he was holding a large metal jug. Nalah heard it sloshing. She could see her reflection in the metal. More eyes, all around her head like a crown of flowers. They blinked at her judgmentally.

"It's not my fault," she told them in a half sob. Some of them rolled.

"Oh no," said Malek, clearly thinking she was talking to him, "it's not your fault you were born with power you don't deserve. Luckily, you won't have to bear that burden much longer."

Malek's cronies entered the room, and Nalah tried to focus on their faces, but she couldn't. They all looked as if they'd been carved from obsidian, like they were the figures from the shrine that had come to life and stepped out of the rock. But each of their faces had been smashed or scratched away.

"Not real," Nalah mumbled. "It's not real."

One of the black glass men took the jug full of Nalah's blood. The other was dragging Soren behind him. His hands and legs were bound, and there was a bloom of purple across one side of his face where he'd been struck, but at least he had the right number of eyes. He flopped to the ground, his eyes closed and his mouth open, as if he were half unconscious too.

"Prepare the thread," Malek told one of his followers. "We will have the cloak ready by the time the master's ritual begins. Leave these two here. We'll decide what to do with them once the work is finished."

Something was happening to Nalah's wrist. Cool water ran over it, and Nalah winced. One of the obsidian men was washing and bandaging it, stopping the flow of blood.

He doesn't want me to die, Nalah thought. *Not yet, at least.*

The glass people all left the room with their many-eyed master. Nalah shifted her weight again, groaning a little as she felt a muscle in her back spasm.

Halan, she called out again, although there had been no answer the last four or five times. *Halan, where are you? I need you. Please, I need you.*

There was still no response. It was as if Halan was far, far away. But how could she be? Nalah was still within the city walls. She closed her eyes, and at once she could see the black tips of the Talons again, the shrine with its floating eye right below her . . . but she ignored it and climbed upward, spreading out her thoughts as far as she could, like ink dropping into clear water.

Halan was . . . *nowhere.*

Then Nalah's eyes snapped open as a familiar smell seemed to waft through her subconscious.

Gasoline and sea salt.

New Hadar!

Nalah groaned again and slumped over the table, her forehead resting against the wooden surface. Could it be true? Could Halan have traveled to Nalah's world?

But why would she go through the mirror? Why now? It must be serious.

Nalah shuddered as a theory came to her.

Please let Marcus be all right.

She looked up at the window and was strangely unsurprised to see a white eye with a burning blue flame at the center peering in, watching her impatiently.

"I'm trying," she whispered.

"Nalah?" Soren sat bolt upright, opening both eyes, and wiped the drool from his chin off on the shoulder of his robe as best he could. "I'm all right—I was just faking. They've gone. Are you all right?"

"I'm seeing a lot of eyes," Nalah answered honestly.

". . . Okay," said Soren, clambering to his feet. He hopped over to the table and rested his bound hands against it, wincing as he looked down at Nalah's bandaged wrist. "Oh, Nalah, I'm sorry. I was supposed to be protecting you, and you would've been better off without me." He shook his head. "Hang on. I'm getting you out of here."

He hooked the bindings around his wrists over a sharp edge on one of Nalah's manacles and started teasing the rope out of the thick knot it had been tied in. It finally gave way, and Soren pulled his hands free, wincing at the friction burns around his wrists. He picked up the small pot of water on the table that Malek's crony had used to wash Nalah's wrists and held it to her lips.

"Drink," he commanded. Nalah didn't need to be told twice. Her lips were sticky and her tongue was dry. She let the cool water run down her throat, and when she had drunk it all, the room no longer looked so completely off balance.

"I can't do it, Soren," she said, sagging under the weight of her failure. "I can't be the Queen's Sword. I can't protect Halan. I can't even protect myself."

"Don't say that," said Soren, trying to undo her restraints. But they were locked up tight. The manacles were pressing down on the leather sacks on her hands, so Soren couldn't get her free of either of them.

"Malek's taken my blood, and now Tam's going to come back, Halan will lose her throne, and it's all because of me." Hot, angry tears leaped to her eyes. "All because of me!"

Nalah hung her head, turning away from the glaring eye at the window.

"I can't even make it to the mountains. What use is it having some grand destiny if I can't save myself from this?"

Soren shook his head and gripped Nalah's shoulder. "You have to snap out of it," he said, his voice hard. "Do you hear me? Snap out of it, Nalah."

"Why?" Nalah spat, angry at him and herself and the world. "What good will it do?"

Soren stood up, his arms akimbo. "What good?" he repeated. "You're what, thirteen? Show me another thirteen-year-old who's done as much as you for people she doesn't even know—and don't say Halan, that's cheating. You channeled the deep magic of the universe and deposed a tyrant. Just because you're powerful doesn't mean everything's going to be easy." And then, in a slightly gentler tone, he added, "My father taught me that."

He looked around and then picked up a long metal ruler that had been left on one of the looms. He started trying to work it in between the shackle and the table, attempting to pry them apart. "Father always said that just because we were special didn't mean we were always going to be right. Thaumas, I mean. A lot of people in this kingdom forget that sometimes, but magic isn't everything. Sacrifice. Perseverance. Mercy. That's what he said was important. And you've got that, in bucketfuls. What good will it do for you to get up and keep going? All the good in the world, Nalah. All of it."

Nalah swallowed, fighting tears.

Persevere, said a voice in her head—she wasn't sure if it was just a thought or another interruption from the place where her visions had come from. *Everyone believes you're a legend . . . so act like it.*

Nalah licked her parched lips, trying to think. If this blood magic worked, who was to say some of the other stories she'd read in Lord Helavi's scrolls couldn't be true too?

Some of them weren't much use, of course. She didn't have any need for a pair of magical wings, or a manticore in need of taming. . . . The only escape story she could think of was about a Fifth Clan Thauma who had to make a key in secret with his captors watching, and had done it inside his mouth.

"Oh!" she gasped, realization suddenly dawning on her.

Malek's thinking was so limited—but Nalah could hardly blame him, because she'd thought the same way, and she really should have known better.

Fifth Clan Thaumas were able to change and shape any material with only the touch of their hands. It was instinctive, just a part of being a human, to pick up and work with things with her hands.

But my elbows are Fifth Clan too! Nalah thought. *And my toes, and the top of my head!*

"Soren," Nalah said, "do you have a coin in your pocket?"

Soren blinked at her, surprised by this abrupt change in manner. "Um. Yes . . ." He pulled out a silver piece and held it in his hand. "Why?"

"Put it in my mouth," Nalah told him.

Soren's face crinkled in puzzlement. "You want me to put this money . . . in your mouth . . . ?"

Nalah huffed in frustration. "Yes! Quickly!" She opened her mouth, and Soren, still with a completely bewildered look on his face, carefully placed the coin inside.

Nalah held the cool metal on her tongue and concentrated on the manacles on her wrists, using her fingers to feel for the keyhole in the metal.

Silver, she thought in her mind, and the voice in her head sounded like tiny bells chiming. *Change for me. Take a shape to open these bonds.*

She felt the coin soften and stretch in her mouth like warm taffy, and after a moment, it cooled and hardened again. She spat it out onto her chest, and Soren's eyes widened. Gingerly, he reached for the object and lifted it to his face.

It was a key. A tiny, perfect silver key.

"Nalah . . . ," Soren breathed.

"Yes?" Nalah replied, trying not to smile.

"I would kiss you," Soren said, "but now I'm sort of afraid to."

"Ugh! Soren!" Nalah grimaced. "Unlock the manacles already!"

Soren hastily unlocked the manacles and helped Nalah up off the table, pulling the horrible leather sacks from her hands. She was still a little woozy, but feeling stronger by the minute. "We need something to defend ourselves with," she muttered, and picked the chains up off the floor.

"What on earth . . . ?" gasped a man's voice. Nalah whirled around. It was one of the cronies—human again now, she realized, with his own surprised face. When she glanced up at the window, the eye was gone as well. Nalah looked back at the man and smiled. In her hands, the chains glowed white-hot.

"Hi," she said.

"Malek!" the man cried, drawing a sword from his belt. "The girl's getting away!"

Soren grabbed the metal ruler from the bench and held it out in front of him, twirling it in his fingers like a scimitar. "Come on then! Let's see what you can do in a fair fight!" he crowed. The man lunged at Soren, clashing his sword so hard against Soren's ruler that sparks flew from the impact. Soren parried and managed to slow the attacker's advance, but without a real weapon, Soren's defense wouldn't last long.

With a flourish of her arm, Nalah sent the glowing chain whipping across the attacker's back. His clothing sizzled at its touch, and the man cried out in pain. Nalah pulled the chain back in and whipped it again, driving the man into the corner of the room like a lion tamer.

Just when Nalah thought that they might have the chance to escape, three more of Malek's cronies burst into the room, their swords already drawn. Soren's expression hardened.

"Get to the back door," he called as Nalah gave a curt nod.

Malek appeared in the doorway, his mouth curled into a snarl. "It's too late for that now," he said, and turned to the other nobles. "Kill the traitor and bring the girl to me."

The nobles rushed at them. Soren parried one blow and got a hard swipe in across the shoulders of one of the women, drawing blood. But then he had to duck and roll under the table to avoid the swords of the other three nobles.

Nalah spotted a box full of loose threads and ran over to scoop them up in her hands. Twisting some of the thread around her fingers, she concentrated on imbuing them with magical energy and speed. When a woman vaulted over a table to swing her sword at Soren, Nalah flung out her hands toward her. The threads shot out like arrows, winding around the woman's wrists and waist, binding her. With a tug and a swing, Nalah threw the woman backward. The woman let out a shriek of surprise as she crashed into one of the looms and the threads wove her tightly into the frame, like a fly in a spider's web.

Soren was backing away from the remaining nobles, parrying and dodging their blows. Nalah went back to the box—there were no more of the nice long threads, but there was a strip of silk. She whipped it around and around, concentrating, opening the minuscule gaps between the threads until she had a large net.

"What are you waiting for?" Malek snapped. "Kill him!" Nalah glanced across the room and her heart sank—he had a cloak over his shoulder, the Sword of the Fifth Clan in one hand, and a large glass pot full of thread soaking in a red, sticky liquid under the other arm.

"He's going to run!" Nalah yelled, and started to dodge around the looms, the net swinging in her hand. She had to get to Malek—she couldn't let him get away with her blood and the sword!

"Nalah, I—" Soren started to say, and then gasped. Nalah spun to look. One of the nobles had got under his guard and stuck a short knife right into his belly. Soren choked and doubled up, the ruler dropping from his hand with a clang. The man then raised their knife to stab down into the back of his neck and finish him off.

"No!" Nalah screamed. She threw out her net and it closed over the heads of all three attackers. They tore at it, but the silk was strong and the loose threads at the edges snaked out and bound their hands to their necks. Nalah reeled them in and bound them to the looms alongside the first woman. They spat and swore at her, but she ignored them, running to Soren, her heart beating wildly in her chest.

Soren leaned back against the table, blood seeping from between his fingers. "I'm all right," he grunted. "Get Malek."

Nalah turned on the Thauma lord, dizzy with fury and fear and blood loss. Malek was halfway to the door. She grabbed the first thing she could get her hands on—Soren's metal ruler—and lobbed it over her head toward him. Malek was forced to duck to avoid the ruler embedding itself in his bald head, and in the process he fumbled the things he was holding. Nalah sprinted at him. The Sword of the Fifth Clan was on one side of him, the shimmering cloak and the pot full of bloodied thread on the other. Nalah skidded to a halt, staring him down, ready for whichever way he reached—

He lunged toward the sword and Nalah moved on instinct, throwing herself at it. Her hands closed on the handle and she rolled over, ready to thrust it between her and the villain.

But it had been a feint. Malek had pulled back and gone the other way. He seized the pot, threw the cloak over himself, and vanished.

A shadow cloak!

Nalah staggered to her feet and swung the sword at the place where Malek had been standing, but it scythed harmlessly through the air. She paused, her breath rasping, listening out for footsteps. But there were none.

"Nalah . . . ," panted Soren. She looked around. He was

leaning on the edge of the table, one hand pressed against the wound in his side. "Let's go."

"But he's still got the threads! He'll be able to make his stupid cloak, and—"

Soren held up his hand to stop her and pointed. She spun to look and saw that the door to the outside was now wide open.

"He's already gone," Soren said, panting. Nalah let out her breath and sagged. Now that she'd stopped, she didn't think she could fight anymore. The dizziness was getting worse again, and she could barely lift the sword. She half expected the eyes to be back, but the world stayed disappointingly real. "We're alive," Soren said quietly. "Let's get out of this place while we still can. Don't worry, we'll deal with Malek, but we're not going to do it now."

Nalah nodded and offered her arm for Soren to lean on. He gave her a skeptical smile.

"No offense, my lady, but I think if one of us is going to fall over, it's you."

"*Never*," said Nalah. But she leaned on the sword like a walking stick as they made their way, slowly, out of the workshop.

Chapter Nine

Halan

They're coming for you. Follow the plan, just like we talked about. Take Luca and leave the city, as quickly as you can. Trust no one—there are Enforcers everywhere. Dorya will meet you in the first inn you find outside the East Gate. Write to me when you're somewhere safe. I'll try to come as soon as I can. Remember, wherever you go, you take my heart with you.

A note left under the door of an apartment in New Hadar,
signed Ario

I'm sure there'll be a glass Thauma in the prison, Halan told herself as she and Marcus hurried down a dark street lined with tall, blocky buildings. *One of them will be able to fix the mirror.*

She refused to consider any other possibility.

All the buildings in New Hadar were taller than the ones in the Magi City, and most of the ones in Marcus's neighborhood were perfectly neat, almost identical, with the same smooth exterior and regimented windows. They were mostly white, but here and there one building had been painted in pale pink or yellow or blue. There was no sign of the flat square roofs, ornate carvings, and sand-colored bricks that she knew from the Magi City.

"All the old structures in this area were destroyed in the Great Quake," Marcus said. "These are all new apartment buildings."

They turned onto a new street, though it looked almost exactly like the last one, and up ahead Halan caught another glimpse of the white tower of the Hokmet.

When she'd first seen it, peeking between the streets, she'd thought she was hallucinating. Nothing could ever be that *huge*. Marcus had had to take her hand to prevent her from stopping in the street to stare at it. She'd forced herself to walk on and only glance up casually—she couldn't afford to look like she had never seen anything like it before. After all, there were Enforcers everywhere. Eyes everywhere, watching.

Marcus claimed it had *twenty-one* floors. The very idea gave Halan vertigo. Birds circled it, even in the dark. It was wider across than two of the palace's towers placed side by side, built from smooth white stone, with only a few windows, and Marcus said it had only one massive door right at the base, which opened out onto a public square.

One way in, one way out.

Halan understood now why Marcus had wanted Nalah. Even if she had managed to bring her phalanx of guards, how could they possibly get inside a structure like that, let alone search it for the missing Thaumas?

Soren might have been helpful too, she thought bitterly. *He knows about sneaking around where he's not supposed to be.*

"Here we are," said Marcus, and nodded toward one of the neat, square buildings. It was almost identical to those around it, with large windows and balconies on each floor, some of which were draped with laundry on lines, or festooned with colorful plants.

Marcus led her inside the building and then opened another door at the bottom of a wide flight of stairs. As soon as Halan stepped inside the apartment, she could tell that Marcus's family was better off than Nalah's. Nalah and her father might have had two floors, but their house was ancient and crumbling, and everything inside seemed like it had been there for a very long time, from the furnace to the threadbare chairs.

She could instantly see that you would never find anything threadbare in the Cutter household. The floor of the entranceway was tiled and lined with beautiful, intricate rugs, and through an open archway she could see a lounge where the chairs and couches were upholstered in embroidered silk.

"Marcus?" asked a high, lilting voice from another room. "Is that you?"

A tall woman stepped into the hall and gasped when she

saw Marcus and Halan. She strode forward and gathered Marcus into a shaky hug. She had pale skin just like Marcus's, and fair hair that had been gathered up into a series of rolls at the nape of her neck. She wore makeup, but it wasn't the heavy kohl and bright colors around the eyes Halan was used to. Her cheeks bore a soft pink glow, and her lips were cherry red.

"Marcus, we were so worried!" She seized Marcus's shoulders and planted several big, smacking kisses on his face, leaving pink traces all over his cheeks.

"Mom!" Marcus protested, pulling a face and squirming out of her grip. "Come on. I'm fine."

Mrs. Cutter shook her head, hands on her hips, and Halan saw that behind the pink blush her eyes were ringed with dark shadows. "How was I supposed to know that?" she asked. "God, I was so worried—I thought . . . well, you know what I thought. I don't know whether to hug you or smack you!"

"Why not just feed me instead?" Marcus replied, shooting her a winning smile.

Mrs. Cutter rolled her eyes and tsk-tsked. "You terrible boy," she said, but she was smiling. "You'll be the death of me."

Is this how normal people talk to their parents? Halan wondered, feeling a stab of guilt. *The last words I exchanged with my parents was a lecture to my father on my duty as a queen.*

Marcus suddenly remembered Halan was standing there, and began. "Mom, this . . . um . . ." He trailed off, shooting Halan a worried look. Just as Halan was wondering how to explain who she was, Mrs. Cutter threw her arms around her and squeezed her tight. Halan gasped and froze as Marcus's mother kissed her on the cheek too.

"Nalah, thank the stars you're safe and sound," she said. "We thought the Enforcers took you and your father weeks ago! Come in, come in. Are you all right? Do you need help? I'm afraid we don't have as much to give as we used to, but . . . well, come in." Halan was ushered through the archway and past the lounge, into another large room with a big wooden table in the middle of it.

On one side of the room there was something she realized had to be a small kitchen—she might not have recognized the oven itself, since it was white and absolutely tiny compared to the giant ovens and cooking fires in the palace kitchen, but apparently the design of saucepans was pretty much universal. On the other walls, racks held hanging cloth and drawers filled with buttons and needles and thread and decorations. There was a small loom and a large, slightly precarious stack of rolled cloth. Halan couldn't help but notice that the embroidered stars on one of the rolls of fabric were actually twinkling, and the tiny little green frogs pictured on another were hopping from one side of the silken roll to the other. She might not know New Hadar, but she knew a Thauma fabric workshop when she saw one, even if it was being run from someone's kitchen.

There were also four more Cutters sitting around the table. An elderly woman, with white hair peeking out from the front of a pink head scarf, was embroidering something on pale blue silk, while next to her, a man with short, dark hair and a thin mustache drank strong-smelling black coffee from a mug no bigger than Halan's thumb. A teenaged girl, who had pale skin and a mass of curly black hair, sat nearby in front of a strange machine, wrapping colored thread around a tiny metal spindle, while on the floor next to her, a girl of three or four sat playing with a pile of discarded trimmings. Her shock of pale hair stood nearly straight up from her head.

All the Cutters wore clothes that were finely made. Not showy or elaborate, but beautifully cut to make even the stiff and blocky New Hadar fashions seem quite elegant. The family all looked up as Marcus and Halan came in, and Halan saw them all sag slightly with relief. The old woman placed a hand over her heart.

"Marcus," said the man, getting up and dragging the boy into another hug. "Don't you dare frighten us like that again; you *know* we said that dinner was nonnegotiable right now."

"Sorry, Dad," said Marcus. His father didn't kiss him. Instead he looked at his face and then took out a clean square of cloth from a pocket in his shirt and handed it to

Marcus, who rubbed at the pink lipstick stains. "I didn't mean to miss dinner. I had to go and meet . . . Nalah," he said, and when the others weren't looking, he threw Halan a shrug.

Halan nodded. It was better, for now, that these people thought she was her sister.

"It's good to see you safe, Nalah," said the old woman. "I hope your father is . . . all right?" All the Cutters turned to look at her with hope and dread in their faces.

He's dead. Halan worked to keep her face passive as the heartwrenching words ripped through her, still fresh, still full of pain and regret.

"He's fine," Halan lied, keeping her voice light. "He's safe, out of town. I came back to see Marcus, and I heard about . . . about all the trouble."

"We thought the Hokmet might have got you," said the teenage girl bluntly. "They're taking people in the night now. You go to sleep and the next thing you know there's a Hokmet Enforcer standing by your bed."

"*Marit,*" Grandma Cutter chided her.

Marit tossed back her hair. "It's true, though, Grandma. There's no point pretending it isn't happening."

"No news about Kadir?" Marcus asked, sinking down into a chair at the table.

There was a long and painful silence.

Mr. Cutter rubbed his face. "We've tried everything

short of breaking into the Hokmet. Minister Tir won't even take my calls."

"I've had dozens of promises from people that they'd call us if they heard anything, but so far . . ." Mrs. Cutter shook her head. "Nalah, you shouldn't be here. Marit is right. If you take my advice, you and your father should travel as far from here as you can. We don't get much news from the rest of the world anymore, the Hokmet has such a stranglehold on the papers, but there must be *somewhere* Thauma would be tolerated."

Halan wished she could tell them. *I know a place where Thauma are the ones running the world!* But what use would it be to them now?

"I don't see why we have to run away," Marit said. "This is our city too!"

"This is the Hokmet's city," said Grandma Cutter bitterly. "It has been ever since the Rebuilding. They have never liked us, *jenta mi.*"

"But it was getting better," said Mrs. Cutter, shaking her head. "When I was a girl, there were Thauma stores on Main Street, and Thauma ministers in the Hokmet! There were rules, but they made sense. It wasn't like this. My poor Kadir . . ."

They all fell silent. Mr. Cutter went to his wife and squeezed her shoulders.

"I want to help," Halan said.

Marcus's mother and father looked at each other, confused.

Grandma Cutter was packing up her embroidery, glancing at the clock. "Don't you worry, girl," she said. "Not all is lost. Not while there are still free Thauma in this city. Are you ready, Marcus? We shouldn't be late."

"Where are you going?" Halan asked, glancing at Marcus.

"There's a meeting of the Trust," Marcus said. "It's the organization of Thauma merchants in the city. You, uh—you probably heard your father mention it."

"Of course, it's been dissolved now," said Mr. Cutter, taking another sip from his tiny mug. "Thaumas aren't permitted to assemble in groups of more than four, unless they're related."

"So if it's been dissolved," Halan prompted, a slight smile crossing her face, "where are you going?"

"Why, nowhere," said Grandma Cutter, getting up from the table and adjusting her head scarf. "I'm off to bed—and Marcus, I'm sure, will have a book to read or something."

"That's what they'll say if anyone asks," Marcus said with a grin. "The Trust used to meet in the Council Hall itself, right next to the Hokmet Tower, and talk about things like permits and imports. Now we meet . . . somewhere else. And we talk about other things. They let me and Marit join last week. I'm the youngest member in history."

"It's only because they're desperate," Marit said, rolling her eyes.

"You're welcome to stay here with us while Marcus is *in his room, reading,*" Mrs. Cutter said. "You're almost free and clear—you don't need to take a risk."

"But I want to go," Halan said quickly. "I was serious about what I said—I want to help. Please," she said, meeting Grandma Cutter's eyes. The old woman gave her a long look, then shrugged.

"I won't stop you," she said. "It would be churlish to turn down help so freely offered. As long as you understand the kind of responsibility you're taking on."

Halan gave her a faint smile. "I'm getting used to responsibility," she said.

This is an odd place for a secret meeting, Halan thought, as Grandma Cutter led her, Marcus, and Marit toward the busy, brightly lit building. The big glass windows on the outside were etched with swirling patterns, but she could still make out that there were people inside, sitting around on tall stools or low cushioned couches.

When she opened the door, a blast of sweet and pungent steam hit Halan in the face, so strong her eyes watered. It was loud in there too. Music was coming from a box with a large brass funnel on top, a driving rhythm that made Halan want to tap her foot. A couple dozen different conversations competed to be heard over the song. Men and women sat over more tiny mugs like the one Mr. Cutter had been drinking from. As she passed a table, being sure to stay close between Marcus and Marit, Halan saw a waitress come over and refill a man's cup with syrupy black coffee. On one side, two women were arguing good-naturedly over a game on a checkered board, and it seemed as if everybody was talking at a hundred miles an hour.

Perhaps this is a good place for a secret meeting after all, she thought. *I don't know how anyone can hear themselves, let alone overhear other people!*

A few of the patrons looked over at them as they passed— some of them giving Grandma Cutter a respectful nod. But the old woman didn't stop when she got to a free table; instead, she walked up to a bar where gleaming coffeepots and strange contraptions with seemingly endless knots of glass and copper piping sat steaming and giving off sweet, intoxicating smells. Halan had been in coffeehouses in the Magi Kingdom before, but none of them were anything like this!

"Good evening, Mrs. Cutter," said the man behind the bar, and to Halan's surprise he lifted one section of it and stood back. Marcus's grandmother led them through and around a corner, and then down a dim flight of stairs. At the bottom, there was a large man with stripes of white through his black hair leaning against a door with a cup of coffee and a book in his other hand, as if he was simply on a break from his work.

"Karin, kids," he said with a nod, and straightened to open the door. Then his eyes fell on Halan. "Is that Amir Bardak's girl?"

"Yes," Marcus said, maybe a little too quickly.

"She hasn't been approved," said the man. He turned to Halan. "Where's your father now?"

"Working out of town," Halan said. "I came back to visit Marcus, and I heard about . . . well, I just want to help."

The man frowned, studying her. Grandma Cutter placed a hand on Halan's shoulder but didn't speak. Halan got the feeling she was being vouched for and tried not to let the guilty feeling show on her face. She wished she could do this without lying, but it would be no use trying to convince these people of who she really was.

"Show me a token," the large man said eventually.

"A—a token?"

"To prove you're one of us. Something Thauma."

Halan's heart dropped like a stone into a deep well.

"I . . . I don't think . . ." She put her hands into the pockets of Nalah's tunic, more for show than anything, and her fingers closed around something smooth and hard. She drew it out, hardly daring to hope.

It was a tiny, white glass rabbit, exquisitely made, with delicate floppy ears and a slight blue sheen to the white glass.

It must have been made by Nalah's father.

It was beautiful.

Halan held the rabbit out to the man. He took it from her with gentle fingers, and then nodded and placed it back in her palm.

"All right. I'd know one of Amir's good luck charms anywhere, and so would the Enforcers. You can go in. But if you speak a word of what you hear inside to anyone outside this room, you *will* face the consequences—understand?"

Halan nodded hurriedly. Marcus gave her a grin, and even Marit's permanent frown seemed to lift slightly as the big man opened the door and let them inside. Halan's hand stayed on the rabbit as she slipped it into her pocket and walked through into a dim room that smelled of coffee grounds and old paint. *Thank you*, Halan thought, sending out a message to the spirit of Nalah's father. *It looks like your good luck even works for me.*

"Ah, there you are, Karin," said a voice in the darkness. Halan blinked, her eyes still adjusting.

They were in a large storeroom, piled with crates and stacks of mugs. Some of the crates had been moved into the center of the room to form a sort of table and around it there stood about twenty men and women. The Cutters joined them around the table, and Marcus scooched up to make space for Halan.

"Is that young Nalah Bardak?" asked an old man. His voice sounded choked and his hands were shaking on a polished wooden cane. "How is Amir, is he . . . ?"

"Amir is fine—he's out of the city," said Grandma Cutter,

and there was a general sighing, nodding, and shaking of heads.

"Master Zurvan's son and granddaughter are both missing," said a woman quietly, indicating the sad-eyed man next to her.

"I'm so sorry," said Grandma Cutter.

Halan's eyes were drawn to a small collection of objects in the middle of the table. There was a silver clock, a glass jug, a long wooden flute, a delicate gold bracelet, and more, all laid out on top of a black cloak embroidered with stars.

Marit must have seen her looking at the items, because she bent her head to murmur, "They're mementos. To remind us of the people we've lost."

Halan shivered. She remembered the palace cells, crammed with people who her father—no, who *Tam* had thrown there to rot, simply because they'd dared to question his rule. Their bereft families and friends had been the backbone of Soren's rebellion.

Is this what Soren's secret meetings were like, when he was plotting against the king?

A cold sweat prickled at the back of Halan's neck. It had become a familiar feeling these past few weeks. She would wake up sometimes in the night, cold and anxious, and longing for the days when she didn't know that her father's love was conditional, that it was a lie he told himself as well as her. She had to earn it by being good and quiet and never questioning his dominion. And she'd failed to do that.

There were so many people in her kingdom who knew Tam's true colors before she did. Everyone who attended the rebel meetings or helped them get their weapons. Even regular people off the street who simply had ears to hear the stories of their neighbors and friends being punished by the king's guard, even they knew more about what was happening in her own family than she did. It had been two months, and that fact still cut Halan to the quick.

Not now, she told herself. This was no time to air her old wounds—this was the time to help others with theirs.

"I'm worried about Aleksander and his little brother," a young man was saying. He had long hair and deep-set black eyes, and he looked like he was about to be sick. "They were trying to leave. They did everything right, everything we've been telling people to do. They changed their names, didn't bring *anything* metalwork, not even Luca's artificial leg . . . but they were supposed to be meeting Donya outside the walls, and she says they never turned up."

"How do they keep finding us?" snarled a rotund middle-aged woman, her walnut-brown skin reddening with rage. She slammed her fists down on the crates, making them wobble. "The Trust hasn't submitted an accurate Thauma register in years. We've done everything we can to hide our people from the Hokmet. But despite all that we've done, our worst fears are coming true!"

"They shouldn't have even half of the addresses we know they've turned over," said another woman, fiddling with a glass charm on a chain around her wrist. "And they certainly shouldn't be able to tell Thauma from ordinary people on the street."

"So how are they doing it?" demanded the large woman, striking the crates again.

A miserable silence descended on the group. Halan thought hard, but the only answer that came to her was too horrible to bear.

But she had to say it.

"Have you considered that there might be a Thauma working with the Hokmet?" she said, forcing herself to speak like a queen, slowly and clearly so that there could be no misunderstanding.

It seemed to take a moment to sink in, and then there were gasps of outrage.

"Are you actually saying," quavered Master Zurvan, "that one of *us* is *helping* them do this?"

Halan drew herself up straight. "I'm not saying that's what's happening. All I'm saying is it's a possibility."

Something upstairs went *thump, thump, thump!* against the ceiling.

Halan's blood ran cold as all the Thaumas looked up with horror in their eyes.

"Enforcers!" hissed the large woman. "Get down!"

As one, the Trust scattered. Halan suddenly realized that the piles of crates around the room were stacked up in a way that seemed random, but behind each pile there was a space for a few people to duck down and huddle, so they wouldn't be seen from the door. They scuttled into the hiding places in near silence, like insects under a bright light.

"Well, if you insist, officers," said a loud voice on the other side of the door. There were footsteps, heavy ones, coming down the stairs.

Marcus grabbed Halan's hand and pulled her toward an alcove between two big boxes. But just as she was crouching down, Halan's eyes went wide and her stomach turned over. Nobody had taken the mementos from the central stack of crates. She tore her hand from Marcus's grip and ran to get them.

"Tiger, what are you doing down here?" shouted the voice from the other side of the door. "Your break was over ten minutes ago. Are you still reading this stupid book? What have I told you about that nonsense?"

Halan sent up a silent thank-you to the owner for buying her time. She quickly folded the cloak up over the objects and lifted them in a bundle, as gently as she could, praying that they wouldn't make too much noise as she moved.

She slid into the alcove and sat with her back pressed to the boxes, the precious bundle held tight in her lap. Marcus gave her arm a squeeze and she looked at him and bit her lip, listening as hard as she could. The owner had stopped remonstrating Tiger outside, and Halan could almost feel the entire room hold its collective breath as the door swung open and light from the hallway spilled in.

"There you are, officers," said the owner, "my supply room. Nothing much of interest here, as I said."

There was a terrible silence, and then Halan heard someone step into the room. One step. Two steps. Three.

Halan figured an Enforcer could take only about five steps before being able to spot one of the Thaumas hiding behind the crates.

Four steps.

A drop of perspiration dropped from Marcus's nose onto the dusty wooden floor.

Five.

Suddenly, there was a bang and a series of shouts from the coffeehouse upstairs. Marcus and Halan both jumped, and the bundle in her lap went *clink*. Halan winced and held her breath, but the footsteps didn't come any closer.

"Master Sorna," gasped a breathless female voice from the hallway. "Tiger, you'd better come quick, the Mokris are fighting again!"

"Let us handle this," said a puffed-up sort of voice from inside the room. The man managed to pack more self-importance into a single sentence than Halan had heard since her audience with Lord Esmailian. Several sets of footsteps retreated from the room and back up the stairs, and the door closed behind them.

There were more scuffles and more shouting. None of the Thauma Trust moved from their hiding places. They waited in the dark, hardly daring to breathe. Halan's hands began to cramp from holding the bundle still so that its loose contents wouldn't make any more noise.

Then more footsteps, and the sound of the door opening.

"They've gone," said Tiger. "Coast's clear, Mandana."

For a moment, Halan still couldn't move. What if it was a trick, what if they were making Tiger say that?

Then the large, angry woman who must be Mandana stood up. "Thanks, Tiger. And we must thank the Mokris for that helpful diversion. What happened to them?"

"Kalen's been taken to the Justice Office," Tiger said. Halan looked at Marcus, and together they both got to their feet. The rest of the Trust were coming out too, one by one, all of them looking edgy and worried.

Mandana pressed her hand to her heart for a moment, then said, "It was only a minor disturbance, and they're not Thaumas. I'm sure he'll be released soon." Halan got the feeling she was convincing herself as much as the rest of them. Tiger nodded and went back out, closing the door behind him.

"Those Enforcers have got the scent, I'm sure of it," said the young man with the long hair. "They'll be back. And next time, we might not have the Mokris here to help us. We need to move against the Hokmet *now*."

The Trust all gathered again around the crates, and Halan carefully put the bundle of Thauma crafts back in its place.

"Thank you—that was quick thinking," Marcus's

grandmother said to her. "But Ario is right. We cannot wait any longer to find out if our families will be returned to us. We know they will not. Someone must go to the source, find out whether our loved ones still live and how we can get them back. Someone must break into the Hokmet."

A shudder of apprehension and dismay went around the makeshift table. Even Ario went pale and bit his lip.

"Mrs. Cutter, we've talked about this. It's suicide," said one of the men who hadn't spoken much—a dour-looking man in a sharply tailored gray suit. "If anyone were caught, being arrested would be the least of their worries. If they didn't kill them on sight, they would capture and torture them for the identities of everyone in the Trust. It's not worth the risk!"

"I respect your opinion, Ahmed, but there's simply no other way," said Marcus's grandmother. "I would like to formally invite anyone willing to make this sacrifice to volunteer."

Halan held her breath, looking around at the members of the Trust. Nobody moved.

I can't blame them, she thought. *It sounds incredibly dangerous.*

She was all alone here, apart from Marcus and these people. She had no throne, no soldiers. And yet she felt responsible. And not just responsible, but *ready*. If she was stuck in this world, she was certainly going to try to make a difference while she was here. She owed Nalah that much.

She placed her palms on the crates and took a deep breath.

Am I not a queen? Is this not what a queen is? Someone who will stand up for people, do the hard thing when it needs to be done, even if it means putting her own life on the line?

There was something else too—a hollow-but-full feeling in her chest. It was the feeling of sneaking out of the palace, of breaking out of the rebels' hideout—the feeling she'd had when she stood up at Nalah's execution, threw the first smoke bomb, and started a revolution. She remembered the exhilaration of that moment, knowing that she, the useless princess, could change her fate.

After all, she thought, *a queen does not belong to herself. She belongs to her people.*

"I'll break into the Hokmet," she said.

Every face turned to her.

"No," said Grandma Cutter immediately. "Nalah, you can't."

"Yes," Halan said calmly. "I can."

"I'll go with her," Marcus put in. Halan threw him a grateful smile.

"No! Absolutely not!" Mandana crossed her arms. "You are far too young to make this kind of decision."

"And yet I am making it," Halan said, slipping back into her Queen Voice. "I know my own mind, and I know what needs to be done here. You all want your friends and family back, and we will be the ones to get them. Either you can help us succeed . . . or you can mourn us when we fail, in the knowledge that you did not do everything in your power. It's your choice."

The Trust all stared at her. Halan supposed that they'd never heard Nalah speak like this. She held her head high and stared back, challenging them to deny her.

"No," Mandana said again, shaking her head as if she were coming out of a hypnotic spell. "This is madness. I think we should all go home and give this some serious thought. We'll meet again tomorrow to talk it through— and perhaps, Karin, you should keep the young ones at home this time."

Halan sighed in frustration. She wanted to argue, but she could see there was no point—nothing she could say now would convince them. They were all nodding, pleased to be able to put the decision off for another night. Perhaps tomorrow one of them would agree to go. Perhaps they would just argue it through some more.

Or perhaps tomorrow it will be too late.

She saw Marcus bristle at being called one of "the young ones," but Grandma Cutter placed a hand on his shoulder. "Mandana is right," she said. "It's very brave of you both to offer, but I would never allow you children to be put in harm's way."

But we already are, just walking down the street, Halan thought, but she didn't say it aloud. Instead, she lowered her head meekly and said, "I understand." Marcus frowned at her, confusion quickly giving way to suspicion, then enlightenment.

He began to nod. "Me too," he said.

As they were walking up the stairs, dawdling behind the adult members of the Trust, Marcus turned to Halan.

"We're going to do it anyway, right?" he whispered.

"Of *course*," Halan hissed back.

"Pretty sneaky for a queen," Marcus murmured. "But I guess I shouldn't be surprised; you did knock me out with a brick once."

Halan chuckled. "You are never going to let me forget it, are you?"

"Nope. That's what you get for knocking someone out with a brick. Now, follow my lead. . . ." As they emerged into the coffeehouse, which was still busy with people, he began patting his pockets and frowning. "Nana," he called out to his grandmother, "I can't find my key. I think it fell out of my pocket . . . you know, downstairs. We should go back and look for it."

Grandma Cutter sighed as she adjusted her head scarf in the coffeehouse doorway. "Go, go, children, but be quick!"

Marcus turned and headed back down the stairs, and Halan hurried after him. Tiger had deserted his post now that the meeting was over, and Marcus beckoned Halan inside the storeroom and shut the door behind her.

"What are we doing?" Halan whispered.

"It's not just the meetings they have down here," Marcus

whispered back. "I saw it the first time I came. . . . You're going to like this."

He led the way to the very back of the cellar, and together they shifted two crates aside to reveal a small door. Inside there were shelves stacked high with dusty old mugs, but behind them . . .

Wonders.

Halan grinned. She did like it.

"There have been rules about what Thaumas can make for hundreds of years, but every family had something, some heirloom, that they'd made purely for their own use. All the really powerful, imaginative stuff. When things started getting really bad with the Hokmet, people realized that even their homes weren't safe from the Enforcers. So they gathered them all together, all the best stuff, and stashed it here. It's probably not much compared to the kind of Thauma magic you have in your world," he added, "but it should help us get into the Hokmet."

"*Definitely*," said Halan with a grin, pulling out a small, unassuming leather satchel. It looked only big enough to hold a book, but she recognized the craft at once. She put her hand in, and it kept on going, until her entire arm was inside the bag.

"A hold-all!" Halan exclaimed, delighted.

"Listen . . . Halan," Marcus said, suddenly serious. "Before we start picking out our arsenal . . . I just want to make sure you really want to do this. I mean, Kadir is my brother, and I would do anything to rescue him. But you've never even met him, or anyone else in this world!"

"Marcus—" Halan started to say.

"You could be *killed*," Marcus insisted. "I'm just a market boy; the only ones who will miss me if I'm gone are my family. But you—you're royalty, Halan. I won't be responsible for an entire kingdom losing their queen."

Halan focused her gaze directly onto Marcus's face. "Now you listen to *me*, Marcus Cutter," she said sternly. "Your life and your brother's and the lives of every single soul being held by the Hokmet are just as valuable as mine. If I were to put my safety above that of others, then I would be a very poor leader indeed."

Marcus held her gaze for several moments before looking down at his hands, which were clenched on the cloak he was holding. Then he threw his arms around Halan. She tried to hug him back, but with one arm still inside the bag it was a bit lopsided.

"Tomorrow morning," Halan said, extracting herself and then her arm. "It begins."

"Tomorrow morning," Marcus whispered, and they started packing.

Chapter Ten

Nalah

Many mysteries and tragedies were born during the Year of Storms. One of the enduring and probably apocryphal tales concerns a Thauma neighborhood that emptied overnight, the families who lived there vanishing from their homes. No bodies were ever found, and nobody ever saw them again. The only clue to their whereabouts comes from the testimony of a woman who was sheltering in the shadow of the city wall when she claims to have seen a huge clan of men, women, and children walking out into the desert.

Of course, logic tells us that nobody could have survived the Year of Storms outside the city, but the idea that one might encounter these lost families still wandering the desert is a romantic one.

Lady Fulvia Shah, A History of the Magi Kingdom

It didn't look this big from the air, Nalah thought.

She was standing at the very edge of the Magi City, beyond the wall. Her sandals crunched on bare, rocky earth, and she stopped to stare out at the rolling, endless desert. When she'd been floating above it all in her vision, the searing white fire had reached the Talons in only seconds. But now, even though the air was perfectly clear, she could barely even make out the faint smudge of the black mountains, far away in the distance.

The sun had set, leaving bloody wisps on the horizon, but its light lingered. Now there were no sharp shadows, only an eerily bright twilight that Nalah knew would go on for an hour at least, maybe more. The sky was a deep, perfect blue, but the brightest stars were already beginning to appear.

She was still exhausted, but the sight was exhilarating and gave her strength. After they had escaped the workshop, and were sure that Malek's men weren't on their trail, they had sat down against a wall in an alleyway and Soren had given Nalah food and drink. He'd pointed out that their rations wouldn't do them any good if Nalah died of blood loss and dehydration before they even left the city. Cobalt had found them, and now he was perched on Nalah's shoulder once again. He gently pressed his beak to her cheek, and she reached up to stroke his glass feathers.

"Almost couldn't have planned it better," Soren said cheerily, one hand on his hip, surveying the desert beside Nalah. He was still holding his other hand to the wound in his side, over the top of the fresh bandage Nalah had crafted for him out of part of her own robe. She looked at him with concern, but Soren only waved her away. "Oh, stop worrying over me. It's all right, it doesn't hurt too badly. Anyway, look at this weather. It's light, and not too cold yet. A good start."

Nalah snorted and shook her head. "If these past few hours are what you call a good start, I'd hate to see what a bad one looks like." She pointed to a small huddle of buildings in the lee of the city wall. "Look, there's the stable. Let's go."

As they approached, Nalah heard a familiar grunting noise that was quite unlike that of any horse she'd ever heard, and she began to grin.

"Soren, look!" she said.

"I can see," said Soren darkly.

"Camels!" said Nalah, clapping her hands in delight.

"Oh, *good*," Soren said, clearly meaning the opposite.

Nalah turned to him, surprised. "You don't like them?" she said.

"I *strongly* prefer horses," said Soren.

"Oh, come on," Nalah nudged him, but carefully, in the side that hadn't been stabbed. "I love camels! They're so smart. I haven't ridden on one in years, but I remember going to see the races with Papa a couple of times when I was little. They're really fast when they get going!"

"So are horses," Soren muttered. "And there's the added benefit of less spitting."

When she saw Soren coming, the stablehand flushed

and hurriedly brushed the straw off her tunic. "Lord Ferro, are you going on a journey? I'm afraid we sold our last horse to a merchant traveler from the Delta, but there should be a string returning from the Lower Talons in a few days—"

"Camels are fine!" Nalah beamed and half ran past the girl to the nearest camel. It was a beautiful mottled gold-and-white color, and it looked down at her with its deep, dark eyes, giving her a look of total indifference. These camels were huge compared to the fairly light and sprightly ones brought to the New Hadar Racetrack every week. Nalah guessed they were built for endurance rather than speed. If any creature could make it across the vast and merciless desert alive, it would be these camels.

Soren paid the girl and bought some extra food from her as well. Then they hung their fairly light packs in saddlebags across the animals' humps and climbed on top. Soren's camel was completely black and rather beautiful as camels went. Nalah couldn't help wondering if the stablehand had picked it out for it looks to make Soren feel a little better.

As they set out, Cobalt took flight from Nalah's shoulder and wheeled above them, glittering against the darkening sky. Nalah held the reins of her camel loosely in her lap and enjoyed the rocking motion of the animal's gait as they joined the worn, wheel-rutted path that was the only road out of the Magi City.

✷✷✷

Night came on so gradually that Nalah almost didn't notice it. They traveled for what seemed like days, though she knew it could only have been a few hours. The landscape was stunningly sparse, and Nalah kept her mind occupied by counting the scattered cacti and tamarisk shrubs they passed. Then Soren turned off the road, and the ground under the camels' feet turned from hard-packed earth to rock and sand. The plants grew even fewer and farther between after that.

Nalah was so tired, and the camel's rolling motion so soothing, that she almost drifted off to sleep once or twice. The fear of falling jolted her awake again, and she realized that she was much colder than she had been before, her fingers prickling with it. She reached down into the saddle-bags and pulled out her extra shawl. After she'd wrapped it around herself, Cobalt swept down from the air and landed on the camel's hump in front of her.

All the stars had come out. Nalah had been astonished by their brightness in the Magi City, but here the sense of depth and the sheer number of them made her feel as if she could lose her grip on the earth and fall into the sky.

Ahead of her on his black camel, Soren looked almost like a ghost floating in midair, haunting the sand dunes. He had stopped at the top of a ridge. When she caught up to him, he pointed into the distance.

"Look."

At first, Nalah wasn't sure what she was looking at, but

finally her eyes adjusted to distinguish differences in the shades of dark. Towering into the sky, much closer now, there was an area of starless blackness and very faint suggestions of pointed, clawlike peaks.

The Talons. They were getting closer.

I'm getting there, Halan, Nalah thought out into the world. *We ran into some trouble, but I'm getting there.* Nalah wondered where her sister was right now and what she was doing.

"We should camp there," said Soren, and pointed to his right.

Nalah gasped. After hours of traveling through the desert and seeing less and less plant life, the oasis stood out like a paradise of green.

The camels, probably sensing the presence of food and water, didn't need much convincing to trot toward it. Once Nalah and Soren arrived under the shadows of the palm trees, they jumped down and tied up their camels near some low shrubs, where they could graze all they liked overnight. Then the pair began to set up camp. Cobalt splashed happily in the water, washing away the desert sand from his body, and then flew up to investigate the treetops. First, Nalah unpacked the essential Thauma equipment that they'd been given. There was a small metal plate that only needed to have kindling placed upon it to burst into flames, and a canvas shelter that unfolded from a square the size of Nalah's hand. Soren knelt stiffly by the pool of clear water, shooed a few ruby-red lizards out of the way, and began to fill their bigger-on-the-inside waterskins.

There was a rustle of movement from the thick bushes on the other side of the oasis.

Nalah looked up sharply. "What was that?" she said.

Soren shook his head and shrugged.

Nalah squinted into the darkness. For a moment, there seemed to be nothing there, but then she saw a pair of glinting yellow eyes watching her warily. A large pair of furry ears twitched, and Nalah realized she was looking at a desert fox. Nalah sighed with relief. The animal drank from the oasis, lapping at the water with its pink tongue, then vanished into the undergrowth. The fox wasn't alone—Nalah looked up to see Cobalt cocking his head at a couple of sandpipers that were roosting up in the shelter of the trees. The other birds didn't seem to know what to make of him.

Relieved, Nalah went back to her preparations. But still, she couldn't shake the feeling that she was being watched. *You're just being paranoid*, Nalah told herself.

Nalah pulled out a silver compass and tried to remember how Lord Helavi said it worked. The arrow under its glass face swung this way and that, and she followed it to one of the trees. Sure enough, she looked up and found herself underneath a canopy of ripe wild apricots. Smiling, she picked an armful and carried them back to camp.

"Oh, awesome," said Soren, stretching out beside the

fire and taking one of the small orange fruits. He bit into it and made a small, happy grunting sound as he chewed. It vaguely reminded Nalah of the camels.

She bit into her own apricot and was starting to relax when there was another crunch and rustle from the undergrowth just behind her. Nalah turned to look, thinking it was another desert fox, but there was nothing there.

But while she was staring into the brush, something moved in the corner of her eye. It almost looked like heat haze—like a column of air had rippled, just for a second.

"Hey, Soren?" she asked. "Do you get mirages at oases? At night?"

"I don't think so." Soren frowned. "Why?"

Nalah shook her head. "Maybe it's nothing. . . ."

But then she saw it again, down by the edge of the water. There were ripples on the surface, as if a lizard or something had just jumped in, but right above them there were ripples in the world, too. As Nalah watched, there was a very faint shimmer in the air, as if something invisible was reflecting the flickering light of the fire.

The shimmering, Nalah had seen it before. But where?

In the next moment, she realized exactly what it was.

A shadow cloak.

That's where she'd seen it before. She'd seen it from the other side, when she and Marcus had escaped the palace under his family's cloak of invisibility.

There was someone else here with them. Someone who

wanted to see them but not be seen.

Nalah's whole body tensed. She could barely breathe, but she forced herself to look away from the shimmer and act as if she hadn't seen it.

Was it Malek? Could he have followed them all this way? Or was it someone else, someone who had been absent from the Magi City for a while, biding his time . . . ?

It can't be. Why would Tam be here now?

She scooted across the sand, a little closer to Soren, and handed him another apricot.

Whoever it is, they're watching us. Will they hurt us if they think I know they're here?

Nalah nudged Soren.

"Hmm?" he said, his mouth full of fruit.

Nalah said nothing, but she stared at the spot where the cloak was as hard as she could, widening her eyes. To her relief, Soren didn't start asking her what she was doing—he seemed to understand. He looked toward the same place, frowning. At first, he shook his head. He couldn't see it. Nalah bit her lip and prepared to say something—and then Soren sat up slowly, and he looked from Nalah to the spot by the water and back again.

Nalah nodded. She watched the shimmer for a moment, and it still didn't move. She had to risk communicating more clearly. She pointed to Soren, and then to the water, and then to herself, and then made a circular motion.

You go down there and distract it—I'll creep up behind.

At least, that was what she meant. She could only hope that Soren got the message.

If Halan were here, she thought longingly, *we'd be able to do this with our telepathy, no problem.*

Nalah stood up and wandered over to the bushes, pretending to be using the silver compass to search for more fruit. She waited until Soren had gone to the water's edge and was dipping his fingers in before turning back and, as quietly as she could, sneaking up on where she saw the ripples in the air. She got as close as she dared and then, slowly, reached out a hand until her fingertips brushed against something invisible.

She concentrated, imagining the tight weave of the fabric, the silky threads twisted up into a complex pattern. She wished she'd asked Marcus more about how shadow cloaks were made. This was going to be a pretty crude solution, but it would have to do.

She grabbed a handful of the cloak and sent a blast of power through it. The weave at the edges of the fabric shuddered and loosened, and the hood of the cloak fell down around the figure's shoulders in a cascade of unraveling midnight-blue silk.

"Ay!" said a voice. A floating head appeared in the air in front of Nalah. It glared down at her in consternation, and Nalah was surprised to find that not only was it not Malek, and not Tam, but she didn't recognize it at all. It was a man's head, with very deep brown skin and close-cropped gray hair. "What has the girlchild done?" he snapped.

"Who are you?" Nalah replied, taking a few steps backward. "Why are you watching us?"

"Nalah . . . ," said Soren, "he's not alone."

Nalah turned, and then stumbled back as all around her, heads began to appear from thin air as shadow cloak hoods were drawn back. The effect was eerie. There were five—no, *ten*—people in the clearing, men and women, young and old, even a small child. They all had either very short or very long dark hair, cut to almost-bald or pinned up in elaborate braids.

"Um . . . hello," Nalah said, changing tack as fast as she could. "I'm sorry. We didn't mean any harm. I thought you were going to attack us."

"Why should we attack the traveler?" asked a young woman whose hair was shorn as short as the older man's.

"I thought you were someone else," Nalah said.

Several of the heads turned and muttered to one another. They all seemed to be speaking the common tongue—the language that Nalah knew as Hadari, the only one she'd heard spoken in the Magi Kingdom—but their phrases were all slightly different. She heard "they hail from that city," and one of the women telling the small child "keep you back," and "see the man, he ben hurt."

"You have unrobed Father!" said the same young woman, and although Nalah couldn't *see* her put her hands on her hips, she got the very strong impression that she had done so. "His robe must rewoven be!"

"Mantis, you miss the vital point," said an older woman, the one whose floating head was closest to the child's. "The girlchild ben a *Star*! We must bring them to Falcon." Her head bobbed closer to Nalah. "What ben your names?"

Nalah glanced at Soren, who shrugged. "I'm Nalah Bardak," she said. "This is Soren Ferro. We're on our way to the Talons. Where . . . ?" But she trailed off. What should she ask these people who had appeared out of thin air?

"I ben Jackal," the woman said. "Our people ben the Shadows. Come you on and meet our Weaver, Falcon."

"All right," Nalah said, partly because she suspected she didn't have a choice. "Is it far?"

The young woman called Mantis snorted. "Far? We ben afraid the travelers might ride right through us," she said. She pulled up her hood and her face vanished. One by one, each of the Shadows melted back into the air with a shimmer—except for Mantis's father, who gave Nalah a last irritated look, then turned and bobbed away toward the edge of the oasis.

Jackal stayed behind, and her head began to move in a strange way, twisting this way and that. Suddenly Nalah realized what she was doing—a shoulder became visible, then an arm, and then the rest of her. She was wearing a loose, sleeveless black tunic that stretched from her neck to her bare feet. Her braided hair was piled up on her head, but the longest ends still stretched almost down to her knees. She threw the shadow cloak over her arm, and now that it was in its visible state, Nalah saw that it wasn't a cloak at all, but a robe with sleeves, a full skirt, and a huge hood. No wonder these people were able to remain completely invisible!

"Follow you," she said, beckoning. After a moment of confusion, Nalah realized she meant *you should follow* and hurried after her. She picked up her pack and her sword, but quickly slung it across her back, making sure to show that she wasn't planning on using it.

Jackal isn't armed, she thought. *Maybe none of them are.* Nalah had a strong feeling that these people could be trusted.

As they followed Jackal farther and farther from the fire, the starlit desert spread out in front of them. She seemed to be walking toward nothing, a flat and open space. Nalah frowned. Where was the head of the old man? She should be able to spot him if he'd gone this way, shouldn't she?

Jackal clapped her hands and proclaimed to the empty desert: "Hiyo! I bring visitors. One of them ben a Star! Open your doors!"

As she watched the scene in front of her unfold, Nalah's mouth fell open in awe. She knew, of course she did, that the Shadows *must* be using the shadow cloth to hide themselves, and that they couldn't have come to the oasis on foot with no supplies. But she wasn't expecting *this*.

A shard of light appeared in front of her, as if the air

itself had split. A small girl, visible in the same kind of long tunic as Jackal wore, stepped out through the light. She held a corner of seemingly nothing and tied it up to seemingly nothing, leaving a glowing portal in the air. Inside, Nalah could see the interior of a tent, warmly lit by glowing Thauma lanterns and lined with rugs.

One by one, all across the desert, the tents of the Shadows were opened. People came out to look at Nalah, some floating heads and some floating torsos of people wearing their shadow robes open to the waist, and others completely visible in the same long tunics, their shoulders and feet bare. Glowing doorways opened in a scattered constellation around a larger central doorway. Jackal led them toward it, and as they passed one of the outer tents, Nalah peered inside and saw that it held a whole stable—a large cart and a string of camels with silvery-pale coats.

Nalah tried to imagine how many yards of shadow cloth must have been made to hide an entire encampment and clothe all its people. Then she thought of how much money all that cloth would fetch in New Hadar, where the Cutter family cloak was a rare and precious heirloom, and she felt rather dizzy.

The dizziness only got worse as she stepped through the large tent's doorway into a bright, exotic-smelling space. A small crowd of people sat in a circle around a Thauma fire, again showing various degrees of visible skin, reclining on furs and beautifully embroidered cushions. Some of them were making crafts of various kinds, embroidering fabric, carving wood, or twisting lengths of metal wire into fascinating shapes. One of them was Mantis's father, still just a grumpy-looking floating head.

Nalah looked up, and she could see the shimmering tent above her. Like being under a shadow cloak, it was visible but slightly see-through. The stars shone clearly overhead. She glanced back at Soren, and he was looking up too. Awestruck, but with worrisome dark rings under his eyes.

"Weaver," said Jackal, with a sweeping gesture that brought her hand in a graceful circle around her face, palm out. "I bring the girlchild Star, Nalah Bardak. She and her man ben traveling to the Black Thorn Mountains."

All the faces around the fire turned to look at Nalah, staring with unconcealed amazement.

"Does . . . does Star mean Fifth Clan Thauma?" Nalah asked. "That I can make things with my hands?"

Jackal nodded.

"But . . . how did you know?" Nalah asked.

"How could you not know?" Jackal responded.

"Approach you, Starchild," said a deep, commanding voice.

The man who had spoken wasn't dressed any differently from the others around the circle. He wasn't wearing a crown or any distinguishing mark. He wasn't even particularly old—perhaps forty or fifty.

Still, as soon as he spoke, Nalah knew she was in the presence of a leader. This must be Falcon, the Weaver. He sat with the kind of poise she recognized from watching Queen Rani. There was a pile of shadow cloth at his feet, and in front of him there was a sort of low, lap-sized loom. His hands worked all the time as Nalah walked slowly toward him, the shuttle speeding back and forth, silvery-black threads weaving together to create the fabric even as Nalah watched.

"We not seen a Star in many generations," said Falcon. "Very welcome be indeed, Starchild." He dipped his head in a gesture of respect.

There was something strange about this reaction, and in the next breath, Nalah realized what it was—the Weaver was happy to see her, but he wasn't especially surprised. Even though they hadn't encountered a Fifth Clan Thauma in probably hundreds of years, there was no doubt in the Shadows' eyes when they looked at her, and no shock.

"Understand I that you unwove Spider's hood," Falcon went on with a wry smile. "Tell me, who did you think he ben, that you needed to treat him so?"

Nalah swallowed. How much should she tell him about Tam and Malek? How much of Magi City politics did these Shadow people understand?

"There's a Thauma lord, a fabricworker, who kidnapped us when we tried to leave the city. He hurt us," she said, and waited for his reaction, to see if "Thauma lord" would need explaining.

Apparently it didn't, because a look of deep distaste crossed Falcon's face. He spat into the fire.

"The *Thauma lords*," he said. An echoing grumble passed through the men and women in the circle, and even Spider seemed to be glaring at Nalah with slightly less of an angry scowl. "From the Thauma lords, you ben safe among the Shadows. Sit you down in the Circle, children," said Falcon. "And tell I the story of our clan."

The men and women in the circle shuffled to make room for Nalah and Soren, and they sat down on a large, soft black fur. Nalah noticed Soren wince as he sat, and she threw him a worried look, but he smiled back at her and gave her a thumbs-up.

"Just a flesh wound, remember?"

Nalah rolled her eyes and focused on the Weaver.

"Listen you well," said Falcon. "Before the world ben broken, lived our ancestors all in the Magi City. They ben Thauma, some of them *lords*, but many common folk, crafters and traders. When the storms raged, the sky ben choked with sand, and the power flowed more fierce than ever before. In that time, the city turned on itself. The lords hoarded food and water in the palace. Mad with power and fear, raided they the city and killed any who would deny them their looting."

Nalah frowned. "I thought . . . sorry," she said, "but all

the stories I was told are about how they persevered and rebuilt the city."

"Doubt I not," said Falcon, shaking his head. "And some, indeed, some helped the needy and forged great works. But many more turned to tyranny and fear to rule over the powerless."

"The royal family," said Soren. He glanced at Nalah. "My father looked into Tam's ancestors when he first realized he was becoming a tyrant. He discovered that the royal family were some of the worst during the Year of Storms. Asa Tam came from a long line of despots."

Falcon was nodding. "And so, instead of digging down, abandoned we our ancestral homes, lord and commoner alike, and swore that no more division of rank would ever be among our people. Ever since, traveled we the world, under the canopy and protection of the stars."

All the Shadows in the circle looked up at the constellations through the shadow cloth, and a slight sigh went through the tent.

"Now come you to us, Starchild, and talk we of your journey—but first . . ." He looked up at Jackal. "Tell you the clan, gather they for the meal. We will have song and dance beneath the stars and welcome we our honored guests."

Nalah and Soren were ushered outside the tent and found themselves beside a large cooking fire that had sprung up while they were looking the other way. Twenty or thirty people were already there, young and old, and more were coming in from the outlying tents. All of them had taken off the shadow robes and were wearing the same long, black, sleeveless tunics. Some of them tended to the fire and the food, passing around morsels of seared fruit and meat whenever they were ready. On one side of the fire, a group began to sing.

"The color of fate ben gold and black,
To push you on and call you back,
Knows the wise woman the length of the thread,
But knows not the end, except for the dead."

The song was so beautiful, it caught in Nalah's throat, and she found tears springing to her eyes. Their voices were a mix of pure and wobbly and tuneful and not, but the murmuring voices of those who couldn't sing so well didn't seem to take away from the song itself—it made it feel more real. Harmonies wove around each other, taking the song in new and unexpected directions.

Falcon emerged from the large tent and sat down with the singing group, lending his deep, rumbling voice to the song. Soren and Nalah sat down nearby and ate hot, sweet goat's meat served on salty flatbreads. And they listened.

The song was about fate and loss and prophecy. It finished, and another started up, and this one was about the pleasure of life, of food and drink and friends and family.

At the next song, Soren gasped.

"I know this . . . ," he said. "At least, I know the tune, but the words are different. This is an old, old Thauma song." He swallowed and then hesitantly began to sing along. His voice, Nalah noticed with a smile, was just as lovely as his face. The group of singers beamed and gestured for him to come over and join them. Nalah nudged him very gently.

"Go!" she said.

Soren got up and joined the singers. The songs were so captivating, and some of the Shadows began to dance, ecstatic grins on their faces. A young woman with beautiful dark eyes and her hair cut down to a shadow on her scalp came over to where Soren stood and grabbed his hand, pulling him into the dance. Soren laughed as he spun with her, the firelight dancing in his eyes reminding Nalah of the dashing, mischievous young man she'd first met.

"So, Starchild," said a voice, and Falcon sat down beside her. "What brings you to the desert? How bides the Magi Kingdom?"

Nalah took a very deep breath, deeper than she thought she had taken in a long time, filling her chest with pure, chilled desert air. The Shadows had welcomed her and Soren so warmly, she knew she owed Falcon the truth about her journey. But where to start?

"It's a long story," she said. "Do you know what a tawam is?"

She told him everything. About the two worlds, about

New Hadar, about Halan and the rebels, about Tam and Malek's blood cloak, and then about the fire and the vision in the crystal orb.

"I am Fifth Clan—a Star," she said finally. "And I should be able to do so much, to *help* people. But every time I try, I just make everything worse."

Falcon nodded, considering her story. He had listened intently to all of it, and now his large face creased into a frown. "It hurts my heart to hear a Star speak so," he said. "Tell you me, Nalah. You ben afraid of your power, yes?"

The question hit Nalah deep in her chest, and she almost broke out in tears, but she looked down at her feet and tried to hold it together. She nodded.

"Look you up," said Falcon gently. "Look you to my brother bird, up above."

Nalah wasn't sure she could raise her eyes without crying, but she made herself try. Up in the sky, glinting silver and gold from the starlight and the firelight, Cobalt wheeled and swooped.

"Ben he afraid of falling?" asked Falcon.

Nalah swallowed. "I don't think so."

"No, he ben not." Falcon chuckled. "It is very clear. Your bird . . . he ben a bird, and knows he how to fly. You, Nalah—you ben a Star. Have faith, child. When the time comes, you will know how to shine."

Tears spilled over Nalah's cheeks, hot and clean, but she was surprised to find she didn't disbelieve him.

Falcon left her after a while and went back to the singing. The fire burned low, and the air became cold. The singers' breath clouded in front of their faces as they started up what sounded like the last song of the night.

"Wherever the wind and the sand may blow
Know we this truth, wherever we go
Keep we our memories, keep we our love
And see you again under blue skies above."

Soren was still singing along, picking up the tune and the words as he went, and when the song finally came to an end, the singers embraced him. The young woman he'd been dancing with even kissed him on the cheek, and for once, it was Soren who was blushing.

"Come you both," said Jackal. "Start your journey early tomorrow—sleep in our camp. A tent ben prepared."

Nalah grinned with relief—the songs and food and talk had been exhilarating, but now her eyelids were drooping. She forced them open long enough to follow Jackal on a path that wove across the desert, moving between the invisible tents. Jackal opened a door, and inside there was a small space, dim and warm-looking, just large enough for her and Soren to stretch out comfortably side by side on a thick and inviting pile of furs. She crawled inside and lay there, looking up at the stars through the shimmering canopy of the tent.

Soren lay down next to her with a grunt of pain that sent a jolt of wakefulness through Nalah.

"Are you all right?" she said.

"I'm fine. It hurts, but that's probably just from all the dancing."

Nalah tsk-tsked.

Soren grinned wolfishly and shrugged. "Hey, a dance with a pretty girl is worth a bit of pain. I'll be fine, little mother—I just need a rest." He rolled onto his back with another small grunt and then let out a long, deep sigh. "This is incredible," he said. "These people . . . Scorpion told me that they've traveled thousands and thousands of miles across the Sand Sea."

"Scorpion?" Nalah asked. "Is that her name?"

Soren smiled at the sky. "Yes," he said dreamily. "She said they've met people out there from other places! Your Provinces, and the other one, Ihktiyan. They're out there, Nalah. Somewhere."

He sighed again.

"Look, do you see that constellation there, the tight circle of stars with the line trailing off to the left? We call that the Spinning Wheel. I used to lie out on the roof at night sometimes, when I was small, with my father. After Mother died, he—" Soren paused and swallowed. "We used to look at the stars together a lot. I wish . . ." He trailed off.

Nalah didn't need to hear the end of his thought. She knew exactly what it was. The pain of losing her father was still fresh, like a deep wound that never healed. She used to hate how protective he was of her, but now she missed that feeling of safety that she used to feel in his arms.

"I miss my parents so much," she said, hugging herself. "I just hope that I'm—I'm doing the right things. I think I am." She thought of what Falcon had told her, and another tear ran slowly from her eye and tickled her earlobe as it fell. "I think they would be proud."

"They would," said Soren.

Soren led an entire revolution just to avenge Lord Ferro's death, the beloved father whose life had ended under Tam's tyrannical rule. "You know what, Soren?" she said.

"What?" he said, his voice soft with sleep.

"I think your father would be proud too."

If he said any more, Nalah didn't hear him. Her eyes drifted shut once more, and for a moment she was flying over the desert with the rising heat under her feathers, and then she wasn't anywhere at all.

Chapter Eleven

Halan

The Hokmet Tower was built during the reconstruction after the Great Quake. Originally meant to replace the royal palace, which had been almost completely destroyed, it was finished after the last king died and the first minister, Master Kalhor, took power. Its design is ambitious and modern, debatably an intentional move to intimidate its citizens. Tours are available by appointment.

From A Guide to New Hadar, Jewel of the Hadar Sea

"Are you ready for this?" Marcus asked. He pulled the Veil of Shadows gingerly out of his bag, the midnight-blue silk wavering in the air.

Halan swallowed. She looked down at the Thauma artifacts laid out on the floor of the little room above the men's clothing store.

The morning sunlight was streaming in through a dirty window, diffuse and strange. The daytime in New Hadar was just as cloud streaked and cool and damp as the night had been. Marcus and Halan had gotten up before the sun and snuck out of his family's apartment, the Thauma satchel heavy at Halan's side with the various things they had stuffed into its deceptively roomy interior. Marcus had led her to a side street that lay in the immense shadow of the Hokmet Tower. He'd namedropped the Trust to the shopkeeper, and the man had paled and ushered them upstairs.

Now it was almost time. Halan wriggled her shoulders and pulled at the strange shapes of the formal dress Marcus had "borrowed" from Marit—it was stiff and square shouldered, and a single plain creamy beige color with no trim or buttons or *anything*, and it didn't fit properly in a couple of places. Halan looked at herself in the dusty mirror that'd been propped in the corner of the room and thought it made her look old. Which was perfect.

She sighed. "Let me do the shoes first," she told Marcus, and sat down on a creaky chair to pull on a pair of unassuming flat shoes. They didn't look like anything special, but the enchantments laced into them were powerful Thauma magic indeed. She remembered the advice Marcus had given her earlier and did not look down at her feet as she stood up again. She knew if she did, they would appear to be touching the floor even though she felt as if she was standing on wedges about six inches high.

It felt very odd to have suddenly grown as tall as her mother. At least now the bottom of Marit's dress didn't drag along the floor when she walked.

"All right," Halan said, turning to Marcus. "Let's do this."

"Okay, here we go," Marcus said. He had to reach up to tie the Veil of Shadows around her head. Halan suppressed a deep shudder.

The last time I wore one of these, I was a hostage, she thought. Soren had made her a prisoner in her own body, with the face of a girl who'd been scarred by Dust. Even Tam hadn't recognized her. He'd almost killed her.

And yet, as painful as it had been, she was grateful too. Without that glimpse into life as an ordinary citizen, one who'd been mistreated and abused, she might not have realized that Tam had to be stopped.

"Like I said," Marcus muttered, tying the ribbon around the back of Halan's head, "this is *much* less strong than the ones in the Magi Kingdom. It'll wear off in a couple of hours. So we need to be in and out by then."

Halan closed her eyes, trying to control her breathing as the veil's magic took hold. The skin across her face tingled and rippled, rearranging her features. It wasn't quite as awful as the last time, but that wasn't saying much—it still left Halan feeling weird and a little sick. She took a few deep, steadying breaths and leaned on Marcus's shoulder as the feeling passed. Then she opened her eyes and looked into the mirror again. The woman who looked back at her was middle-aged, with lines around her eyes and dark brown hair that fell in a short bob to her chin.

"And you're sure this woman is a member of the Hokmet? And it really looks like her?" Halan asked.

"It's the best I could do," Marcus said, and Halan threw him a *really?* look. Marcus grinned back. "Don't worry. I'm good."

Halan rolled her eyes and picked up the satchel. "All right. Queen Halan, rebel and Thauma spy, reporting for duty. Put on your shadow cloak and let's go."

Even though she knew he was following close behind her, invisible underneath the Thauma fabric, Halan felt very alone as she stepped out into the sunlit square in front of the Hokmet Tower. From this close, it looked even more forbidding. Its shadow stretched for what seemed like miles—from the top of the tower you could have used its position to tell the time, like a sundial the size of an entire city.

There were other people in the square, all of them heading into the building—adult men and women in stiff fabrics and muted colors, a sea of hats and head scarves and satchels and square cases.

They seemed so . . . mundane. Just ordinary people, going to their workplace to do their job. Halan glanced around at the faces and wondered which of them were going to some everyday task and which of them were looking for ways to wipe out the Thauma who shared their city. Did they all believe the Thauma were inferior and dangerous? Or did they just not care as long as they and their families were safe? They were just regular, innocent people.

Weren't they?

Or was witnessing evil and doing nothing about it just as bad as doing it yourself?

Halan steeled herself for what was coming and walked toward the huge open doors in the base of the tower—not too slow, not too fast. She tried to look important and bored—luckily, she had quite a bit of experience with that.

The enormous double doors were wooden, painted gold, and carved with elaborate geometric patterns, reminiscient of something from the Magi City. Inside, the entrance hall was cavernous, with a paved sandstone floor that sent her footsteps echoing off the bare white walls. Little groups of people stood all around, talking in low voices. A spiral staircase rose in the center of the room, and Halan suspected it went all the way to the top, like the screw in a cork about to be pulled from a bottle.

"Papers," said a bored voice. Halan saw the man in the Enforcer uniform, and her heart lurched in fear. It was the same Enforcer who had followed Marcus to the Magi City. *It's over and I'm barely through the door!* Halan thought in a panic. *He'll recognize me for sure!* It took a few seconds before Halan remembered that she was completely disguised by the veil. She ordered herself to calm down, arrange her face into a mask of indifference, and reach into one of the pockets of her satchel, taking her time about it. She pulled out the folded paper and held it out to him with a look she hoped said, *I know there are no problems with my papers, because I don't have time for you.* Inside, her heart was trying to climb up inside her mouth, and she could feel sweat collecting around the rim of the invisible veil.

She distracted herself by studying the man's face as he looked at her papers. He had a large and colorful bruise half hidden underneath his cap where she had hit him with the glassworking pole. He must have been found in Nalah's house, and now he was assigned to door duty. He didn't look very happy about it.

I hope he's miserable, Halan thought, and the flare of fear turned to anger. *This man broke my mirror! He's the reason I can't go home!*

The Enforcer sighed and handed her papers back to her. "Thank you, Minister Torabi," he said, and his gaze slipped to the person walking through the doors behind her. "Papers?"

Halan walked away, counting five steps before she allowed herself to breathe again. She started slipping the paper back into the pocket.

"Nice work," whispered Marcus's voice close behind her, and Halan jumped just a little and dropped the paper. She bent down and scooped it up before anyone else could see it. It would *probably* have shown them the same as it showed the Enforcer: official Hokmet papers that matched the face they were looking at. But she couldn't be completely sure. It might have been blank!

"You can tell Master Ansari his Thauma paper works," she said into her sleeve as she stood up.

"Like a charm," said Marcus. "Now, there should be—"

"Minister Torabi!" called a young woman's voice. Halan froze. She *knew* that voice. Plastering her face with the most self-important frown she could muster, she turned and saw a figure hurrying across the entrance hall toward her.

It was Ester, her friend from the laundry back in the palace—but it wasn't. The real Ester was still there, somewhere in the Magi City, probably enjoying some time off with her new fiancé, the handsome armsman she'd fallen in love with many months ago.

This girl was New Hadar's version of Ester—her tawam!

Not everybody from the two worlds had a tawam— Ester's ancestors must have survived the quakes, met and had children, and their children met the same people and had children, and on down the generations, for hundreds of years. Halan was strangely pleased for Ester that she had a sister she had yet to meet.

She only hoped this girl was as kind as her twin.

The girl was dressed in a style that reminded Halan of Marcus's mother: a white blouse and long brown skirt, her dark hair rolled up into large curls at the nape of her neck.

"Minister Torabi, do you have a moment?" she asked. She was carrying a board with papers clipped to it and was avoiding direct eye contact. *Does she work under me? Am I her boss? What does she want?*

When in doubt, Halan thought, recalling her mother's advice during uncertain moments like these, *just act like you know what you're doing*.

Halan drew herself up to her full, magically augmented height and tilted her head.

"Yes, what is it?"

"Have you had a chance to read my report about the vultures? I wondered if you had any thoughts about the funding problems."

Vultures. Funding problems. Okay. Halan covered her nerves with an impatient sigh.

"You know, I really agree with you, but I'm just not sure there's money in the budget for it," she said, with a sad shake of her head, parroting something she had heard surprisingly often in the few weeks she had been queen. *Bless you and your ideas about economic responsibility, Lord Helavi.*

Ester's face fell, and Halan tried to remind herself that this wasn't Ester. This girl worked in the Hokmet of all places, the source of who knew what terrors for Marcus and his family! She gazed into her friend's face and wondered if she even knew what was happening elsewhere in this building.

"But what about the Cultural Fund," Ester pleaded. "Are you sure there's no money to be had from them? This is so important!"

"That may be true," Halan said, keeping up her

impression of Lord Helavi's patient, considerate, but iron-firm grip on the purse strings of power. *Bless your sandals and your books and your entire family, unto the tenth generation.* "But the budget is what it is. I understand that the vultures are a real problem, so I suggest you look into other ways to reduce their number. . . ."

A suspicious frown crossed Ester's face, and Halan's mouth immediately went dry.

"*Reduce?*" she said. "Minister, did you read my report? We need to *increase* the number of vultures in the city; losing any more would have untold effects for the other wildlife, not to mention what it would do to the—"

"Y-yes, yes, of c-course—I . . . ," Halan stuttered, trying to recover from her mistake. Then suddenly there was an almighty crash from the other side of the room. A large and probably very expensive vase had fallen off a plinth and shattered on the floor. A crowd was gathering around it, and Ester's tawam cringed when she turned to look. "I really need to be going," Halan said, desperately casting around for an escape.

"Yes, Minister, I should . . . ," Ester said, gesturing toward the scattered porcelain.

Halan didn't stick around to say good-bye. She hurried, as fast as she could while still wearing the Thauma platform shoes, toward the spiral staircase.

"Boy, that was fun," whispered Marcus's voice behind her as she started up the steps. "Not often you get to throw a priceless vase on the floor! That'll keep them scratching their heads for a while."

They reached the second floor and found themselves on a landing, surrounded by doors.

"Quick," Marcus muttered. "While there's no one here, try it out!"

Halan reached into the satchel, as far as her arm would go, and pulled out a pair of spectacles with perfectly round, blue-tinted lenses. She slipped them on and immediately found herself in darkness so complete there seemed to be no up or down. She could see only one thing: Marcus. Or rather, she could see a bright yellow light in the shape of a person, standing right in front of her. The figure was surrounded by a softer blue glow, which must be the shadow cloak he was wearing. Both shapes were wavering slightly at the edges, giving out a sort of trail like an ink pen pulled through water. The yellow trail led to her right and then down and around in a spiral pattern, tracing the path Marcus had taken up the stairs. As she watched, the oldest end of the trail started to fade.

She pulled the glasses off again and blinked in the glare of the artificial lighting.

"No other Thauma on this floor," she muttered. "Come on, let's keep moving up. We've got to hurry."

They climbed to the next floor, and Halan put the glasses on again. This time she did see some colored light, but it was very faint and unmoving—too small to be a person.

"There are Thauma artifacts in one of these rooms," she said.

Marcus snorted, and she saw his yellow Thauma shadow fold its arms. "Of course there are. The Hokmet are such hypocrites. Perfectly happy to use Thauma *things*; they just don't want the *people*."

There was nothing at all on the fourth, fifth, or sixth floors. When they reached the seventh floor, they had to keep going up to the eighth, because there was a group of ministers having a fiery argument at the top of the stairs. Halan looked down from the eighth floor and couldn't see anything. Then she thought to look up and saw there were a few faint traces of Thaumaturgic energy on the floors above, various colors standing out against the blackness. How many of them were just objects and how many might be people?

There was only one way to find out.

They kept climbing, stopping whenever it was safe for Halan to put on the glasses and scan the area for more Thauma energy. But at every floor, she still saw only traces of light—nothing definite.

Then suddenly, on the thirteenth floor, a faint blue trail that she had been seeing from below was laid out in front of her. Here it was strong and bright, and they followed it up the stairs to the next floor and then to the door of one of the rooms, where it coalesced into the form of a man inside. He was moving back and forth—pacing, Halan thought—filling the room with swirling Thauma essence.

She tore the glasses off and stood next to the closed door of the room, panting with exertion. "Found one," she whispered to the empty air, uncertain just where Marcus was standing.

"What? Where?" asked Marcus from right next to her ear.

"Inside this room," she said.

"Only one?" Marcus asked, the disappointment clear in his voice. The likelihood that this one Thauma was Marcus's brother was slim to none—and the fact that the person was found on this high level of the building was suspect. Could Halan's guess have been correct? Was there, in fact, a Thauma working for the Hokmet? There was only one way to find out.

Her fingers found a smooth metal funnel in the bottom of the bag. She tried to control her breathing and move silently as she approached the door and placed the wide end of the funnel on it, and then pressed her ear to the small end.

"—more you expect from us, Obsidian," said a sardonic man's voice, as clear as if he had been standing right beside Halan. "Thanks to you, Maktum is almost full, and the city streets are virtually free of Thauma. But how many more of them could you possibly need?"

Maktum? Halan thought.

"I don't like it," said another man's voice, this one weak

and anxious. "That many Thauma all in one place . . . what if they all band together? They could blow up Maktum, take out the forest and half the Warehouse District with it—"

"Dejagah, I've told you," the first man broke in. "Obsidian has the situation there completely under control. What I want to know is, when are we going to start seeing the results of this marvelous new process? I don't mind telling you, the ministers are getting quite impatient, and some of them are very unhappy about this whole business. They feel it's . . . *inhumane*, and we should go back to just keeping a register and enforcing the regulations."

"Nostalgia for the old days," said the one called Dejagah dismissively. "Or else they have Thauma friends and relatives they haven't disclosed. It's sentimental garbage, if you ask me—but if you have a way to get rid of these Thauma scum once and for all, I'd feel a lot better if you got on with it already."

A voice replied, but it was muffled. Halan gritted her teeth in frustration, held her breath and listened as hard as she could, her heartbeat pounding in her throat. But the voice was still muffled. She thought she might have heard words like *patience*—unless it was *patients*—and *reward*. But it was no good. She pulled back and glared at the funnel in her hand. Was the man calling to the first two from another room? Perhaps it didn't work if—

Then she heard footsteps, even without the funnel, and

she threw herself away from the door so fast she didn't bother to work out where Marcus was standing. "Go go go," she hissed, then she reached the stairs and hurried down them as fast and as quietly as she could in the Thauma shoes. Thirteenth floor. Twelfth. She slowed down, listening. Someone else was on the stairs, but she couldn't see who it was.

"We've got what we need to know," she whispered, hoping Marcus would hear. "Let's get out of here!" She walked down the rest of the stairs, trying to recapture her air of importance, while her heart beat like a drum and her mind raced.

Maktum. The forest. The Warehouse District. That must be enough for someone who knows this city well enough to know where to look!

The Thauma are being kept there. They're together, and for now—they're alive.

And a Thauma called Obsidian has been helping the Hokmet locate and capture them. It sounds like he has some sort of plan for them . . . but what?

She wished that she'd been able to hear the man's voice or see his face. The face of someone who would sell out his own kind.

I'll get my chance, before this journey is over, she thought. *And I'll be sure to give that traitor a piece of my mind.*

She crossed the hall slowly, half hoping that Marcus would say something so she would know for sure he was still with her. The sun was streaming in through the huge doorway, and after the dim artificial light inside, it called to Halan. She made a beeline for it. Just as Halan was heading out, there was a woman coming in. She was presenting her papers to the Enforcer on the door.

Halan's heart lurched as she recognized the woman's face—it was the same one she was wearing right now. The *real* Minister Torabi.

No, Halan thought, her mind racing. *I'm so close. . . . I can't get caught now!* She quickly turned her face away, pretending to pick at a loose thread on her dress while she tried to think.

To make matters worse, she began to feel the veil on her face ripple—the magic was starting to wear off. What would happen if someone caught a glimpse of her face changing from one to another?

Nothing good, she thought.

"Marcus," she whispered into the air, hoping he was close. "Minister Torabi, she's here. You have to tell me when she's looking the other way so I can sneak out."

Several tense moments passed in silence. Halan tried to keep breathing.

And then, a small voice in her ear saying: "Now."

Halan put her head down and strode toward the door. Because of the crowd, she had to pass directly by Minister Torabi, who was bending to speak to the Enforcer about something. Just as she was walking by her, a man pushed through the crowd, bumping into Halan—who then bumped into Minister Torabi.

The minister stood up to glare at Halan, and for a split second, their eyes met.

Halan muttered an apology before turning away and hurrying out of the building in a flash. With the New Hadar sunshine on her face, Halan was about to breathe a sigh of relief when a woman's voice called out.

"Hey! You there!"

Halan froze in place. She could feel the veil rippling on her face, and she reached up and frantically tore at the ribbon holding it in place. Her face had just finished rearranging itself when she felt a hand grip her shoulder.

There was a look of confusion on Minister Torabi's face when Halan turned around to face her. "Oh . . . ," the woman said, her eyebrows furrowed. Halan balled the veil up in her fist and did her best impression of a bewildered, innocent girl.

"Yes?" Halan said. "Is there something wrong, ma'am?"

"No, I . . . ," the minister said, shaking her head. "I'm sorry, young lady. For a second, I thought you were somebody else."

Halan simply shrugged, smiled, and turned away. After a few steps, she snuck a look back to see Minister Torabi making her way back into the Hokmet, still shaking her head. Just like they'd practiced, Halan strolled around the corner and waited until she was all alone on a shady side street. After a minute or so, Marcus appeared beside her, and they stuffed both the veil and the cloak into the small satchel.

"Whew," Marcus said, leaning against the building. "That was close."

"Too close," Halan agreed.

"So?" Marcus asked quietly as they set off at a stride to put as much distance between themselves and the Hokmet as possible. "What did you hear in that room upstairs?"

Halan grinned at him, enjoying the feeling of wearing her own face once again. "Enough," she said. "I know where to find your brother, Marcus. I know where to find them all."

Chapter Twelve

Nalah

The Talons have long been a site of great geographical, social, and spiritual importance to the Magi Kingdom. As well as the mines and quarries on the lower slopes where the mountains meet the Delta, the peaks are said to be sacred places where a brave and persistent traveler may encounter spirits and find enlightenment.

Lord Artu, The Geography of the Magi Kingdom

Nalah opened her eyes and found herself lying under a dome of perfect pale blue. Under the shadow cloth tent, it was like sitting in the shade and in the sun at the same time, cool but bright. She sat up and glanced around, and saw one or two partially unrobed Shadows moving across the desert and the still-smoking remnants of the feasting fire, but mostly she saw the bending palm trees around the oasis and, over her right shoulder, the black peaks of the Talons.

She smiled. "Soren, look! We're so much closer. How long do you think it'll take us to reach the shrine?"

"Nalah . . . ," Soren whimpered. Nalah's head whipped around and her stomach turned over. Soren was lying next to her on his side. His skin had turned ashen gray, and sweat was pricking all over his body. His handsome face was twisted in agony.

"What is it?" Nalah choked. "What happened?" She rolled him over onto his back, and he groaned loudly, his head flopping back, as if even feeling the pain was too exhausting.

It was obvious that his wound had become infected, even before she pulled aside the bandage. There was an oval-shaped yellow stain that had soaked all the way through to the top layer. Underneath, Soren's flesh was pink and swollen. When she gingerly touched it, it was hot, and a thick white substance oozed slightly from the wound.

"Soren!" Nalah moaned, fear and anger briefly overwhelming her panic. "You knew something was wrong! You knew last night and you didn't _say_ anything!"

"You're too . . . important . . . ," Soren said through gritted teeth. "You . . . need to get to . . ."

"Oh, shut up." Nalah shook her head. "Nothing is more important than your _life_, you idiot!"

She held her hands over his chest, her fingers tingling with the heat of the infection.

Suddenly, she remembered the infection that had ravaged her as a child. She remembered the weakness, the feeling of her body trying to fight a battle it wasn't ever going to win. She remembered the metal bracelet her mother had slipped around her wrist, how cool it had been against her hot skin. And she remembered her mother trying to get out of the room again before Nalah saw her tears, but she hadn't succeeded.

I could make something like that to draw it out of him, she thought. *Just like Mama did. I know it's possible.*

But the fire . . .

If her mother couldn't control the power she'd created, how could Nalah ever hope to? Especially when someone's life depended on it?

She leaped to her feet.

No. It's too risky. I'll just make it worse. I need help.

She shoved aside the flap of the tent and stumbled out into the heat of the desert. She filled her lungs and yelled at the top of her voice.

"Help! Help, please!"

Shadows melted out of the air all around her, throwing back their hoods or climbing out of their tents, staring in fright.

"Starchild, what ben wrong?" gasped Mantis, running over. Her near-bald head gleamed in the morning sun, and her shadow robe was tied around her waist so they could see her arms and chest.

"It's Soren," Nalah gasped. "His wound's infected. It's bad—"

"Stand you back," Mantis said. "Let us see him." She peeled back the flap of the tent and pinned it. Soren looked over and blinked, wincing at the light. Nalah pressed her hands to her mouth. She was afraid if she so much as breathed on the tents, her panic would set them aflame.

Jackal and Falcon came running up next, Jackal's long braids swinging loose around her knees. Falcon ducked inside the tent with Mantis, his big shoulders only just fitting through the small doorway. A moment later, the dark-eyed girl who Soren had been dancing with—Scorpion—appeared in front of the tent, lowering her hood to reveal a face full of fear. She leaned in to listen to the two older Shadows, who were talking very fast in an undertone. A moment later, Scorpion sprinted away across the desert and vanished inside a different tent.

Nalah watched all of this, her terror rising, power swirling inside her like a captive storm. She closed her eyes and balled her hands into fists, not wanting to touch anything or be touched, for fear that the storm would be released onto the world.

"Nalah," said Jackal's voice softly. "Give to me your hands."

Nalah opened her eyes and shook her head, but Jackal held out her own hands, palms up.

"You will not hurt me," she said.

Nalah slowly lowered her hands into Jackal's, and Jackal

held them gently but firmly. Nalah exhaled and felt the storm within her subside. They stood together outside the tent, while inside Mantis and Falcon went on talking in urgent, low voices. Scorpion reappeared and sprinted past, her arms full of supplies. Nalah tried to get a glimpse of what she was bringing, but her vision was blurred with tears and she couldn't seem to focus on anything at all.

"There, there, Starchild," said Jackal, and before Nalah could tense and pull away, she found herself enveloped in a hug. "Come to the Weaver tent. Falcon and Mantis will do everything they can for your friend. Come you."

Nalah had no energy to protest. She let herself be led to the cool shade and sat down, alone in the circle of cushions around a blackened wooden bowl that must have held the flame. People brought her cool water and fruit. She drank but didn't eat. Time seemed to stop moving.

Soren is going to die. The thought just wouldn't go away, no matter how she tried to ignore it. *He's going to die, and it's all my fault.* Thoughts of her father's body, limp in her arms, roared back into her mind, and Nalah felt light-headed with sorrow and despair.

When Falcon's broad form crossed the doorway into the tent, Nalah looked up at him and thought, *This is it. This is how I find out.*

"Your friend will be all right," said Falcon. Nalah gasped so hard, she choked and started coughing and then crying.

He will be all right, Nalah chanted to herself, the words

like a salve. *He will be all right.*

Falcon sat down beside her, leaning his large forearms on his knees.

"He ben very sick," he said. "But he will not ben moved, not for a few more nights. Come you and see him. Say your good-byes."

"Good-byes?" Nalah croaked, wiping away her tears.

"Go you must, on to your shrine," Falcon said, nodding solemnly. "Find you what the Seer has to tell. Your destiny ben the destiny of all of us, Starchild, and it must not be delayed. Read I this in the stars—but know you this already, I think," he added with a wry smile.

Nalah let out a heavy sigh. Then she climbed to her feet and turned to look through the shadow cloth toward the Talons.

"How am I going to do this without him?" she wondered aloud.

Falcon stood, and he leaned over and tapped her gently on the forehead and the chest.

"Listen you here, and here," he said. "And you will be all right."

Nalah ducked into the small tent. Mantis and Scorpion were both in there, still tending to Soren. His wound had been cleaned and closed with stitches that were tinier and neater than those Nalah had seen on clothes, even machine-made New Hadari clothes. The swelling had already gone down, and Mantis was preparing a new dressing while Scorpion pressed a wet rag to Soren's lips.

He looked up at Nalah, and his eyes were more open and better at focusing than they had been.

"I'm sorry, Nalah," he croaked. "I *was* an idiot."

"You were such an idiot," Nalah said with a grin, trying not to cry again. "Soren, I . . . I have to leave you here."

Soren nodded slowly. "I know. You need to find your answers," he said. "I'll be fine. Scorpion's taking care of me," he said, and a silly grin crossed his face as he looked up at the girl. Scorpion reddened and brushed a lock of Soren's wavy black hair from his eyes, a secret smile touching her lips. Beside them, Mantis rolled her eyes hugely and shook her head.

Nalah grabbed Soren's hand and squeezed. "I'll be back," she said. "I promise."

"I know you will," Soren said. "I don't think there's much you couldn't do if you tried."

Nalah flushed and punched him very, very gently in the shoulder. "Shut you up," she said.

"Thank you all, thank you so much," Nalah said, looking down at Falcon and the gathered Shadows from the saddle of her camel. She wrapped Falcon's gift around her face—a blue head scarf as soft and light as a cloud, which would keep her cool in the day and warm at night.

Falcon solemnly waved his hand in the same gesture

Jackal had made the previous night, circling his face palm out, and each of the Shadows who'd come to see her go made the gesture too. Nalah returned it as gracefully as she could and saw a broad smile cross the Weaver's face.

Then she swiveled in the saddle and focused her gaze on the Talons. Despite her earlier optimism, right now they seemed a very long way away. She had never been alone in the desert before. Would she be able to make it?

Cobalt landed on her shoulder and let out a chiming cry that sounded to Nalah like a challenge. She took a deep breath, held the reins of the camel lightly, and urged it forward.

All she had to do was follow the white fire in her memory—one rolling camel step at a time.

For the first few hours, Nalah occupied her thoughts with Halan. Like messages in a bottle, Nalah sent her thoughts out into the void, hoping that perhaps they would reach her sister somehow. She made sure to eat and drink regularly and kept her mind as alert as she could.

But by the time the sun was setting, Nalah's spirits had begun to fade. She felt wrung out and empty, like a dry sponge. The endless, unchanging desert lulled her into a stupor, and she had to struggle to keep her mind focused on the task at hand. That was why when the muffled sounds of her camel's hooves on sand turned to a louder crunching as it changed to a rocky path, it took Nalah a full ten minutes to even notice she had arrived.

She stopped for a moment, dismounting to stretch her aching legs and back. She looked up and saw the spires of the Talons rising high above her, black against the bloodred sunset. "Well, we made it," she said, turning back to the camel. She'd been having short conversations with her steed as they went, simply to fill the silence. "Are you ready for a climb?"

The camel grunted.

"I'll take that as a yes," she said. And so, leading the camel, Nalah started to climb.

The wind up on the Talons was wild and unpredictable, striking her from one angle and then another, tossing her body to and fro like a rag doll. She held the camel's reins in a tight grip, hanging on when the worst of the winds buffeted her virtually off her feet. More than once, she had thought they were completely lost among the sharp jutting rocks. But each time she would walk a few steps farther and find something that felt familiar—a particular formation in an outcrop, a new angle on the desert below, even the dry and twisted skeleton of a dead tree—and she knew she was on the right track.

"At least someone's happy," she muttered, looking up at Cobalt swinging and dipping through the air as if he were having the time of his life riding the breezes.

There was a lot more mountain below her than above now. The desert stretched away on all sides, and she could see the dark green stain of the Delta Lake to her left and the Magi City to her right. It looked so small, perched on the edge of the white Sand Sea. Most of the people who lived within those walls never left them their whole lives.

Nalah stretched out and felt her back and shoulder muscles pop in a satisfying way.

"One more push," she told the camel, picking up its reins again and urging it away from the tasty leaves of a scrubby bush that had grown out of the rock wall beside them. "Almost there."

They climbed a little longer, and when Nalah turned a sharp corner in the path, what she saw made her jaw drop. The wind immediately blew her hair into her mouth, but she didn't care.

The shrine. It was real. And she had found it.

Just like in her vision, the immense structure was nestled into the peak of the mountain, a flat, open courtyard in front of it. Its doorway was in shadow, framed by tall white pillars, cracked and half covered in hardy mountain ivy. It was a beautiful sight, but what really took Nalah's breath away were the giant figures carved from the black rock of the mountain.

They were Thauma. Four of them. Even though a couple had cracked and lost hands or noses, it was quite clear—here was a man blowing a glass bowl on a long pipe, and there was a woman with an axe in one hand, the other laid against the trunk of a tree. There was another woman with a hammer raised above her head, about to bring it down onto an anvil, and on the other side, a man sat at a loom, hand-braiding a twisting rope. The four clans, all working at their elements.

But there was a fifth figure too, placed higher up, above the rest. And it was with the sight of that figure that Nalah knew she had come to the right place. The figure was a woman with her arms open, arms that were large enough to hold all the Thauma below her. Her hands were covered in stars, and her face was upturned, staring forever into the sky above with a beatific smile.

A fifth figure, for the fifth clan. Her clan.

Cobalt flew down and flapped a few tight circles in front of the entrance, then landed on Nalah's shoulder, his talons clutching onto her tightly, his glass body tinkling as it trembled.

"You're nervous too, huh?" she said. She tied the camel up to a post that might well have been made for that once, and fed it some water and a handful of apricots. Then she took a deep breath and slung the Sword of the Fifth Clan over her back and stepped forward, climbing uneven steps into the murk beyond.

She felt the size of the cavern before she actually saw it. Something about the change in the taste and feel of the air, from the dry heat and wind outside to still, cool dampness, gave her the idea that it was an immense space. Her footsteps echoed, and then her eyes finally adjusted to the darkness.

Her whole house in New Hadar could have fit easily within the cave. The walls and arching ceiling were featureless rock, but the floor was smooth, paved with regular and polished black flagstones and coated in a layer of dust that kicked up behind Nalah as she walked.

There was only one doorway besides the one she had come in through: an archway in the far wall behind a small, empty altar.

Her heart in her mouth, Nalah set her shoulders and approached the altar. There was something written on it, underneath the dust. Nalah blew on it, sending the dust spiraling away into the darkness and revealing a message carved underneath.

"Whoever wishes to face the challenges of the Shrine, enter," Nalah read. "But you must enter alone and unarmed."

She turned her head and looked at Cobalt. He looked back, his head tilted to the side and his feathers puffing up as if in outrage. She imagined him saying, *Surely, it can't mean me!*

"I think I have to leave you here, boy," she said, pulling the sword from her back and laying it on the altar. "I must obey. Go on."

With a huff that sounded like a breath being blown over

the mouth of a bottle, Cobalt hopped onto the altar and settled down, lowering his neck into his hunched wings so that he looked more like a grumpy pigeon than a noble falcon. Nalah smiled, despite the fact that her heart was beating harder now that she would be so completely alone.

"It's okay," she said, walking around the altar and facing the door. There was even *less* light on the other side. "I'll be back soon."

She hoped those wouldn't be her famous last words.

Nalah stepped forward through the archway and found herself in a narrow corridor. It turned to the left, and then to the right, and then right again, growing so dark that Nalah had to run her hands along the walls to stop herself from walking into them.

Then suddenly she stepped into a pitch-black room, and something blue flared in front of her eyes, making her blink and shield them from the light.

There was a lamp hanging from the ceiling of this room, and it held a bright blue Thauma flame that had sprung into life as soon as Nalah had stepped inside.

Nalah noticed immediately that the room smelled woodsy, like the forest back home in New Hadar. She realized, after her eyes adjusted, that the walls and floor of this room were built with wooden panels, and that all around her, a tangled forest of trees had been painted there. The flickering light made the shadows dance between them, as if the branches were waving in a breeze. On the far side of

the room there was a door—also wooden, and heavy looking, with a silver keyhole that glinted in the light of the
Thauma lantern.

The only other object was a small wooden box, sitting
on a pedestal in the middle of the room.

Nalah cautiously moved to pick up the box, turning it
over and over in her hands.

Something rattled inside it. She noticed that there were
two small slits in the wood—through them, when she held
the box up to the light, she could see that it contained a
gleaming silver key.

But there was no lid, no hinges, not even any joins where
the wood had been put together. It was as if it had grown
on the tree in this shape, complete with the key already
inside it.

Nalah could feel her heartbeat in her fingertips as she
held the box. It was the first thing that she had ever held—
other than the Sword of the Fifth Clan—that *must* have
been made by another Fifth Clan Thauma. There was no
other way to have gotten the key inside—and there was no
other way to get it out. She was going to have to open up
the wood herself, using only her hands.

A prickle of cold sweat formed on the back of her
neck as she recalled the last time she'd tried to work with
wood.

I have no choice, she thought. *Either I am a Star, and I
pull myself together and complete this test, or I give up and*

*return to the Magi City with no answers and no hope of ever
controlling my powers.*

It should be simple. For Fifth Clan Thauma in control
of themselves, it would be the work of a moment. In fact,
she should be able to do this hardly having to think about
it, the way she had folded a plank of wood into a crude
chest on command for Soren when she had first arrived in
this world, or the way that she'd unraveled Spider's shadow
robe.

But for some reason, that thought hurt more than anything. Nalah stood holding the box between her hands,
staring at it, trying to make herself do it, but a voice in her
head kept saying, *This is so easy, this should be easy for you,
all you have to do is open it, why can't you just—*

"All right, okay," she said. "No need to be afraid. It's only
wood."

She concentrated on the feel of the grain and let the
power flow through her hands into the box. She tried to
feel the way the sap had once flowed, the rings of the tree
that showed its great age. If she could only persuade it to
warp and split apart—

It's so easy! the voice chided her again. *Why can't you
do this?*

And then, in the heat of the moment, a thought that had
long lain hidden in the depths of her mind came out, cruel
and unmerciful.

Is this what your mother sacrificed her life for?

Nalah gasped, and her hands clamped down hard on the box and twisted. The wood creaked and warped, and she felt it grow hot under her fingertips.

"No, no, *no!*" Nalah yelled, and threw the box to the floor. As it fell, it caught fire, and a few small flames licked out of the slit in the side. The flames spread to the dry wooden floor below, and before Nalah could even realize what was happening, one of the walls had caught too. The paintings of the trees cracked and blackened, as if a whole forest was burning too.

"Oh stars, no . . . ," Nalah breathed, and again, like a recurring nightmare, her world smelled of smoke and burning. She looked at the box and had a horrible thought—what if the heat of the fire melted the key? She would be stuck here, unable to move on. Quickly, she kicked dust over the box, putting out the flames. She picked it up in her hands and stared at it.

She felt paralyzed. And around her, the world burned.

Why did she have to think that, just then? Why couldn't her mind seem to let the fire go?

Forget the times it's all gone wrong, she told herself. *What about when it's gone right? When I spoke with the voice of the wind, and when I changed a coin into a key in my mouth?*

How had she done it? Had it just been that she was desperate and tired and scared for her life? She wasn't sure she wanted to re-create that state of mind.

What was it Soren had said to her?

Sacrifice. Perseverance. Mercy.

Her heart ached with longing to live up to that mantra.

"What *did* Mother sacrifice herself for?" she whispered.

The answer came to her, as clear as the answers had always been in her head when she'd looked into Rina's photograph and told her about all her problems.

For me. She gave her life for me.

If she were watching me now, Nalah wondered, *what would she see?*

And again, the answer was right there in her own heart, buried under a layer of fear and self-doubt, but it shone out clear in the darkness.

A girl who's not just alive but has done wonders, traveled to other worlds, ridden across a desert. A girl who's survived more than she could possibly have imagined.

A girl who isn't afraid to try.

Because that's what I learned from you, Mom.

Sacrifice. Perseverence. Mercy.

Her cheeks were wet with tears, but it felt good to let the feeling out.

All around her, the walls continued to burn, but Nalah ignored the heat and the smoke. She focused only on the box in front of her and what she wanted to do.

She blew out a long breath and simply let the power flow with it into the wood. She didn't grab or twist or tear. She just let go. The wood already knew how to be a box. All she needed to do was help it remember how to be a tree.

With a blast of cool air that extinguished the flames around her, the box opened up, petals of wood peeling back one at a time like a flower opening. It was beautiful. Even the scorch marks were beautiful. Nalah reached in and plucked the silver key from its heart, and smiled as she held it up to the light.

Without the heat of the flames, the room became cool and still again. Nalah slipped the silver key into the door and opened it into yet more darkness. *One down,* Nalah thought as she walked through.

As in the first room, a light flared as soon as she'd stepped over the threshold. But instead of the blue Thauma light, this was the dim orange glow of a furnace burning.

This room was a forge, equipped with an anvil as well as a roaring fire in a barred hearth. But there were no tools, no metal to melt or reforge. There was only a large clear glass jug sitting on the anvil, reflecting the dancing flames.

Strange . . .

Suddenly there was a sound—a sort of ringing, scraping sound, like a sword being sharpened. Nalah froze, looking around at the room for hidden blades coming at her from the darkness, but instead the shadows shifted and something stalked out from behind the forge.

It was a wolf. The flickering light picked out the hundreds of tiny blades that formed its coat, two serrated metal ears, and a jaw that disguised rows of metal teeth. Yellow eyes glowed like embers in its pointed face.

Nalah had never seen anything like it. Horror and awe mingled in her mind as she stood frozen in place, waiting to see what the creature would do.

The wolf crouched back, blades grinding against each other, and Nalah yelped and dived aside as it pounced, snapping at the air where her throat had been.

She landed hard and rolled to her feet as fast as she could, but the wolf was much faster, and it cornered her against the wall of the chamber. In a panic, Nalah kicked out as the wolf lunged again. The creature's snarling head twisted in midair, and its teeth closed on Nalah's leg.

She screamed. The pain spiked up through her body as the wolf's fangs sank into her flesh. Half blind with agony, Nalah threw back her head and channeled her breath into a burst of heat that struck the wolf right in the mouth. It yelped and let her go, recoiling, pawing at its face.

Nalah took the opportunity to dive for the door back into the forest room, her leg buckling and screaming as she forced it to take her weight, just for one step—two, three— and then she was slamming the door shut. She shrieked and braced herself against the door as the weight of the metal creature hit it again and again, but the wood held.

Nalah slid to the floor with a long, groaning cry, stretching her bleeding leg out in front of her.

Her victory had lasted ten, perhaps twenty seconds.

I can't, she thought. *How can I beat this thing—unarmed, alone?*

The door shuddered as the wolf threw itself against the wood once more, and Nalah flinched. Blood was pooling underneath her calf, and her head swam.

"Mama, I'm so scared," she gasped. "What do I do now?"

There was no reply except the metallic growling of the wolf.

Chapter Thirteen

Halan

In the time before the Great Quake, a man came to Mak-tum. He was different from the other woodwork Thauma who made pilgrimages to the place, to study or to give thanks for the bounty of the forest or for the talents they had been given. He was wild-eyed and raving, saying he had seen a vision of the future. He insisted on being brought to the Chief Thauma of Maktum, a man named Darvish. They met in private, and the legends do not tell what the man said to Darvish, but whatever it was, it must have been convinc-ing. Maktum was abandoned at once and left to rot, visited only by the curious, the foolhardy, or the forgetful.

Ali Dacosta, **Myths and Legends of the Old Kingdom**

Halan was high on life, and it wasn't just because of the magic shoes she was wearing. Their mission into the Hok-met had been a success—now they just needed to figure out their next steps.

"But we don't know exactly *where* in the forest," Marcus mused as he and Halan hurried back toward his family's apartment. Halan was walking just slightly ahead, and she heard him say, "We could be lost for days in there. We'll have to—*mmmf!*"

She spun on her heel, her heart pounding and her hand reaching into her satchel for something, anything she could use as a weapon. Marcus was being held by a dark figure in a black head scarf, a hand clamped over his mouth.

"What the *hell* do you two think you're doing?" growled the figure softly. Marcus's eyes went wide with recognition. Then the attacker took her hand away and grabbed Marcus by the ear before stepping out of the shadows.

"Ow ow ow—Marit, stop!" Marcus batted at his sister, and she tweaked his ear before letting him go. She folded her arms and glared at Marcus and then at Halan from underneath her thick black eyebrows.

"Answer me! What did you do? And is that my dress?"

"Not here, all right?" Marcus muttered, casting his eyes up and down the street.

Halan frowned. She could understand that Marit was worried about her little brother, but she wouldn't let her chide them.

"We were doing what the rest of the Trust wouldn't do!" she retorted. "I told them all last night, I wasn't just going to wait for someone else to fix things. And now we know . . ." She stopped, nervous of the man and woman strolling down the street toward them. They were paying no attention, as far as she could tell, but who knew how much they might hear and understand?

Marit rolled her eyes. "You think I don't agree with you? You should have told me. I would have helped, you idiot! Come on, we're going for coffee."

"Right now?" Marcus's eyebrows shot up.

"Yes, now." Marit turned and strode away, and Halan and Marcus had to hurry to catch up with her.

The coffee shop was not so full this time, and the atmosphere was a lot more relaxed. But there were still plenty of people sitting at the tables with cups of steaming black coffee and sticky pastries placed in front of them. Marit nodded and said, "Morning, Kalen," to a young man with a black eye who was sitting near the door, then led the way downstairs to the storeroom. The guard on the door wasn't Tiger this time, but a rangy woman with a nose that reminded Halan of Cobalt's beak. Luckily, the woman didn't question Halan's presence; she just sniffed and opened the door.

The whole Trust was already inside, and as Halan stepped in, they all stopped talking and turned to stare at her.

News must travel fast around here.

They all seemed to take a breath and hold it while the door was open, then as soon as it was shut they all spoke at once:

"How could you?"

"Of all the dangerous, stupid—"

"Incredibly brave—"

"What did you find?"

Grandma Cutter pushed past another old woman to envelop Marcus in a tight hug. She murmured something in his ear that Halan didn't catch.

Mandana clapped her hands, and the rest of the Trust fell quiet, eventually.

"Marcus. Nalah," she said. "I'm glad you came here of your own volition, instead of forcing one of us to seek you out after your . . . ill-advised mission."

Halan stared at the woman, openmouthed. "But it just happened a little while ago—how did you know?"

"One of the Trust spied you coming out of the Hokmet, pulling the veil from your face and almost getting caught by Minister Torabi," Mandana said. "Then we checked the armory closet to see that many items had been taken—it was a simple matter from there to figure out that you two had gone against the wishes of the Trust and gone into the lion's den yourselves."

Marcus looked at the floor. But Halan would not be shamed for her actions—she looked back at Mandana with defiance and waited to hear what she had to say.

Mandana took a deep breath and began. "We all agree that you should *not* have done this. Going alone into the Hokmet—it was pure madness." Halan thought it sounded like she was saying it partly for the benefit of the other members of the Trust—some of them were frowning, some nodding along. She paused a moment to let the scolding sink in before continuing. "However, what's done is done. You managed to survive the attempt, so tell us: What happened in there? Do you know . . . the fate of the Thauma?" Her expression softened at the end, a quavering note of suppressed hope in her voice.

"Yes," said Halan. "They're alive."

Several of the Trust let out shaky breaths or turned and squeezed each others' hands. Halan swallowed, suddenly almost overwhelmed by their relief.

"They're being held somewhere called Maktum. It's in a forest, probably outside the city, on the side closest to the Warehouse District."

"*Maktum?*" asked Master Zurvan. "I know of it. . . ." He picked up a crate full of rolls of paper and began to go through them, frowning.

"We found out something else, too," said Halan. "Do any of you know a Thauma called Obsidian?"

She was half glad and half disappointed when everyone in the Trust shook their heads.

"It may be a code name of some sort," she mused. "Well, whoever he is, he's working with the Hokmet, finding and capturing Thauma. And I don't think we have much time to get them out. They were talking about Maktum being full and asking when the Hokmet were going to see the *rewards* of their plan. . . ."

Mandana groaned and pinched the bridge of her nose.

Master Zurvan pulled out a roll of paper and spread it on a table. It was a map, and Halan leaned in to look, her heart in her mouth. She knew that this world and her own were almost identical, in their bones, but it was strange to see the shapes laid out like this—the city, the shoreline, and the mountains were all where she remembered them, but there were green forests and farmlands instead of desert, and an actual river delta that ran all the way to the ocean, instead of pooling to form the Delta Lake miles from the city.

It was this river that Master Zurvan pointed to. One of its tributaries, to the northeast of New Hadar, was labeled the Maktumi River. He circled the area of forest the river ran through with one finger.

"Here," he said. "There's an ancient temple named Maktum—it's a shrine from the days before the Quake. Hardly anyone ever goes there anymore. Plenty of ghost stories to keep them away."

Halan stared at the map, thinking of all the things waiting for her there. The lives of the Thauma—including Marcus's brother—waiting to be saved. Perhaps a glass Thauma among them, who could remake the mirror and get her back home to her family and to Nalah. And maybe—just maybe—the answer to her world's problems.

She hesitated to put all her faith in this one mission, to think that it held the solutions to so many of the problems that plagued her life right now. It was a difficult path, perhaps an impossible one—but it was her path to walk now. And walk it she would.

She looked up, steeling herself for a fight. "I know you didn't want us to go to the Hokmet without telling you. So now, this is me telling you. I'm going to Maktum, and I'm going to free the Thauma who are trapped there."

"I'm going with her," said Marcus.

There was a moment of silence as the Trust looked around the room, each of them not wanting to be the first to respond.

Finally, Ario stood up and broke the silence. "The Trust will do everything it can to help you," he said. At this, the other Thauma around the crate-table all started to talk at once again, half of them agreeing, with desperate hope in their eyes, the other half muttering their reservations.

"You got lucky last time," said the man in the gray suit. "Do you really think you can break into a Hokmet facility and rescue a hundred prisoners?"

"There's no other choice!" Ario shot back. "You heard Nalah—the place is *full*. What if they're moved, or *killed*, while we stand here arguing?"

"You can't go by yourselves," said Master Zurvan. "It's a suicide mission. You're just children!"

"But I think perhaps they must," Mandana said slowly, raising her hands to command silence. The hush that descended was shocked, full of people holding their breath.

Halan held hers too. "The fact of the matter is, every one of us has a target on their head. There's no denying that the Hokmet know who we all are and are simply biding their time before picking us up with the rest. If any one of us tried to leave the city—no less a group of us!—then the Hokmet's spies would be onto us before we reached the city gates. But if two children left . . . perhaps they would have a chance." Mandana paused and looked at Marcus and Halan with worry in her eyes. "I admit that allowing this gives me no pleasure. The mission of parents is to protect their young ones, not to send them out into danger. But I read somewhere, perhaps it was a book about the legendary Seer Cyrus. . . . He said that sometimes we must put our faith in the children—that someday, a child will lead our kind into a bright future. Perhaps that day is today."

Halan blushed and smiled.

"Therefore," Mandana continued, "I propose that the Trust grants these two its blessing, along with whatever help it can give, to find out what is going on at Maktum and bring our families home. All in favor, raise your hand."

Some hands shot up immediately. Others crept up slowly, as the mood of the room began to change. Master Zurvan and Ario both raised their hands. Grandma Cutter planted a kiss on Marcus's temple, then raised hers too. A few kept their hands down—but not many. Mandana nodded.

"The majority rules. The motion is carried. Go quickly,

and with all the luck of the stars."

Halan gave the Trust a smile and a stiff nod, fighting the urge to sweep them a gracious, Soren-esque bow. This place was not her kingdom, nor were these people her subjects.

Yet she wanted to serve them all the same.

Master Zurvan bent over the map again. "You should leave the city here, from the North Gate. We will get one of our non-Thauma allies to drive you as far as they can. With the Cutters' shadow cloak, you should be able to slip past the checkpoint. Then you will have to make your own way through the forest on foot. Find and follow the river, and you should reach Maktum in a day, perhaps."

Halan nodded.

Ario was rummaging in the secret cupboard where they had left the Thauma crafts that wouldn't be any use to them. He pulled out two things and set them down on the crate-table in front of Halan and Marcus.

They were weapons: a knife with a tarnished blade in the shape of a teardrop, and a long metal staff that rang with a strange note as he laid it on the table. "My family made this long ago," he said, tapping the knife and meeting Halan's eyes with an intense stare. "It will render anyone it cuts unable to speak for at least an hour."

"Useful," said Marcus, reaching out to gingerly take the knife.

"And this, Aleksander and Luca made together," Ario

said more softly, touching the staff. "It strikes with twice the force you put into it and will bear almost any weight without bending. And when you don't need it anymore—" He touched a small oval of black metal that had been set into the grip of the staff, and it telescoped into an impossibly small cylinder that fit snugly into the palm of his hand.

"Thank you," said Halan with feeling, taking the cylinder from him. "We'll find them," she added. "And we'll bring them home. I promise."

Halan gritted her teeth and held on to the front seat of the motorcar for dear life, her knuckles white.

"Are you sure you're all right?" Marcus asked, throwing her an amused grin. She didn't dignify him with an answer.

She wasn't sure what had been more frightening, the Enforcers peering right into the backseat where she and Marcus were huddled under the shadow cloak, or the way the motorcar bumped and shook as it drove over the uneven ground. The sheer speed of the machine was breathtaking. Buildings and people—and now trees and bushes—whipped past so quickly that Halan couldn't even really see anything but colorful blurs. The motorcar had seemed fairly comfortable when she'd first climbed in and felt the smooth leather of the seats, but that was before they had started moving. Then the motorcar filled up with the smell of burning oil, which made her head spin.

Pouring flammable liquid into a metal box and setting it alight doesn't sound like a particularly brilliant method of transport to me! she thought desperately. *What idiot even came up with that idea?*

"Okay," said the man in the driver's seat. He turned the wheel and the machine swerved slightly and then finally, blessedly, rolled to a stop. "This is as far as I can get you."

"Thanks, Mr. Daei," said Marcus. He pulled the shadow cloak off and they climbed out of the motorcar. Mr. Daei lifted his hat and scratched the balding patch on top of his head.

"Kids . . . I don't know what you're doing, but be careful," he said. "It's dangerous out there."

Halan nodded. "We will."

Outside the motorcar, Halan found herself standing on a dirt path in the middle of a forest.

She had heard of forests. She'd seen pictures. And she'd seen trees as large as small buildings—Nalah's Hedgehog Cypress, for instance.

But she had never set foot in a forest before, and she realized that she hadn't been prepared for just how *many* trees there would be. She didn't say this to Marcus—he would laugh at her, and he'd be right! Who went into a forest without expecting there to be a lot of trees?

But there were *so many.* And they were so tall, their narrow trunks festooned with sprays of dark green leaves high up in the canopy. At ground level, the bushes were mostly ferns, their elegant leaves as bright a green as she'd ever seen. What's more, it was all so wet—the air was humid and thick with woody, heavy scents that Halan couldn't even identify. It wasn't quiet, either—the cries of birds and the hum of insects were all around them. It was as if the whole forest was breathing.

Mr Daei's motorcar turned around and drove off, back down the bumpy road, and was swallowed by the greenery in seconds. Halan hit the black oval on the handle of the staff and it unfolded with a *pop*. She stabbed it into the ground by her feet and stared into the forest.

"The river should be that way . . . ish," Marcus said, gesturing. "Come on."

It was slow going at first. Halan's sleeves were soon damp with dew from the ferns, and she flinched as a buzzing insect zipped past her ear. The ground underfoot was soggy but solid—most of the time—until she stepped on a glossy green mound of moss and sank a few inches into the sucking mud. She pried herself out with the extending staff and wiped the worst of the mud off her shoes with big flat leaves, but for a while she still walked with a *squish squash squish* sound. Marcus managed to avoid the mud, but once he tried to push through a clump of ferns and found himself tangled up in a thornbush so thick he had to keep perfectly still while Halan cut him out with the teardrop knife.

Eventually they both seemed to find their forest feet,

and the going became easier.

Then Halan heard a roaring sound and froze, afraid that it was another motorcar somewhere close by, that they'd been seen and the Enforcers were on their trail. But then the trees parted in front of them, and she gasped as she saw a flood of rushing water, tumbling over rocks and around trees, splashing and churning the earth around it.

The ocean was still probably the strangest thing she had ever seen in her life, but she had to stop and stare at the river, leaning on the staff. Where was it all coming from? Where was it rushing to? It was crystal clear, and as she watched, silver and blue fish swam past, carried by the current, their scales flashing in the sunlight.

This world holds so many wonders, she thought as they set off again. *Imagine if my world had access to such amazing resources! Our problems would be solved.*

Thinking about her kingdom made her heart hurt. She had tried, in all the time she was here in New Hadar, not to think about them too much, but here in the quiet of the forest, she couldn't stop her mind from wandering.

What would her parents be doing? Rani would be out of her mind with worry, and so would Omar. Perhaps they had all the best glass Thaumas in the kingdom trying to figure out a way to get to New Hadar.

And Nalah, was she back from her quest? Did she even know Halan had gone?

My tawam, my twin, Halan thought, sending a message out across the worlds. *I promise I'll see you again soon.*

She prayed to hear that familiar voice answer in her head, but as before, there was nothing.

The sun was starting to go down. It was a clearer night tonight, not so many thick clouds, and Halan could see the moon peeking down on her over the tops of the trees.

"We'll camp in a bit," Marcus said. "We can't be far off now, but we shouldn't try to find it in the dark."

Halan nodded. She was staring at the moon.

Is the moon different here too? she wondered. *Or is the same moon shining down on Nalah right now, wherever she is?*

They slept side by side, with their backs against the trunk of a huge tree and the shadow cloak draped over them. They cradled their weapons in their laps like baby dolls and were lulled to sleep by the constant rushing of the river.

In the morning, they were woken by the dawn chorus, a sound unlike anything Halan had ever heard before. It was as if every bird in the forest had its own urgent news that it needed to broadcast as far, as fast, and as *loudly* as possible. They stretched out their stiff limbs and drank and washed their faces in the river, and then they set off again.

They walked for about another hour. Halan had a few

bad blisters now, and she was just about to ask Marcus if he thought they could possibly have missed Maktum when he grabbed her arm and pointed.

"Look!" he hissed.

Halan followed his gesture and gasped. Peeking out between the treetops up ahead there was the spire of a tall, pale stone tower.

Just the sight of the spire made Halan's heart ache. It looked like a building that would have been at home in the Magi Kingdom. They crept closer, and the more she saw of it, the more homesick Halan felt. It was set up on a hill, and it looked a little like the royal palace on a much smaller scale. There were the elaborate carvings and pillars around the large stone doorway, and there were the beautiful jewel colors baked onto the tiles of the roof. They were brighter even than the ones in the Magi Kingdom, less faded from the constant sun, but they were cracked and had vines growing up between them.

She had seen a few shrines like this in the kingdom since her coronation, ancient places that had been built to give thanks for the powers of the Thauma and the continued thriving of the kingdom. Tam had ignored the places completely, and the hunched old women who maintained the Shrine of the Weaver in the Magi City had been shocked and ecstatic to receive a visit from their new queen.

Halan pulled the Thauma-sensing spectacles out of her bag and slipped them on. She gasped. The whole building had a shimmering aura of blue Thaumaturgic energy. Was that from ancient worship? Was this place, itself, a kind of Thauma artifact?

Either way, she knew they were in the right place, because underneath the shrine itself, somewhere inside the hill it stood on, there was blazing ball of energy in a constantly shifting, swirling rainbow of different colors.

"They're here," she breathed. "Lots of different energies, all together, under the building. I can see figures, I think . . . but it's too hard to make out." She took the glasses off and grinned nervously at Marcus. "Are you ready?"

Marcus nodded. "Let's go find Kadir and shut this place down."

They hid themselves underneath the shadow cloak and snuck as close as they dared to the big stone doors. There were people there, Hokmet Enforcers standing at attention but looking rather wilted. *It must be very hot and sweaty in their stiff uniforms and square blue caps*, Halan thought. They looked as ill at ease with the forest as she and Marcus had been.

She nudged Marcus and pointed to the knife hanging from his belt, then bent down and tapped the side of her ankle. Marcus nodded with a grin.

They snuck up on the Enforcers slowly, approaching them sideways through a patch of scrubby grass, keeping low to the ground. Twice, Halan thought one of the Enforcers had heard the rustle of the grass and was about to investigate, but they always turned back to their conversation or to staring out at the forest with wary distaste.

They edged closer, closer, until Marcus was within striking distance. He readied his blade, and Halan very carefully lifted the edge of the cloak. She saw Marcus steel himself and wince in sympathy before he struck, stabbing the tip of the knife into the soft exposed flesh where the Enforcer's shoe met the bottom of his stiff trousers.

The Enforcer doubled up in pain and Marcus and Nalah scampered away from him. He opened his mouth and tried to yelp, and then tried to curse, but there was no sound. He gripped his ankle and hopped on the spot, looking down at the bleeding pinprick.

"Azmoun, what are you doing?" snapped the second Enforcer, turning to stare at his comrade's dance of confusion and pain. The officer Marcus had stabbed tried to say something, but no sound came out—he tried to mouth the words, and then pointed to the long grass, flapped his hands at his sides very fast, and then made a stabbing motion with one hand.

"Something bit you?" the other Enforcer guessed.

Officer Azmoun slapped his forehead sarcastically and then nodded.

"What's happened to your voice, man?"

Azmoun flailed, pointed at the grass, pointed at the forest, tried to yell at his companion, flapped his hands at his sides again, and then turned an incredible dark purple color and bent over to catch his breath. The other Enforcer gave the whole forest a frightened look and then took Azmoun by the arm.

"Come on, you need a medic," he muttered. "And it's nearly time for the shift change anyway."

They went inside, Azmoun hobbling painfully. Marcus and Halan followed close behind them through the doors, the shadow cloak sweeping the dusty ground as they hurried into the dim, cool shrine.

They were in a long corridor, and at the end there was an open archway into a wide chamber. Marcus and Halan pressed themselves against one wall and waited for the two Enforcers to vanish into a side room and shut the door.

"So," Marcus whispered, "where are they?"

"Down," Halan whispered back. "We need to find the stairs."

She led them through the hall and looked into the large chamber. There were ancient, rotten rows of benches arranged around a cracked stone plinth in the center. If she concentrated, she could see how the bones of this place were similar to the shrine she had visited in Magi City, with its altar covered in a beautiful Thauma tapestry and its old but polished wooden benches.

Halan suddenly thought of the ancient Thauma Lady who had kept the place running.

Her office was underground, in a maze of stone passages, and the door was . . .

Halan led Marcus over to one corner of the chamber, and sure enough, there was a small wooden door. She opened it and found a staircase leading down, lit by artificial yellow lights that looked like they'd been strung up recently across the sconces that would once have held Thauma flames.

They snuck down the stairs, staying under the shadow cloak as much as they could. The passage at the bottom was long and dim, lined with dark archways on one side and a few more wooden doors on the other.

Marcus's hand found Halan's, and he squeezed it reassuringly. Halan wondered if he was really feeling as confident as he seemed. She wondered if he, too, had noticed that there was barely room for two people to walk abreast in this corridor. If one person came past, they might be able to press themselves against a wall. If two people came walking toward them, though . . .

She tried not to think about it.

They stepped forward, and all of a sudden her nerves melted away and she squeezed Marcus's hand back.

"Look!" she whispered. "Bars!"

The archways were, in fact, cells with barred doors across them. Halan and Marcus hurried toward them, and yes, there were people inside, sitting with their backs to the walls or lying on the floor. They looked filthy and haggard, but they were alive.

"Kadir!" Marcus gasped. He threw off the cloak. Halan

winced and drew it around her own shoulders, looking up and down the corridor, but there was nobody coming.

The Thauma prisoners stared at Marcus as he appeared from thin air in front of them, their mouths hanging open.

"*Marcus?*"

One of the prisoners sat up. Kadir had dark blond hair and a messy, half-grown beard to match. He ran to the bars, leaping over the legs of his fellow Thaumas. "What are you doing here? How did you find us?" Then he shook his head, as if to clear it, and held up a hand. "Later. Can you get us out of here, little brother?"

"I'll figure it—" Marcus began, but then one of the doors banged open and two Enforcers ran out. Halan's breath caught in her throat and she instinctively backed away.

"I thought I heard something out here!" one of them yelled. "Get the kid!"

Marcus drew his knife, and the Enforcers paused, drawing their long, polished wooden truncheons.

"Leave him alone!" Kadir yelled. "Marcus, run!"

Halan wanted to throw off the cloak and fight them, or throw it over Marcus and whisk him away before they knew what was happening, but she didn't get a chance. Marcus lunged wildly at one of the Enforcers with his knife and then tried to bolt around them, but the other one was too quick and gave him a stunning blow across the back of the neck with his truncheon. He sprawled on the floor and the knife skittered out of his hand.

Halan, her breath coming in short gasps, gripped the shortened metal staff and crept up behind the Enforcers as one of them snatched up the knife and the other one hauled Marcus to his feet. Could she take them both out in one blow? What would happen if she didn't? What would happen if she did?

"Let my brother out!" Marcus shouted, struggling against the grip of the Enforcers. "Please! I don't care what you do to me. I'm here to free my brother, and all the others, that's what counts!"

Halan stumbled to a halt in the middle of the corridor and pressed a hand over her mouth.

That wasn't for the Enforcers. He's saying that to me.

Marcus was right. She needed to stay out of this, to let them take him, so that she could still free the prisoners somehow. Moving silently, Halan backed away down the corridor.

I'll save you too, Marcus. I swear I will.

She waited, pressing herself into the smallest corner of the passage she could find, until the sounds of the Enforcers' footsteps and Marcus's struggling had faded.

It wouldn't do her any good to reveal herself to the prisoners, not right now. She still had a few tricks up her sleeve, but none of them would get her through those bars. What she needed was a key, and those weren't just left lying around. Halan sighed, her frustration building.

If you were a Thauma, like Nalah, those prisoners would

be free by now, Halan thought.

It was true. If Marcus had brought Nalah on this mission, as he had originally intended, they might have had more success by now. Nalah knew more about this world, and she had her powers to boot. What did Halan have?

You have your wits, a voice answered. *Your resourcefulness. Your courage. You are the queen of your kingdom for a reason.*

For a moment, Halan thought it was Nalah's voice, finally getting through to her somehow. But then she realized no—that wasn't Nalah. That was her own voice.

I want Nalah, Halan thought. *But I don't need Nalah to succeed. I can do this alone. I must.*

Halan got up and squared her shoulders. She needed more information to formulate a plan. She needed to explore.

Staying quiet and keeping watch over her shoulder, she followed the corridor around a corner and then down another very short flight of stairs. At the bottom, there was a turn to the left and a doorway straight ahead. The door was open, and inside she heard voices. Halan drew the shadow cloak tight around her body and pulled down the hood, making herself as small as she could. Then she edged into the room, moving one footstep at a time.

The room was a little like the one where she'd met the old lady in the Magi City shrine but far more neglected—it contained a variety of half-broken chairs and a large desk.

More New Hadari lamps had been set up on the desk and strung from the ceiling.

There were two men in the room, one in a dark green suit who was standing with his hands on his hips, reading one of about twenty pages that had been pinned to the wall, thick with writing and diagrams. The other was sitting behind a desk, wearing a crisp, cream linen suit. He had his back to Halan, and his head of dark hair was bent over as he wrote something on a piece of paper.

"I need to know, Obsidian," said the man in green, turning and wiping his brow with a handkerchief that matched his horrible suit. "All *this* . . ." He waved a hand at the notes on the wall. "What does it mean?"

So the man in the cream linen suit is Obsidian, Halan thought. *The Thauma who is betraying his own people to the Hokmet.* She took a few more steps along the wall, craning her neck to see the face of such a man. Such a traitor.

"You would not understand the workings of it, Minister Dejagah," the man called Obsidian said, his voice as smooth as oil. "A mind as simple as yours could not grasp it even if I devoted the next ten years to teaching you."

Halan's blood ran cold.

That voice.

Another two steps, and the face of Obsidian became clear to her. It was a strong face, with piercing dark eyes and a perfectly trimmed beard that was waxed into a point. It was a familiar face.

The face of a man she had called Father for twelve years. *Tam.*

Halan choked back a gasp as the world seemed to rock under her feet.

It wasn't enough for Tam to try and rule my kingdom through tyranny, Halan thought with growing rage. *He had to come to New Hadar and begin sowing his evil seeds here as well?*

Halan's hands began to shake as fear and fury all welled up in her heart at once.

She backed carefully into a corner, making sure her feet were covered by the cloak, and wrapped her arms around her body. Seeing him like this brought back too many memories—memories of him sweeping through the palace corridors in his bright Magi robes, giving commands; memories of countless feasts, where she'd sat next to him while they ate and swayed to the music; memories of his face lighting up when Halan appeared in his doorway, and his arms open for an embrace.

You loved me, once, Halan thought as she looked at him, sitting there at the desk with his head cocked to the side, as he always did back home. *Or rather, you loved the idea of me. You loved the Halan who was of your blood, the Halan who obeyed, the Halan who would have allowed you to kill in my name.*

But I am not that Halan. Not anymore.

She squeezed her eyes shut and forced herself to breathe

in long, slow breaths. She needed to uncover Tam's plan for the Thaumas. Nothing else mattered.

She'd had a feeling since the moment Marcus appeared out of the mirror that it was her fate to come to New Hadar. Now she knew it for certain.

I stopped you once, she thought, opening her eyes. *I can do it again.*

"Now look here!" Dejagah snapped. "I may not be Thauma, but I'm not an idiot. The Hokmet have been very patient with you, *Zachary,* but if we don't start seeing results soon, I'm authorized to warn you that our support may be withdrawn."

Tam huffed in apparent disgust.

So, Halan thought, taking note. *They think he's Zachary Tam.*

Halan hadn't met Asa's tawam from New Hadar, because Asa had murdered him for his powers before she even knew that New Hadar existed. But Nalah said he was a good man, a recluse, a friend of her mother's. Halan tried to imagine Asa Tam and her mother Rani being friends, but she couldn't. They had been married for fifteen years but had never been friends. It was all just a facade, kept up for the sake of the throne.

Dejagah drew himself up and looked down his nose at Tam. "Where would you be then, eh? Without our help to round up the Thauma scum and bring them to this forsaken place?"

Tam was up in a flash, rounding the desk like a lion pouncing on a tiny, green lizard. Tam grabbed the man's wrist with his right hand, on which he wore a glove made of deep green iridescent fabric, like a beetle's shell. As soon as he touched the bare skin, the man's hand spasmed and turned ashen gray, the flesh seeming to sag and shrink away. Dejagah screamed in pain and tried, unsuccessfully, to wrench his hand out of Tam's grip. "Let go of me!" he screeched. "Let go!"

Tam didn't flinch or look down at the hand, which continued to wither with each passing second. Instead he leaned in to the minister, not breaking eye contact the entire time.

"Never. Threaten me. Again," Tam said softly.

For a second Dejagah seemed hypnotized, like a rat staring down a cobra. But then Tam let go, and Dejagah tore his hand away and held it to his body, trembling.

From the doorway there was a soft cough. Halan turned to see an Enforcer standing there, looking uncomfortable.

"What is it?" snarled Tam.

"I'm so sorry to interrupt, sir," said the officer, sounding genuinely sorry. "I need to report an intruder."

"*What* intruder?"

"Just a kid," said the Enforcer, shaking his head. "I don't know how he got in here, but—"

"A kid?" Tam took a few quick, long strides across the room, directly toward Halan. She ducked back, her heart pounding in her throat, and Tam passed barely inches in front of her to come face-to-face with the officer.

"Who was this kid?" Tam snapped. "A girl? About twelve years old? Or twins, were there *twins?*"

Halan's breath caught in her throat. *He doesn't know, but he suspects.*

"N-no, no girls or twins, sir!" The Enforcer snapped to attention under Tam's fierce glare. "Just a boy. Kind of pale. Came to try to rescue his brother, sir. I've thrown him in with the others."

"Pale," said Tam quietly. Halan shut her eyes for a moment.

Now he knows. . . .

Tam turned away from the Enforcer and stared at the plans on the wall, seeming to consider them for a long moment. Then he turned back. "It's too much of a risk. I won't let anything get in the way of my plans. We must begin the ritual at once."

He didn't wait for Dejagah's agreement. He swept out of the room, almost bowling over the Enforcer on the way.

Ritual? What kind of ritual?

Halan scoured her mind for anything that she'd learned or read about that would apply to someone gathering a large number of Thauma. Was Tam planning on killing them all to get their powers, as he did with the other tawams in New Hadar? But in that case, their powers would go to their tawams in the Magi Kingdom—if they even had them—not to Tam himself. So it couldn't be that.

Suddenly, Halan remembered something she and Nalah had been talking about back in the palace gardens. About how objects imbued with the blood of Thauma can have great power.

If one Thauma's blood can give power—what would the blood of a hundred Thaumas do?

Halan shivered at the thought.

Dejagah stood in the room for a moment, massaging his wrist.

"Madness," he murmured to himself. "This whole enterprise is madness. . . ." But he hurried after Tam all the same.

Halan sank to her knees and then sat down in the middle of the floor, the shadow cloak pooling around her.

What do I do now? she thought. *I've got a little bag of Thauma tricks, but I've no power of my own, and I'm alone here. How can I figure out how to stop him in time?*

Halan threw her head back and closed her eyes, sending another message out into the ether. *Nalah!* she shouted in her mind, putting her entire heart and soul into the call. *If you can hear me—I need you! I don't know if I can do this without you. Please!*

She waited for a few heartbeats, but there was no reply, not even a distant whisper.

Nalah was too far away to help her now. Everyone was. Halan was on her own.

Chapter Fourteen

Nalah

Destiny does not just happen. Fate must be seized. A prophecy holds no power simply because it is understood—it is not the events themselves, but how we react to them that shapes our destiny.

Cyrus, *Prophet of the Sands*

Nalah . . .

Nalah's head snapped up. She held the makeshift bandage tight against her leg for a moment and held her breath, listening.

I need you. . . .

The words appeared in Nalah's mind, like a voice calling from within a deep well. If Halan really was in New Hadar—was it possible Nalah was hearing her sister from across the worlds?

We have an unbreakable bond, she thought. *And if she's in New Hadar, fighting for my world . . . what am I doing?*

We're both alone. I don't even have Cobalt.

Nalah's eyes widened as she thought of her glass falcon.

"Halan," she whispered aloud. "Thank you. Now I know what I have to do!"

The wolf was still prowling behind the door. It had stopped throwing itself against it, but she could hear it growling and the scissor-snip sound of its paws on the flagstones. She pushed herself up, not daring to let go of her hold on the door. She had stopped the bleeding, but her leg still throbbed with pain. Parts of it had gone numb, and other parts burned as if they were being stabbed with hot needles. Wincing, she grabbed the handle of the door and tried to ready herself.

I don't have help now, she thought. *But I can make some.*

The people who built the shrine, whoever they were, had given her everything she needed. But she had been too blind to see it.

Now her eyes were open.

She pulled off the beautiful Thauma head scarf Falcon had given her and paused a second to silently thank him again for his gift. Then she flung open the door and rushed at the wolf, throwing the scarf over its head.

Bull's-eye! The wolf tossed its head and snarled as the head scarf covered its face, while Nalah hobbled past it, pushing herself off from the chamber walls, and grabbed for the empty glass jug.

Already the wolf's sharp fur and gnashing teeth were cutting the scarf to ribbons. She took a deep, centering breath and squeezed the jug between her palms. The glass melted in her hands, and she balled it up as if it were made of taffy. It glowed white-hot, and Nalah could feel the heat on her face, but her bare hands felt nothing but the warm flow of her power.

She had to think fast. The wolf was turning to her, one yellow eye staring out through a tear in the head scarf. She grabbed the ball of glass and pulled it into a long tapering shape. With her fingers she pinched out a flat head and dug in two beady eyes.

The wolf hunkered down to pounce. She bent down, clapped her hand onto her leg, and squeezed. She moaned in pain as blood oozed out of the wound and onto her fingers. She wiped it onto the back of the molten glass snake, and it glowed all the brighter, stripes of red against the white. Then she threw the snake down in the dust between her and the wolf.

The glass twitched, then curled, and then the king cobra reared up in front of the wolf, puffing out its hood and hissing through sharp, furnace-hot fangs.

The wolf shuddered at the sight of it, backing away. Its growl took on a high-pitched edge, like two sharp knives scraping together.

And then the snake struck, like a bolt of lightning, and the fight was on.

The cacophony that rose from their battle was so terrible that Nalah had to cover her ears. As they fought, she took the opportunity to sneak around them along the wall to the doorway on the opposite side of the room, as fast as her wounded leg would carry her.

She burst through the door and slammed it shut behind her, panting in the dark. She was about to walk out into the room when the Thauma lights flared on, and she screamed.

She was standing on a narrow ledge, about as wide as she was tall. Beyond that, there was nothing but an unending blackness below.

If she had taken even three steps into the room before the lights came on, she would have toppled over the edge and fallen to her death.

The challenge of this room was clear. There was a doorway about thirty feet in front of her, set into the opposite wall—the only problem was that there was a chasm in the way. It was as wide across as the great hall in the royal palace and there was no bottom to it, or at least, not one Nalah could see.

The world began to spin and she recoiled from the edge, her heart thumping in her ears. She backed up against the door she'd entered the room through and sank down with her back against it, trembling all over.

They give you what you need to get through, she thought. That had been true in the previous two rooms, so it must be true here. But when she looked around, her heart sank. The only thing in this room was a small heap of fabric, pale and ordinary linen. She pulled it into her lap and looked at the weave of it and then looked over at the chasm.

She had already accomplished more than she'd thought possible. But she was exhausted now, gasping and dizzy from the pain in her leg, and if the Prophet Cyrus thought she could fashion a rope from this linen and then climb down the chasm or up the wall and across the ceiling with it, he had another think coming.

"I haven't given up," she said out loud, just in case the prophet was listening. It was an absurd thought—Cyrus had lived at the time of the splitting of the worlds. Whoever had set this place up would have been dead for a hundred years. But still, she carried on speaking aloud, even though her voice was cracked and dry. "I just need to sit here for a while. I need to catch my breath and fix my leg that your wolf nearly chewed off."

The leg was not all that bad, actually. It hurt, but she could still move her ankle and wiggle her toes, even though she really didn't want to, and it wasn't bleeding aside from where she had made it bleed herself.

She sighed and laid her head against the cold stone wall behind her. As she looked up at the ceiling, she saw something she couldn't quite understand at first. It was a line of perfect bright blue drawn across the dark stone. Then a black shadow passed across it. Then another, and another, arrow shapes flying in formation.

Birds.

That blue line was the sky!

Nalah found herself smiling as she watched the birds wheel in and out of sight. It was good to remember that there was a whole world outside this dim temple. Then she heard a glassy cry and sat up straighter.

"Cobalt?" she cried, her voice echoing all the way down the chasm. "Can you hear me?"

A series of excited chirrups and whistles came down to her in reply. She couldn't see him, but hearing his voice was enough to give her a burst of energy.

"I'm alive!" she yelled up. "I'm almost there! I've just got to—"

She looked up at the shadows of the birds overhead and then down at the cloth in her hands.

The Weaver, she thought. *What was it that he said? Stars aren't afraid to shine, and birds aren't afraid to fly.* . . .

She flung out the linen, watching the way it caught the air underneath it.

She knew what she had to do, and instead of the intense emotion of the wooden box or the pure adrenaline of the glass snake, now she just felt *certain.*

Is this it? she wondered. *Is this what not being afraid is like?*

She was *definitely* afraid of falling into the bottomless pit, but for the first time, she felt as if she could channel that fear, turn it into something better than raw, undirected force.

She flung the linen into the air once more, and this

time as it reached the highest curve of its arc, she blew out a breath and let a burst of power travel down her arms, through her fingertips, into the threads of the cloth. It stiffened and froze into a hard sheet, with a creaking, pinging sound, and then she pulled and tweaked the fabric until it grew to nearly twice its size and curved around in a wide sort of M shape. The shape of Cobalt's wings when he was hovering, floating on the air currents. Last of all, she pulled out two handholds on the fronts of the wings and a strip to go around her waist.

She struggled to her feet and wriggled herself into the white makeshift wings.

Will this work? she wondered, testing her grip on the handholds. She flapped once, bending the stiff fabric, and felt the resistance of the air against it.

Have faith, she told herself.

She stared at the door across the chasm and took a deep breath.

Be the Star.

Then she threw herself toward the edge of the chasm and leaped.

Shine.

For one terrifying moment, Nalah felt herself plummeting down into the abyss. But then the wind caught in her wings and she swooped high up, riding the thermals like Cobalt. Nalah let out a scream of mingled fright and joy as she soared into the air, her stomach turning somersaults.

The moment seemed to last an eternity, but it was probably only five seconds before she crashed down on the other side, flopping onto her belly on the hard flagstones. For a moment she just lay there, breathing and embracing the blessedly solid ground.

As she did, she realized that apart from a few practice things like the tree gazebo, she hadn't really had *plans* for what she wanted to do with her powers. Now, as she was wriggling free of the linen wings, she was making plans.

One day, Cobalt, you and I are going to go flying!

She hardly felt the ache in her leg at all as she stood up and faced the door. *Well,* she thought. *Here goes nothing.* And with that, she took a deep breath and stepped through.

The light that struck her was blinding, so bright that she threw her arm up over her face, half afraid she'd been caught in some kind of blast. But then she felt a familiar warmth on her face, and smelled the fresh mountain air, and her eyes began to adjust.

She stepped outside onto a black dirt path that wound through what looked like a well-tended desert garden, bathed in sunlight. It was in a small dip that had been carved out of the very peak of the mountain, with blue sky above and black stone walls rising all around. A few gnarled trees and scattered flowering cacti grew alongside the path. It was beautiful in a sparse kind of way.

She followed the path around a tree, then stopped dead in her tracks. There was an old man, with brown skin like gnarled tree bark, sitting on a carved stone bench. He was wrapped in a cream-colored robe, his white hair in long, thin braids cascading down his back.

Nalah hesitated, feeling strangely shy. Just as she was about to call out "Hello?" to him, she realized that Cobalt was perched on the bench too. The glass falcon was rubbing his beak against the man's finger, but when he saw Nalah he gave a chiming cry and took off, flying around her head and finally landing on her shoulder.

"A lovely bird, that one," said the man, rising to his feet. "I see he has a little crack in his heart, though—much like his maker."

The man turned to face her, and Nalah's jaw dropped slightly at the sight of his face.

His eyes were cloudy white, but not the way that a blind man's would be—she could see the clouds in them, swirling, glowing faintly as if the sun were shining out from behind his pupils.

"My heart?" she asked numbly, as if in a dream.

"For one so young, you have already lost so much," said the man, the wrinkles around his eyes deepening with concern. "And yet, like your bird, you heal. You persist. You soar." He smiled. "Welcome Nalah Bardak, to the Shrine of the Seer."

Somehow, it didn't surprise Nalah that the man knew her name.

"You're a seer?" she breathed.

The old man's smile widened. "I am *the Seer*."

Nalah's neck tingled. "Not—not *Cyrus*?"

"The very same."

"But you—" Nalah broke off. It would probably be rude to tell Cyrus that he ought to be dead. Stunned and breathless, and uncertain what else to do, Nalah knelt and bowed her head. "My lord," she said. "You summoned me here, and I came. I completed your tests. I wish to know, please—what is my purpose? My powers, more often than I'd like, do as much harm as good. Please . . . help me."

Cyrus nodded at her words, as if she had said exactly what he'd expected her to. *He is a seer, I suppose*, she thought.

"Rise, and walk with me," he said.

Nalah got to her feet and followed him through the gardens, weaving between the dry trees before stopping to sit down on another bench, this one overlooking a gap in the high black stone wall so Nalah could see the Magi Kingdom far away below them like a distant jewel.

"I am not alive, Nalah," Cyrus said. "Not quite—not the way you would understand it. I exist here. I have existed here since before I was born, and I will exist here for a long time after you are dead. In my short time as a mortal being, I was a Fifth Clan Thauma named Cyrus, also called the Prophet, the Blind Seer. I was blind, then, although it might be more true to say my eyes were simply . . . elsewhere."

Nalah thought of the eyes in the fabric workshop. "Have you been watching me?" she asked.

"Since you picked up my prophecy orb, I have not left your side," said Cyrus. "I stowed that orb in the palace for you to find. I knew that, at the right moment, it would bring you here." He turned and looked Nalah straight in the eyes. "There is much I want to teach you in the coming years, child. But already, you have learned one of the greatest lessons from yourself, have you not?"

Nalah stared out at the world below, thinking about everything that had happened since she'd left the palace. Escaping from Malek's prison with Soren. Finding the lost Shadow Clan and learning from the Weaver. Traveling across the desert and scaling the mountains with only Cobalt by her side. Completing the three trials alone.

A theme, like the melody of a song, began to emerge from it all. It was in every challenge that she conquered and came out of the mouth of every friend she met along the way.

I didn't need to prove my own worth to everyone else, Nalah thought. *I needed to prove it to myself. So that I can stop being afraid.*

She suddenly remembered what her papa had said to her in those last moments, there in that dark cell at the bottom of the palace dungeon.

Nothing was ever going to be able to hide the light within you.

A single tear rolled down Nalah's cheek. *Oh, Papa. I was the one who was hiding it, all this time. Afraid that I wasn't good enough for the powers I was given, like Malek said. But now I think I finally believe that I am.*

Nalah sniffed and looked up at Cyrus. "Yes," she replied. "Yes, I think I have."

"You will be a powerful woman indeed," said Cyrus with an air of satisfaction. "And I look forward to speaking to you more. But not now. Your people need you. You may be the only one who can stop what's coming."

Nalah shuddered. "What's coming? What do you mean?"

"There is no time for more explanation," Cyrus said. "You must go, my child, and quickly. Your great work begins at once."

Chapter Fifteen

Halan

There's something that's been living in my mind lately. A terrible secret that I can't share with anyone. Not Omar, not Mother—not even Nalah.

The secret is this: I miss my father.

Asa Tam raised me. He loved me. Sure, it was the wrong kind of love. A love that killed, and could have killed many more had we not stopped him. But . . . it was love nonetheless.

Sometimes these thoughts drift into my mind, and I hate myself for thinking them.

Sometimes I wonder, if he had succeeded, if he had killed Nalah and I had gotten her powers—would he have stopped hurting people? Would he have changed? Was it my weakness, my lack of power, that drove him to violence?

It's too easy to feel like everything is somehow my fault. It's a trap, one that I find myself falling into all too willingly. There are so many traps when it comes to Asa Tam.

He was a monster. A murderer.

But he was my father.
I wish I could forget that.

From Halan's diary

Halan sat in an invisible heap on the floor in Maktum, praying for a miracle.

Then, suddenly—the sound of voices and heavy foot-steps coming down the short flight of stairs nearby. Halan pressed herself flat against the wall behind her as several Enforcers passed, pushing one of the Thauma prisoners in front them in handcuffs. She got to her feet as soon as they'd gone and rushed to the doorway to follow them, but another pair of Enforcers came up behind her in the nar-row corridor, and she almost ran right into them.

She ducked back inside the chamber and sagged against the wall, panting.

I need to do something! she thought, her frustration mounting. *I need to help those people! But the longer I stay here, the more likely it will be that I'll get caught. I need a weapon. . . .*

She fished in her bag—she had the staff, the spectacles, and—

Her fingers closed on a pointy, jagged object, wrapped in cloth.

The shard.

Halan pulled it out and unwrapped the piece of

Transcendent Glass carefully, making sure that it stayed completely hidden under the cloak. Halan held it up and stared at her own tearstained reflection in the mirror, the shifting sheen of colors passing over her face.

And then, suddenly, it wasn't her face at all.

Nalah!

She was standing somewhere bright and sunny. The wind was blowing her hair around her face, and her mouth was set in a hard line. She looked so grown up—like a true Queen's Sword—her expression so fierce and determined, that it made Halan feel a little stronger herself.

Wherever you are, whatever you're doing, I believe in you, she thought. And as she thought it, the mirror switched back to reflecting her own face.

She wiped away her tears and stared into her dark, frightened eyes.

If Nalah was a true Queen's Sword, she would need a queen.

But what kind of queen was Halan Ali?

It was the same question she'd been asking herself ever since the coronation. Certainly, she wouldn't be the kind of sovereign Tam was. But neither would she be the formal, stiff kind of queen Rani had been.

And then Halan realized that she—with every action she had taken—had already answered her own question. She was the kind of queen who would try to help everyone in her kingdom, even if it meant doing it one at a time. She was the kind of queen who traveled to another world to save people she didn't even know from a man whose power was much greater than her own.

She was the kind of queen whose power didn't make magic—

It made justice.

These Thauma are people I've sworn to protect, and every moment I stand here is another moment that I leave them to the mercies of Asa Tam.

So, she thought, *how do I beat him? How did I beat him the first time?* She cast her mind back to the plan she'd made with Ironside's rebels to come up through the tunnels under the palace courtyard and storm Tam's guards with a surprise attack. *I did what he least expected,* she realized.

Halan looked around the room and saw that there were papers tacked up to the walls. Papers with drawings on them and diagrams and handwritten notes. They looked like Tam's writing. *His plans . . .* And Halan realized that Tam must have assumed that there was no way for anyone to get into this room without being detected—certainly no one who had enough knowledge of arcane Thauma to understand what these notes were about.

I'm what he's least expecting. Me.

She quickly wrapped up the shard again and dropped it back into the bottom of her bag, before starting at one end of the room and studying each page of Tam's writing. Every few minutes she heard another set of footfalls on the stairs and glanced through the doorway. More and more people were marched past—men, women, children as young as six, elders whose backs were bent and knees knocked as they were shoved along. Many of them were fighting back, but without much success.

She tried to hurry, but the writings were dense, the sketches complex, all the terms were unknown to her, and half of it seemed to be pure speculation. . . .

Someone who hadn't had the right education might not have been able to make heads or tails of it. Luckily, Halan had had exactly the education her father had wanted for her, and her knowledge of arcane Thauma magic and history was vast. The irony tasted bitter in her mouth, but she smiled anyway.

Thank you again, Lord Helavi, she thought. *Stars bless you from your toenails to your wispy beard. If I ever get home, I'm finding a way to promote you. Again.*

But after reading Tam's notes, her smile quickly faded. She read the third page three times, checking that she hadn't made some kind of mistake, but she had not.

"The Undoing," the heading read, and next to it, Tam had drawn a picture of sand running through an hourglass.

A weapon to reverse the act of the great mistake—when the worlds were split, leaving one world with bountiful

resources and the other with magic. One a world of water,
the other a world of sand.

Only one world can live and thrive.

One must die so the other can live.

Break the veil between worlds, and drain the magic from
the parasite dimension. That world will wither and die, and
leave only one to rise from its ashes, whole once again.

Halan felt dizzy.

Tam was planning to destroy her world and everyone
in it.

The girl you thought was your daughter. The woman you
married. The kingdom you claimed to love. You would destroy
them all for a chance to have all the power for yourself!

Feeling disgusted, Halan tried to read on, to make sense
of the notes about the ritual itself and find out what he was
using the Thauma for. He was drawing power from them,
that was obvious, but the specifics were in arcane scribbles
that probably meant nothing to anybody but Tam.

Halan stepped back, pulling the telescoped-in metal
staff out of her bag. She would just have to go and find out
for herself.

She waited by the door until a pair of Enforcers went
past, holding another prisoner. This one was a young boy,
only seven or eight. He already had a black eye, but it hadn't
broken him. He was still wriggling and yelling in their grip.

Halan slipped out of the room, her heart in her mouth, and followed close behind the two Enforcers. She wasn't sure if she could simply follow them all the way to wherever they were going, but for now they weren't going to notice an invisible girl when they had the belligerent boy to contend with.

"I'm gonna bite you," he snapped. "Let me go!"

"*Sure* you are," one of the Enforcers replied, before turning to his partner. "I'm glad this is the last one. I've had it with these uppity Thauma scum. *Stop that!* Or shall we put you down and see how far you get?"

"I bet he can hop pretty good," said the other. "I bet he can hop all the way home, like a little frog, can't you kid?"

"I'll hop up and down on your head," the boy snarled. "See how you like me then!"

Halan looked down. The boy had only one leg. She bit her lip. Could this be Luca, Alexsander's little brother with the artificial leg, who had been mentioned at the meeting of the Trust? *Now I know why they never made it out of the city*, Halan thought. So Luca was the last Thauma to be brought to Tam. The ritual must be about to begin. And she still had no idea how to stop it.

They turned a corner, and Halan's heart sank. At the end of the corridor there was another door, much larger and more impressive looking than the one into Tam's office chamber, and it was being guarded by four more Hokmet

Enforcers. They opened it to let their colleagues and the struggling Luca inside.

"Having trouble there, Parvin?" One of the door guards snickered, folding her arms and leaning on the door as they passed. "Shall I tell Captain Kamya that the one-legged kid was too much for you two?"

"Enjoy your scintillating door duty, Nouri," the one called Parvin muttered under his breath as he dragged the boy inside.

Halan hung back. She caught a tantalizing glimpse of blue Thauma fire in the room beyond before the door was closed again.

I'll never be able to slip in there unnoticed, she thought, chewing her thumbnail. *I have to distract these guards. But how?*

"That Parvin." Nouri shook her head. "What an amateur."

"Oh, lay off him, Nouri," said one of the other three.

"He's not wrong about door duty," said another one darkly, picking at his fingernails.

Nouri rolled her eyes. "I'm surrounded by morons," she muttered.

Not exactly the best of friends, are they? Halan thought. Halan's eyes narrowed as a plan began forming in her head.

She started to edge around the walls, making sure to move slowly and keep her feet covered with the cloak.

Creeping as close to Nouri as she could, Halan waited, holding her breath. Finally, the door opened. Parvin and the other Enforcer who was with him appeared in the doorway.

Halan readied the telescopic staff in one hand.

Then she heard a cry from inside the doorway and almost gasped out loud. It was the sound of a boy in pain. "Get off me!" Luca whimpered. "Please . . . don't . . ."

Then he was silent.

Halan's stomach turned over in horror. What was Tam doing to him in there? To all of them?

I have to get in there!

Halan steeled herself, and just as Parvin passed Nouri, she reached out and tapped her on the back of the head with the telescopic staff.

Nouri's head bounced forward, her hat tumbling to the floor. Halan cringed back, pressing herself against the wall—she had forgotten that the staff multiplied force two-fold!

"Yow!" Nouri cried. She turned around, saw Parvin coming through the door, and shoved him hard. "What in blazes are you thinking, Parvin?" she demanded. "You want to start something?"

"What?" Parvin snapped back. "I didn't do nothing to you!"

"Oh no?" Nouri jabbed a finger at her hat, lying on the

ground in front of her. "You're too chicken to admit you hit me?"

"Parvin, come on," muttered his companion. "She's imagining things—it's not worth it."

No! Halan couldn't let them walk away from this, or she'd never get inside. Thinking fast, she leaned close to Nouri and altered her voice to be lower than normal. "That's right, run away, you coward," she said.

All the guards turned toward her. Nouri jumped at the sound, looking around, confused.

Parvin's face flushed purple and he drew his truncheon. "What did you say to me?" he demanded, but he didn't give Nouri a chance to answer—he shoved her backward, and Halan dived out of the way just in time.

Rage overtaking confusion, Nouri took a swing at Parvin and clocked him square in the jaw. With that, all the rest of the guards joined in, trying to separate the two fighters. One of them caught a flying elbow that was meant for Parvin and lost his temper, and at that point Halan couldn't tell anymore who was fighting who.

She grinned as she daintily slipped past them and through the door into the chamber beyond.

What she saw on the other side took her breath away.

Before her was a cavernous circular space lit by flickering Thauma torches with wide columns stretching up to a vaulted ceiling.

In the center of the room, Tam was standing at an altar, his eyes closed and his mouth moving constantly as he muttered incantations. Placed on the altar was a large crystal bowl filled with a liquid so dark it was almost black, and giving off an eerie ghost light that hurt Halan's eyes to look at. All around the room, Thauma prisoners lay on tables side by side, their eyes closed. Halan felt a huge wave of relief as she saw that they were breathing. Kadir, she noticed, had a bandage hastily slapped around his inner elbow, as did the woman next to him. *No, wait—all of them.* They had all been cut; that must have been what was happening to Luca when she heard him cry out. And whether it was because of the ritual or something like the teardrop knife, all of them were unconscious now.

Halan's stomach churned as she looked back up at the liquid in the bowl and realized exactly what Tam was doing in order to perform the Undoing ritual.

Blood.

He's drawing power by drawing blood.

Tam suddenly raised a hand, and Halan froze, thinking that somehow he knew she was there. But instead, he dipped the other hand into the bowl and began to write in the air, symbols that seemed to burn on the backs of Halan's eyelids when she blinked, written with the blood of innocent Thauma.

Tam closed his eyes again and tilted his head back, mumbling more incantations under his breath. Behind him, something was forming. It was faint at first, but then grew larger and brighter with every symbol he burned into the air. It became a red nimbus cloud, glowing slightly from the inside, pulsating with light and stretching out to fill the room behind Tam's head.

It's not too late, Halan thought. *He's not finished. I can still stop this.*

But how? Her fingers itched to simply take the crystal bowl from the altar and smash it, but would that be enough? And what if she didn't make it that far? Tam would catch her, one way or the other, and then he could restart the ritual, draw more blood, and he would have her as well.

She looked down at herself, still wearing Nalah's clothes, underneath the cloak that belonged to Nalah's best friend. Even if Tam did catch her, would he even recognize her now? She looked so different from the decorated princess he'd once known.

And with that, a thought came into her mind.

If I were Nalah and he caught me, what a precious addition to his Thauma collection I would be. More precious, by far, than his powerless, useless daughter.

It hurt to think those things about herself, but she knew it was how he truly felt about her. She stood for a moment and watched his face, the face that she'd longed to see again, twisted with the vicious anticipation of destroying a whole world for his own benefit.

The only thing he cared about was power. Not her, not

anyone else. She could see that now, once and for all. The promise of even more power might be the only thing that could make him slip up and make a mistake.

Halan shut her eyes and took a few deep breaths. She could do this.

"Asa Tam!" she exclaimed, throwing off the shadow cloak. She stood there in front of him, visible, her fists clenched. Tam's eyes went wide and his hands drooped to his sides as he saw Halan appear before him. "Stop this ritual," she said. "Or I will summon up the winds and stop you myself!"

Hello, Father, Halan thought. She forced her face into a scowl.

Perhaps that way he wouldn't see that her heart was breaking.

Tam only paused for a moment. Then he smirked and held out his hand, fingers coated in the blood of the Thauma.

"Welcome, Nalah," he declared. "I am very glad you could join us!"

Halan scowled harder, so as not to show her relief.

Got you.

"I won't let you hurt these people," Halan said. "You have done enough damage as it is. My father's death will be avenged." The words struck home hard as soon as they were out of Halan's mouth.

Nalah wasn't the only person who lost a father that day.

Tam took the father I knew and loved, and he murdered him too.

Tam circled the altar, cracking his knuckles.

"I don't think I'll ever get used to how much you look like Halan," he observed. "I shall try to kill you quickly."

"Halan is in the Magi Kingdom right now!" Halan bit back. "If you cared at all about her, you wouldn't be trying to destroy the world with her in it."

Tam's eyes turned sad for a moment, and Halan's chest squeezed painfully. "A king cannot tolerate betrayal," he said with disgust. "That girl is not my true daughter. And even though I offered her everything—power, a throne, everything she could ever want—she still chose to defy me. She is a barren, useless child. I would rather she died than that I should go on living with that shame."

His words stung, each one like a shallow cut across Halan's heart.

And with that, the last of Halan's love for him leaked away.

How could this man stand in front of her and talk about shame and betrayal in his crisp suit with his hand dipped in blood?

She pulled out the staff and, being careful to keep the oval button turned away from Tam, she pressed it and made as magical a gesture as she could with her free hand as the staff folded out of itself. "You will destroy no more lives today," she growled. "Not today, not tomorrow—never again!"

She lashed out with the staff and it hit one of the columns, sending shards of smashed marble flying through the air. Tam ducked, feinted left, and then leaped to the right. He was going for one of the metal tables beside Luca's elbow. Halan saw, too late, the gleaming knife lying there. She brought her staff down, but she wasn't fast enough. Tam grabbed the knife and pulled back, and the table collapsed in a heap of scrap.

"I will have to punish Malek for not killing you when he had the chance." Tam chuckled. "But then again, I was planning on letting him die with the rest, so I suppose that's punishment enough."

Halan's blood ran cold. *What happened with Nalah and Lord Malek?*

Tam took advantage of her hesitation and lunged with the knife. Halan recoiled but forgot to protect her staff. Tam stepped in close and gripped it with his free hand. He wrenched it from her grip and threw it into a corner. She tried to duck under his arm, but he got behind her and seized her wrist, twisting it up behind her back. She gasped as he pressed his knife to her chest.

"Oh, you're not going anywhere," he whispered. "Not when you could be *so* helpful. You let Malek take the blood he needed, and then you come here to present the rest to me. Such a good girl."

He marched her toward the altar, the flat of the knife

pressing hard enough against her skin to bruise through Nalah's high-necked tunic.

"With the blood of a Fifth Clan Thauma flowing in both worlds," Tam continued, "my weapon will be more powerful than the old king could possibly have imagined. Say your good-byes to the Magi Kingdom while you can, Nalah, because as soon as that cloud breaks, neither you nor anybody else will ever see it again."

Chapter Sixteen

Nalah

Is there such a thing as "the Undoing"? Scholars— inevitably—disagree. Perhaps the magic that ended the war could be reversed. Perhaps the Sand Sea could be turned back into an ocean of water and the damage from the Year of Storms could be undone. It seems unlikely, and more to the point, it seems too dangerous for anyone but a maniac to try. After all, the full effects of the weapon are still unknown to this day. Who knows what else we could find ourselves facing?

Lady Nazhanin, The Role of Magic

As if in a dream, Nalah walked down the sunny path beside the prophet Cyrus, with Cobalt's comforting weight on her shoulder. Cyrus had refused to say more about what trouble she'd be facing, but as soon as she remembered hearing Halan whispering her name through the worlds, calling out to her, needing her, she had a feeling it was big.

First, I have to find Soren and the Shadows again, she thought. *Whatever's coming, I have to warn them.*

She couldn't help shooting Cyrus curious glances as they walked—he was dead, or at least not quite alive, and yet here he was right beside her, as real and physical as any living person. And he was blind, or at least not quite seeing, but he navigated the treacherous paths without hesitation.

"I have much more to teach you," Cyrus was saying. "But you have begun your journey toward mastery, and you have accepted the responsibility of being Fifth Clan in this world. That is far more than most of our kind have done by the time they were your age."

He stopped suddenly and held out a hand for Nalah to stop too. For a moment, she wondered why, but then she saw it—a huge flock of birds cresting the mountaintop. They rushed past, incredibly close and ridiculously fast, the wind from their wings buffeting Nalah's face. If Nalah and Cyrus had been standing just a few feet ahead, they might have been knocked right off the path.

"It's hard to condense all the necessary knowledge into the time between here and where we must part," Cyrus went on, continuing to walk down the path as if nothing very interesting had happened. "So, let me say this: the true path lies in *balance*. Skill and talent. The learned and the innate. Craftsmanship and sorcery. Fear and faith. Yes—fear plays a vital part, but you have had too much fear and not enough faith. Some Thauma have too much faith in their own work and not enough fear, and that too is an imbalance. Remember this, Nalah."

"I'll try," Nalah said.

"And remember this, too," said Cyrus more quietly. "Fire is not always your enemy. I know your history with that element is fraught, but fire can purify and heal, and there is a fire inside your soul that drives you and fuels your passion. Your mother knew this. It may be the most important lesson she has to teach you."

Nalah nodded, her heart full to bursting with the day's events and the memories of her parents now so fresh in her mind. In that moment, she missed them more than ever.

They turned another corner, and now Nalah could see the whole kingdom laid out below her once again. "Nalah, take my hand," said Cyrus. She did. "Look at this world and tell me what you see."

"I see the Magi City . . ."

But there was something wrong. The city didn't seem real, somehow. Nalah's scalp prickled, and she leaned forward, dread rising in her throat.

She gasped.

The Magi City was tearing open, as if it were a photograph that someone was ripping down the middle. Red clouds rose from it like steam from an erupting geyser. Cracks ran out from the deep in the heart of the city, farther and farther, rifts like the ones that had torn down the length of New Hadar. They even opened up in the sky, great tears in the fabric of reality itself. The color began to drain from the Magi Kingdom and into the rifts, and then the light itself, until Nalah was standing on a black ledge staring out at nothing at all.

And then, in the darkness, with a sound like glass shattering, a speck of golden light appeared. She reached out for it, and it spoke with Halan's voice.

"Take my hand!"

Then Nalah gasped and found herself standing right on the edge of the high path, her hand outstretched. She stepped back hurriedly, but then she realized she couldn't have fallen—Cyrus still held her other hand in a firm grip. He gave it a squeeze.

She looked around, checking for red rifts in the earth, but there were none. The vision wasn't real.

Not yet.

Nalah felt the electric energy in her hands begin to grow, prickling at her skin, waiting to get out. But instead of being afraid, she took a deep breath, allowing the electricity to flow into her arms, her legs, into her whole body until she felt it sparking even at the corners of her eyes, illuminating the world before her with the light of the power within. "I need to go back," she said, and her voice crackled with captured energy.

"Yes," said Cyrus, and let go of her hand. "It's time."

She hurried down the path, Cyrus keeping pace next to her. "Is this the way back to the shrine entrance? I left my camel there—oh stars, it will take forever to get back to the kingdom!"

"Do not worry," said Cyrus. "I will take care of your camel for you. You won't be needing it today."

"Won't be needing it? But how will I—" Nalah turned to look for Cyrus, but he was gone. "Cyrus!" Huffing impatiently, suddenly not at all in the mood for his mystical wise man antics, Nalah hurried onward down the path and found herself outside the shrine entrance. Her camel looked up from nibbling at a bush and eyed her with interest.

"Your steed, Nalah," said Cyrus's voice, and Nalah turned.

What she saw may have been one of the most astonishing things she'd seen that day, and that was saying something.

It was a horse, but no ordinary horse. Its curved body was made of smoothly interlocking bands of steel, and it wore a saddle carved from wood and padded with thick, black woven fabric. As she approached, the horse looked at her with black glass eyes and shook its out its silken mane in the hot breeze.

It's alive like Cobalt or Chestnut, she thought, *but made with all the elements. It must be the work of a Fifth Clan Thauma!*

"This is Forge," said Cyrus. "He has been a companion of mine for many, many years, and now I would like you to have him." He handed the reins of the horse over to Nalah, and she took them, still stunned by the creature's odd beauty. "He is five times faster than his flesh-and-blood brethren," Cyrus went on. "And as long as he likes you, it's very hard to fall out of his saddle. Also, he hasn't had a proper run in several hundred years, so I expect he's as keen to get going as you are." Forge tossed his head and nudged Cyrus affectionately with a whicker from deep in his throat that sounded like wooden sticks rattling together.

Almost in a trance, Nalah reached up to stroke Forge's smooth steel nose and then climbed up into the saddle, swinging her leg over and settling back into the wooden seat. She wasn't particularly surprised to find that it fit her like a glove.

Cyrus patted Forge affectionately on the flank, then picked up the Sword of the Fifth Clan from where it had been resting against a gnarled tree and handed it to her.

"Don't forget this," he said. "You will need it."

Nalah nodded. "Good-bye, Cyrus. And thank you . . . for everything."

"Farewell, Nalah. We will meet again. If you wish to repay me, then fulfill your destiny and stop the oncoming storm. Now, ride!"

Nalah slung the sword over her back and spurred Forge forward, holding on tight as he sprang from a standing position directly into a full-on gallop. Cobalt lifted off Nalah's shoulder and into the air, shrieking in surprise.

Forge sped down the narrow mountain path, his steel hooves striking sparks off the black stone. Nalah's hair whipped out behind her, and the air buffeted her face and chest so hard she could barely breathe. She gasped as Forge turned a sharp corner, his hooves sending up a wave of black scree behind him, and then they were descending again. Any normal creature would have taken the steep drop with caution, but not Forge—this horse was completely fearless. Adrenaline coursed through Nalah's veins as they thundered down the precipice, as unstoppable as an avalanche.

They were down the mountain in a few terrifying, exhilarating minutes, and Forge set out across the desert without a moment's pause. Nalah bent over the saddle and murmured into the horse's ear. "We're looking for the Shadow camp. It should be by the oasis, about halfway across."

She figured the horse might understand, and sure enough, Forge slightly adjusted his course.

They shot across the desert, Forge's hooves barely seeming to touch the ground. Nalah gripped the pommel and put her head down into the wind. *I'm coming, Halan,* she kept thinking. *Whatever's happening, just hold on, I'm coming.*

When Nalah saw the oasis just up ahead, shimmering in the sunlight, she thought she must be seeing a mirage—but as they drew closer, and she could see the wavering palm leaves on the trees, she realized that they had actually arrived. Forge really *was* that fast.

For a moment she feared that the Shadows might have moved on, but then there was a split in the air and a floating torso ducked out, and then another, and another. Forge slowed as they approached, and Nalah could make out Jackal and Mantis, and then Falcon, greeting her from a distance with his graceful salute. She thought about returning it but decided against taking her hands off Forge's saddle.

Then Soren appeared from between the tents, dressed in the same black sheath tunic as the Shadows. Nalah breathed a sigh of relief as she saw that the color and the mischief had returned to his face. He looked more himself, in fact, than Soren had in a long time. Nalah grinned, taking a certain pleasure in the way his jaw dropped at the sight of Forge.

"Starchild," Falcon called out as she drew Forge up beside him. "We ben happy to see you returned safe." He approached the steel horse and patted his steaming neck. "Your new friend ben very beautiful, but think I you do not come just to visit with us. Sense I a change, a *wrongness*," he added quietly, urgently.

Nalah nodded. "I had a vision at the shrine. I'm on my way back to the city. I just stopped to get Soren—if you're well enough," she added, turning to him. She was happy to see him walk to Forge's side with perfect ease.

"Falcon's told me what he's seen," Soren said. "Whatever it is that's going on, I'm coming with you." He glanced behind him, at the bare heads of the Shadow Clan and their shimmering invisible tents. Scorpion had pushed to the front of the crowd that was forming and slipped her hand into Soren's, giving him a smile and a firm nod. "But when we're done, I plan to return here and join the Shadow Clan. They're going to set out again soon. They'll travel far beyond anything I know, and I'm going to go with them."

Nalah had had a feeling this was coming, ever since she'd seen the way Soren and Scorpion had looked at each other across the bonfire that night. And it made sense— Soren had been longing for adventure since the end of the rebellion. Longing to see the world beyond the kingdom. Now, he could do all that and more.

"That's wonderful! I'm so happy for you," she said, though inside, her heart hurt. Soren had become a true friend to her. "Everyone will miss you so much," she added, looking at the ground.

"Of course they will," Soren said with a shrug. "I'm sure all your lives will be completely dull without me around to brighten the place up. But that's for later," he said, swinging himself up onto Forge's back behind Nalah. "Let's go and save the world, and then we can talk about my going-away party after we're done."

Nalah looked up into the sky and saw Cobalt wheeling high above.

"Cobalt!" she called up. The glass falcon replied with a ringing cry. "Fly to the palace! Tell them the Queen's Sword rides!"

Cobalt shot off at once, his wings glittering in the

sunlight, and Nalah urged Forge after him, as fast as he could go.

Forge clattered through the gates and into the Magi City, drawing astonished gasps from the guards and the people milling in the streets. Nalah found her eyes drawn to the air.

It was foggy. There was a chill that she had never felt in this world during the daytime. The sun beat down on the city, the same as it always did, but it couldn't seem to penetrate the cloud. All around her the bright colors of the Magi City were muted. Nalah thought of the way the color had drained from the world in her vision and shuddered.

"We have to get to the palace," Soren muttered, and Nalah nodded and pressed Forge forward. The streets were packed as citizens emerged from their houses and work-shops to stare up at the mist in awe and apprehension, but they parted when they saw Forge trotting up the street, tossing his silken mane.

"The Queen's Sword!" A cry went up from the crowd as they cantered up the hill toward the palace. Nalah heard the guards take it up too. "The Queen's Sword has returned!" Nalah's heart swelled with happiness—despite all the mistakes she'd made, the people still turned to her in times of need. They trusted her to help them. She could not let them down.

Forge came to a screeching halt in the palace courtyard. It, too, was full of fog. Nalah jumped down from Forge's back, her knees trembling as she landed. She felt dizzy suddenly—could it just be the long ride?

"Nalah!" came a choked cry, and Nalah was barely able to catch sight of Rani and Omar's figures dashing across the way before she found herself enveloped in a hug. They held her tight for a moment before pulling away, their faces drawn and pale. "Nalah, thank the stars you're back," Rani said. "What is happening? Have you—have you spoken to Halan?"

Nalah's stomach turned over as if she were still on Forge, thundering down the steep mountain path toward the ground.

"No, I haven't," she said. "Not really. I think I heard her saying that she needed me, but she sounded so far away, She went to New Hadar, didn't she?"

Rani's face was a mask of panic. "Yes—and now she's stuck there, all alone!"

"What?" Nalah gasped.

"The Transcendent Mirror stopped working," Rani said. "Nobody can get through, and we've heard nothing from the other side."

"But why did she go through?" Nalah asked.

"It was your friend Marcus Cutter," said Omar, and Nalah's heart gave yet another great lurch.

My instincts were right—but what's happened to Marcus?

Omar looked as if he hadn't slept in days. "He came to ask for help. He said people in your government had taken his brother. I didn't want her to go . . ." He shook his head. "But she had to. She couldn't leave your world to suffer. She—" He stopped, choked up.

"She's alive," Nalah said quickly. "I'm sure she is." Omar and Rani both let out shaky breaths and nodded.

"But now . . . this!" Rani gestured to the sky. "Nalah, I don't know what's happening. I've never seen anything like it."

"Yes, I saw a vision on the mountain," said Nalah. "If we don't stop it . . ."

They looked at her expectantly, but Nalah just shook her head.

"Failure isn't an option," Nalah said, injecting her voice with as much confidence as she could muster. "We must figure out how to end this and quickly."

"Queen Rani! Lady Nalah!" It was Lord Helavi. He was running across the courtyard, his gray beard fluttering behind him. He came to a halt and sagged against Forge for support, hardly seeming to notice that he was made of metal. Forge sniffed his yellow hat. "I have been watching from the East Tower," Lord Helavi gasped. "The fog, it is thickening. Whatever curse is upon us, it is strengthening by the minute."

Looking at him, Nalah was reminded of something he'd said the last time they'd been together in the East Tower. Something about a scroll that seemed to be a lost prophecy from the Seer. From Cyrus.

Perhaps, even then, she thought, *he was leading me toward my destiny.*

"Lord Helavi," Nalah said. "The scroll you were trying to decipher, the one about . . . door and dust. You said you didn't understand exactly what it meant, but I have a feeling it might be connected to what's happening. Can you tell me more about it?"

The vizier looked perplexed for a moment. He looked up at the cloud above them and then back at Nalah, his eyes widening. "My word . . . ," he breathed. "You might be right."

"Please," Nalah urged him. "Tell me more."

"Well," Lord Helavi began, "as with many of Cyrus's prophecies, it was written a bit like a poem. Full of symbols and hidden meanings. Let me see if I can remember. . . ." The old man closed his eyes and began to recite some of the words from memory:

> *"The Undoing shall come quietly, unseen,*
> *From a world of water blue and forests green,*
> *A fallen king who wears a mask*
> *There will go about his fatal task.*
> *And all the while in the world of sands,*
> *Great blood be spilled by idle hands,*
> *And from that blood a vile robe be made,*
> *To cut the world's veil as with a blade.*

And when all the fires go out, the dust will rise:
A cloud of hate and bleeding lies.
The choice is left to balance, love, and trust:
A parasite or sister? Door or dust?

Lord Helavi stopped and looked up at Nalah as if waking from a dream.

"The Undoing," Nalah whispered, looking out at the fading world all around her. "That certainly sounds like what's happening here."

"Yes," Lord Helavi agreed. "I have read references about this ritual elsewhere, but it was always considered just a myth—just a story."

Nalah chuckled humorlessly. "Stories can end up being more real than we'd like to think."

"Indeed," Lord Helavi said. "Well, the Undoing was said to be a ritual that would undo the work of the old king's weapon, the one that split the worlds in the first place. But doing so would sacrifice one of the worlds altogether, causing the life and power of one world to be sucked into the other. It would be destroyed."

Nalah thought of the rifts she had seen opening in her vision, the color draining from the world, and now she had to lean on Forge to catch her breath too.

"If the Magi Kingdom is fading, that means that someone in New Hadar is doing this," she said. "All the magic here will flow back into my world. If that happened, they'd have it all—the water, the machines, the magic—everything."

"But who is doing this?" Omar asked. "And how?"

Nalah thought back on the words of the poem.

A fallen king who wears a mask . . .

Blood be spilled by idle hands . . .

"It's Tam," she finally said as the truth dawned upon her. "Tam and Malek. They must be working together. After all, Malek kept mentioning how he was making the cloak for 'his master.' I was foolish not to realize it sooner."

"Asa . . . ," Rani whispered, rage and terror mingling in her voice.

"He couldn't have ultimate power here in the kingdom, so he went to my world to get it there. And get revenge on all those who betrayed him in the process."

"He'd kill a whole world, just out of spite?" Omar exclaimed.

"If it meant he'd get power out of it," Soren broke in, "then yes—I think he would."

There was a moment of silence as that revelation sank in.

"And what of Lord Malek?" asked Rani. "He was banished from this land—how was it that you saw him, Nalah?"

Nalah sighed. "He captured Soren and me before we even got out of the city. He used me to make a blood cloak."

"A *blood cloak*?" gasped Lord Helavi. "Nalah, he didn't . . .

not your blood, not the blood of the Fifth Clan?"

Nalah nodded. "We escaped with our lives, but not before he got what he needed," she said. "It's just like the poem said: *from that blood a vile robe be made, to cut the world's veil as with a blade.* Malek must have used the power of the cloak to open a portal between the worlds, allowing the ritual to begin from the other side."

She frowned. She felt a prickling tightness in her head, like a headache that was just starting to get going.

"Nalah, your hands," Soren said. Nalah looked down. Her hands had turned very pale, the scuffs and scars standing out white against her skin. Her fingers felt stiff when she tried to flex them. "It's the cloak! You're right, Nalah. It's drawing on you to give him power."

Nalah curled her shaking hands into fists.

"We *will* stop this," she said through gritted teeth.

"But the seals are broken," muttered Lord Helavi, shaking his head. "If Malek has torn the fabric of reality—the barrier between the worlds can't be rewoven now!"

Nalah tried to think through the stiffness in her neck and the fatigue that seemed to be seeping into her bones. Up on the mountain, she'd seen the world go dark, but even in that nothingness there was a light.

Halan. She's on the other side.

And what was it that Cyrus had said?

"The true path lies in balance," Nalah gasped. "Without Tam's ritual, what is the rift? It's just an opening, like a window or a door. It lets the light in."

The others were all staring at her, and even Lord Helavi was frowning as if she was making no sense at all. Maybe she wasn't.

But then again, maybe she was.

"I know what I have to do," she told them. "I just hope it's not too late."

Chapter Seventeen

Sisters

One is an important number. One is the point of a sword, a length of rope, a sovereign nation, a journey with a destination. But one is also an unstable pivot, a lonely girl, a last chance.

With two, you can make a bridge, give and take advice, forge alliances, return home after a long journey. Two eyes grant perspective.

Two is the number of second chances, and that makes it perhaps the most important number of all.

Cyrus, Prophet of the Sands

The pain was worse than what Halan had been prepared for. She let out a sobbing yell as Tam dragged his knife across her arm, holding it out over the crystal bowl. Blood cascaded down the blade and dripped into the black pool in long, viscous strings. Halan weakly tried to wrest her arm from Tam, but he held it firm.

"Now," he crowed, "the blood of the Fifth Clan will

draw the magic from that world straight into my hands, and then—"

He stopped. Halan looked up, hardly daring to hope that her risk was paying off. The red nimbus cloud above their heads was shuddering strangely. As Halan watched, it contracted suddenly, and a flash like lightning passed through it. She glanced at Tam, waiting for his reaction.

"What is this?" he snarled. He dropped Halan's wrist and raised his hands to the sky, bloodstained fingertips reaching toward the cloud expectantly.

But nothing happened.

The cloud contracted again, and then billowed out and turned a dark, sooty black.

Halan pushed herself away from the bowl and staggered back, clutching her arm to her chest. Blood dripped on the stones at her feet, but despite the pain, she began to smile at the sight of the dismay on Tam's face. Whatever was happening, it wasn't what he had planned.

"What kind of foul trick—" Tam began, wheeling to face her, brandishing the bloody knife.

"What's the matter?" asked Halan. "Not what you expected, *Father*?"

Tam's eyes widened.

"No . . . ," he whispered.

"Yes," she growled. "It's me—your powerless, useless daughter. And you've just added a big helping of completely unmagical blood to your ritual."

For a moment, Tam's face paled and he looked down at the knife in his hand with something like grief and regret. "Halan," he said. But Halan steeled herself, closing off her heart to his lies. He was more upset about his spell than he was about her. She knew it with a cold, sad certainty.

"Was I a good liar, Father? Was I as good as you?"

Tam looked up at her with revulsion in his eyes. "My plans. My *power*. You have no idea what you've done!" he said, and lunged at her, slashing wildly with the blade. Halan ducked and tried to scramble away from him, but her foot slipped on the flagstones and she fell. Her back thumped against the ground and she let out a grunt as the air flew out of her lungs. For a moment, she couldn't think or breathe, but she tried to push herself away from Tam. He advanced and raised his knife—

Then something hit the side of his head with an almighty *clang*. Tam went flying, rolling over and over, the knife flying out of his hand and skittering across the floor.

"Whoa," gasped Marcus's voice. "This thing packs a punch, doesn't it?"

Halan gasped as she saw him, still trying to force her lungs to breathe again. He took her hands and helped her to her feet.

"Marcus," she panted, and flung her arms around him. He had dark rings around his eyes, but he was alive and holding the Thauma staff. Behind him she saw Kadir on his feet, leaning weakly against one of the columns, and

Luca and the others all sitting up, rubbing their eyes.

My blood disrupted the spell, she thought. *It woke them up.*

"How do we stop it?" Marcus asked her, peering at the swirling black cloud.

Halan shook her head. "I don't know—but we have to try."

"You can't," croaked Tam. Halan spun and saw him struggling to a sitting position against the wall, clutching his head. He let out a mad, hysterical chuckle. "You think you're heroes? You're too late! The veil is open, and there is no way to reset the balance. You've cost me my power, but you haven't saved your kingdom or your precious mother and sister. In a few minutes, it will all be over. The Magi Kingdom is as good as gone!"

We're close, Nalah thought, as Forge pounded down the hard-packed sand street with a group of royal guards in black uniforms sprinting to keep up. *I can feel it.*

She was having trouble breathing, like her lungs had shrunk to half the size they should be. She leaned forward over Forge's neck, as if she could draw strength from him. But she knew she couldn't. There was only one way to get her strength back.

They turned a corner, and Nalah saw it. The upper edges of what looked like a swirling black cloud, pulsating and shuddering inside an open courtyard at the back of a large house. She dismounted and sprint-stumbled through an archway and into a small garden.

Malek was standing in front of the cloud, his blood-red cloak sweeping through the air as a driving wind blew through the courtyard like a sandstorm. He spun around at the sound of her footsteps, scowling—but when he saw Nalah his face lit up.

"What wonderful timing," he said, his black eyes glinting. "I suppose you did this—disrupted my master's spell somehow?" He gestured to the cloud. Nalah stared at it— the light hurt her eyes, and the cloud seemed pretty active to her, but that wasn't what caught her gaze and held it at the center of the swirling mass.

Somewhere on the other side, Halan is still fighting, she thought. *I'm sure of it. I just have to get to her.*

The soldiers arrived behind Nalah with a clatter of mail, and Nalah gave Malek a weak smile.

"You're outnumbered, Malek. It's over. Take off the cloak."

Malek glanced at the guards and laughed, a high, cruel sound. "You are weak! All of you, *weaklings*. With this cloak on my back, I am like a god! I can feel the power of the universe coursing through my very veins like lightning!" He looked back at Nalah, his lip curling in disgust. "This should never have been yours, girl. It resides now in the form it always should have had, the body of a true Thauma lord!"

Nalah drew her sword and leaned on it like a walking stick, working hard to keep drawing breath into her lungs. "Guards," she shouted with effort, "seize him and bring me that cloak!"

The soldiers rushed forward, but Malek just smiled. He reached down and grabbed a handful of sand from the raked garden at his feet. "See, now," he said, "the power of the Fifth Clan!" And with that, he threw the sand into the air.

"Watch out!" Nalah yelled. Most of the soldiers managed to duck and shield their faces, but a few were too slow as the sand melted and twisted into tiny shards of glass and flew at them. Two men fell to the ground, gasping and clutching at their faces, blood beginning to seep from a thousand tiny wounds.

Malek laughed again and reached out to grasp the branch of a nearby tree. Suddenly, all the trees in the garden began to whip their branches around wildly. Two of the soldiers were knocked on their backs, and three more standing too close let out choking screams as the branches wrapped around them, hugging them tight to the trunks of the trees.

Nalah sagged, struggling to stay on her feet, the sword wobbling under her weight.

"I am the true Fifth Clan Thauma!" Malek cried, the wind continuing to whip the blood cloak into a frenzy at his back. "I will stand beside my king in the New World, and you will shrivel and die with the rest of this useless rabble!"

"Tam will never share his power with you," Nalah shot back, though every word seemed to cause her last bit of energy to ebb away. "He's left you here to die with us! Don't you see that?"

Malek let out a wordless howl of fury and pulled a dagger from his robe. He hurled it, and the blade arced through the air toward Nalah. With a grunt of effort, Nalah swung her sword and batted the knife away from her. It spun in the air, and then to Nalah's horror it turned around, its point swinging around to face her again. Dropping the sword, Nalah dived out of the way, seizing the shield that the closest unconscious soldier had been holding. She rolled with the shield over her head, just in time to hear the knife glance off the metal with a *twang*. She started trying to pull herself along the ground, staying low, trying to get even a moment of respite from the onslaught.

"That's right," Malek shouted at her. "Crawl, little worm!"

There was another *twang* as the knife made a second pass, glancing off the shield again.

How can I beat a man who's using my own power against me?

It was all very well for Cyrus to go on about balance when he lived on a mountain and never—she was willing to bet—had magic knives thrown at his head.

"Ready to die, girl?" Malek said with cruel glee.

Twang!

Every bone in Nalah's body ached to give up. Malek was literally leeching the life from her with every second that passed. A flash of anger laced through her. This small, heartless, terrible man thought that stealing her blood made him like her. He had no idea what it meant to be a Fifth Clan Thauma. It was more than just the power. Cyrus had taught her that.

Then Nalah remembered another thing Cyrus had said to her. *Some Thauma have too much faith in their own work and not enough fear, and that too is an imbalance.*

Malek doesn't have enough fear, she thought. *But I still have too much.*

Maybe I need to restore the balance a little.

Dredging up every last bit of her strength, Nalah tossed away her shield and struggled to her feet just as the knife sailed past her head. She watched it begin to turn and fly back toward her, and then Nalah began to run—directly toward Malek. He stared at her in utter disbelief as Nalah, with the knife sailing right behind her, came barreling at him at top speed.

Malek twisted to duck out of the way, and Nalah threw herself at him, one hand reaching out.

Her fingers closed on the hem of the blood cloak.

She gasped. It was like waking up from a dream. The fabric shuddered and pulsated with her touch, and the world seemed to speed up. She sat up just as the knife came flying toward her face, and she reached her free hand out to catch it by the hilt before it could pierce her skin. In her hand, the knife melted into a soft ball, as if it was made of nothing more than clay.

"No!" Malek screamed, clutching the cloak around his shoulders and attempting to wrench it from her grasp. "It's mine!"

"No," said Nalah, slowly getting to her feet and seizing the cloak in both her hands. Her voice shook the garden like a roll of thunder. The trees let go of their captives, and the bricks in the courtyard wall trembled and fell. *"It's not."*

For a moment they stood there, Malek trying to use Nalah's own power to fight back against her grip on the cloak. But the cycle of power flowing through Nalah, the cloak, Malek, and back only seemed to make her stronger.

"You are no Fifth Clan Thauma," Nalah said, her voice roaring through the garden like a summer storm, growing in volume with every passing moment. *"Even if you stole every last drop of blood from my body, you would still never be one. You cannot take my power, just as you cannot take the stars from the sky. It doesn't* belong *to me. It is me!"*

And with that, Nalah sent an electric blast of energy through her hands into the cloak. Malek screamed again as the cloak burst into a floating tangle of threads, unweaving and unwinding in the air in front of Nalah. The threads themselves untwisted, and then they turned to dust and blew away on the breeze. Malek fell to the ground, his mouth open in a shocked O, his hands still curled into claws from gripping the cloak that was now gone, gone.

Two of the guards managed to get to their feet and grab Malek between them. He struggled, weakly. "Master!" he screamed into the sky as they dragged him away. "Save me!" But no one came.

Nalah's whole body felt so light and powerful, she thought she could have lifted a building or swum across the Hadar Sea. She turned to the black cloud, her heart thumping steadily against her ribs.

She had stopped Malek, but the Undoing still continued. How could she stop the swirling rift?

She could see the color beginning to drain from the garden around her. Looking up, Nalah felt her stomach turn over as she realized that above her head the sky was no longer blue but a spreading stain of gray, reaching out farther and farther. The cloud was growing all the time, blackness swallowing the courtyard wall and the bushes. The wind picked up, and leaves started to peel from the trees in the garden, wheeling past her head and into the void between the worlds.

"My Lady," gasped the head guard, her hair streaming past her face as if it were trying to follow the leaves into the cloud. "What do we do now?"

Nalah swallowed. "Get everybody out of here!" she

called, raising her voice as the wind whistled in her ears.

The head guard nodded, but when Nalah didn't follow, she stopped and called back to her.

"But Nalah," she shouted, "how about you? You can't do this alone!"

Nalah looked into the swirling cloud, at the gaping wound between this world and her own, and then back at the captain. "I won't be doing it alone," she replied. "Please! Just . . . trust me!"

The head guard hesitated another moment and then gave Nalah another solemn nod. "Guards!" she turned and shouted. "Everybody out! Go! Go! Go!"

Nalah took a deep breath and began walking toward the rift. She had to brace herself with every step, channeling all her newfound strength into staying upright and not allowing herself to be pulled into the void. It tore at her hair and the loose fabric of her clothes, tiny shards of debris and grains of sand cutting into her flesh as she went. Shuffling now, Nalah got closer and closer, until the black mist was all around her and through watering eyes she could see her own hair turn translucent and vanish as it hit the tear in the world.

She could feel herself being unmade. Her very soul being slowly taken apart, bit by bit.

I know you're there, she thought, sending the message through the void as powerfully as a thunderclap. *You needed me, and I'm here now. I need you, Halan. I need you!*

And with a pained cry, Nalah reached a hand out into the void.

"Get them out!" Halan shouted above the gale. "Go, get them all out!"

The Thauma staggered and stumbled off the tables where they lay. They grabbed each other, helping the old, carrying the children, bracing just to stay still as they were buffeted by the driving wind that had started to blow out of the black cloud. They half walked, half fell through the huge doors, which rattled on their hinges under the force of the gusts.

Halan and Marcus had taken shelter, lying behind the altar. Marcus's knuckles were white on the Thauma staff.

"How do we stop it?" Marcus yelled. "And where's Tam?"

Halan didn't know. She cried out as the wind tossed the crystal bowl full of blood off the altar—it sailed over their heads to splash and shatter against the far wall of the chamber.

Then . . . a voice.

I need you, Halan.

Halan sat up. "Nalah?" she whispered.

Marcus threw her a frightened look.

I need you!

The words were clearer this time, carried on the wind.

Halan turned around and hooked her fingers through a hole in the stone and very slowly raised her head above the altar. She was almost blasted backward, but she hung on, the wind whipping her hair out behind her. She could barely see through the flying debris, but there was something different about the center of the cloud now. There was something there, something bright.

Halan seized the staff from Marcus's hand and used it to brace herself as she stepped out from behind the altar. "What are you doing?" Marcus cried, but Halan ignored him and kept walking. She almost lost her footing but regained her balance and pushed herself across the room toward the swirling black nimbus, using the striking force of the staff against the ground to propel herself one small step after another.

Halan, take my hand! Nalah's voice cried inside Halan's mind. *I need you—we need to reset the balance!*

Halan gasped as she drew closer to the center of the cloud, the black mist whipping around her head, and saw that the bright thing was a hand made of pure light, extending toward her.

"Nalah!" she screamed into the void, reaching out with her own hand. "I'm here!"

She was almost there, but then something knocked the staff away. Halan wheeled her arms, fighting to stay standing, and looked back to see Tam rising behind her, the knife in his hand once again. "Why won't you just die?" he shouted, his face a mask of desperation.

With a great cry of effort, Halan turned away from him and leaped into the cloud, throwing out her hand, reaching for her sister—

Their fingers touched.

For a moment, everything went white.

Then there was a great pulse that rolled out from their clasped hands, passing over Halan like a tidal wave. She looked back and saw it strike Tam just as he was about to bring his knife down, blasting him away from her. His back hit the altar with a sickening crunch, and he wheeled away and struck the wall that was peppered with the shards of his crystal bowl. Tam hung there for a second and then slid down the wall and lay still.

"You first," Halan whispered.

The gale died, and Halan almost toppled over, suddenly unbalanced. The hand that held hers gave a shaky squeeze. Halan turned and saw her.

Nalah stood in a wind-ravaged courtyard garden, the blue sky blazing above her. Halan could feel the heat of the sun radiating from the garden, could smell splintered wood and Thauma smoke and all the million tiny uniden-tifiable scents of *home*.

The black cloud had gone. Where it had been, there was just a hole, like an archway in a wall, encircled by a ragged ring of softly glowing white mist.

"Halan?" Nalah breathed.

Halan stared down at the hand in hers—it was identical, soft, brown, *real*—connecting one world to the other.

"Is this really happening?" she said. "I see you! I see my kingdom. . . ."

Nalah took a deep breath, smiled, and stepped through the hole into her own world. "I see you too, Sister," Nalah replied. "I never stopped seeing you, not since the moment I left."

Halan threw her arms around her sister's neck and buried her face in her shoulder. "The mirror broke," she cried. "I thought I might have lost you forever."

"Nalah?" Marcus had come around the cracked altar and was staring at the two of them and at the hole in the world, his blue eyes and his mouth both open wide. He started to smile, started to run toward them.

Then his smile died. "Halan, look out!"

Something seized Halan's ankle, feeling like a hundred biting insects all stinging her skin at once. She screamed and tried to pull away, but the grip tightened. Halan's vision swam and she reeled, losing her balance and hitting the ground hard. She held up a hand and watched as her skin turned gray and began to wither before her eyes.

Halan barely managed to lift her head for long enough to see that it was Tam, his skin covered in cuts, his outstretched hand once again wearing the iridescent green glove. "If I go," he growled, blood oozing from the corner of his mouth, "I'm taking you with me, Halan."

"Let her go!" Nalah screamed, and kicked him away from Halan. Tam lost his grip on her ankle and fell onto his back, and Halan saw the light leave his eyes.

She lay on the floor of the cold chamber, beside the dead man who had once been her father. She was faintly aware of Nalah and Marcus moving around her, but she couldn't hear what they were saying. She could see blue sky through the portal and feel the warmth of her own kingdom on her face.

I'm home, she thought dimly.

Then everything went dark.

"What is it?" Nalah yelled. "What did he do?" She gritted her teeth and touched the pale skin on Halan's face, her heart thumping painfully in her chest. "Come on, Halan, please. Wake up, wake up!"

Halan lay still, her face burning hot and her breathing coming in occasional, broken gasps.

"Pestilence Glove," Marcus said. "A few seconds' contact can make the victim sick. Any more than that can be . . ." He swallowed and didn't continue.

"*Nalah* . . ." Halan's voice was weak, barely more than a whisper.

Nalah seized her sister's burning hot, trembling hand. "I'm here, Halan. I'm right here. You're going to be all right, do you hear me? I won't let you go."

"*I'm sorry* . . ." Tears escaped from Halan's closed eyes

and streaked down her face.

"No!" Nalah replied, barely holding back a sob. "What for? You saved my world—and yours. We did it together. Look, I can see Cobalt in the sky up there, can you see him? Halan? Halan?"

Halan had stopped speaking, and her face had gone slack.

"No, no, no—please!" Nalah cried out, grabbing her sister by the shoulders and shaking her. "I can't lose you too!" The heat in Halan's skin was getting even worse, and Nalah's own palms burned in answer. A shudder ran through her, a burst of fear, and the faint smell of smoke.

Fire can purify.

Fire can heal.

Nalah stood up. *If there's even a chance of me saving her,* Nalah thought, *I have to try.*

She needed metal. Two pieces.

Stepping back from Halan's body, Nalah sprang through the portal.

"What are you doing?" Marcus yelled.

Nalah didn't reply. She seized the Sword of the Fifth Clan from where it lay and and leaped back into New Hadar. She needed fire, too, but she could make that herself. Her heart already felt as if it were burning hotter than the sun.

I'm sorry, Nalah thought as she held the sword in her hands. *You served me so well. I promise I'll reforge you one* day, *better than before.* And with that, she took the steel blade in her hands and began to rip it in two, as easy as tearing paper, with a sound like a faint scream of pain.

"Nalah!" Marcus cried in alarm. But Nalah couldn't stop to explain now. Not when every breath Halan took could be her last.

She tucked the point of the blade against Halan's chest, folding her thin gray hands over it. Then she gripped what was left in her hands and backed away.

"Stay back," she told Marcus, who was watching her with his mouth open and tears streaming down his cheeks.

Metal and fire.

Love.

That was the dangerous recipe that Zachary Tam had taught his friend Rina, Nalah's mother, when she was desperate and Nalah was dying. That was the spell boiled down to its very essence. The fire had gotten out of control and killed Rina, and Nalah had been too afraid to try it on Soren, but now she understood. Rina hadn't been afraid. She had given up her life for Nalah's and gladly. When your heart was at stake, there was no room for fear.

She held the blade and shut her eyes, breathing hard. Each breath felt like the pumping of the furnace bellows, stoking the fire, sending up sparks that danced behind Nalah's closed eyelids.

"*Draw out the sickness,*" she said, her voice ringing like metal under the stroke of a hammer.

She opened her eyes. The blade on Halan's chest was glittering, glowing from the inside with a faint golden light. Meanwhile, the blade in her own hands burned red, then white hot. The fabric around the hilt caught fire, and then the wooden hilt itself. The glass in the blade melted and fell steaming to the floor.

Nalah held on to the blade, the bellows of her lungs still working. The metal sagged, bent, and melted. Nalah let it run from her fingers, splashing and scorching the flagstones in front of her, burning up the dust and dirt all around it.

"I love you, Halan," Nalah whispered. She could feel her skin and hair begin to burn. But she didn't stop.

"Nalah," Marcus choked. "Nalah . . . it's working!"

Nalah moaned as the burning inside her continued, so hot that she felt as if smoke would rise from each breath she took. She looked down at Halan's body and saw her skin returning to a healthy brown color.

She saw Halan take a breath.

Nalah felt as if in another moment, her body would be a cinder, would simply fall to the floor as ash and blow away in the wind. But she didn't stop.

Finally, Halan's eyes opened. She looked up at Nalah, who was like a great, glowing flame, and reached out to her.

"Nalah," she murmured. "It's okay . . . you don't have to fight anymore. Let it go."

Nalah gasped, dropping the shard of her sword on the ground, the fiery glow dimming. Nalah fell to her knees, and Halan got up to catch her. They both remained there, kneeling in each other's arms for a long moment before anyone spoke.

"I knew you could do it," Halan murmured into Nalah's shoulder. "I always knew. You had it in you all along, Sister. You just needed to believe that yourself."

"I know," Nalah sobbed. She looked up to see Marcus standing a little ways away, his eyes watery, his hands awkwardly at his sides. "Marcus," she called to him, and he dashed to her, throwing his arms around them both. For a long moment all three of them clung to each other, crying with joy and laughing with exhaustion.

"Look," Marcus said finally, through his tears. He pointed down to where a line of white swirling cloud ran right underneath them. "Do you think we're the first people to ever hug in two different worlds at once?"

"Maybe," Halan said. "But I don't think we're going to be the last."

Chapter Eighteen

Sisters

The new First Minister Baharak Tir gave a speech on the steps of the Hokmet Tower last night in an attempt to address the public's concerns regarding the actions of her predecessor and the persecution of Thauma on his watch. First Minister Tir seemed eager to dispel any notion that the Hokmet themselves were to blame but at the same time made many conciliatory promises to the Thauma community, including the immediate return of all confiscated goods, and a Hokmet initiative to revive the Thauma Market and significantly revise the Regulations. She ended her speech with a rousing welcome to the Magi citizens in attendance, and a hope that a free and profitable trade between the worlds would be to the benefit of all.

From the New Hadar Herald

"To Halan and Nalah!" Mr. Cutter said, raising his coffee cup, and the other Thauma echoed the movement.

"To Halan and Nalah!" they chorused.

All the Thauma Trust and a handful of other people

Halan had never met were crammed into the Cutters' apartment, occupying every chair and perching on many of the other surfaces. It had been four days since the opening of the first portal, and New Hadar and the Magi Kingdom were both buzzing with the news. Everywhere the two sisters went in either world, there was an atmosphere of celebration. Urgent questions were being asked and incredible solutions were being proposed, and the air was full of chatter and anticipation. Even the two royal guards who had accompanied Halan to the Cutters' party were fairly relaxed, their helmets and cloaks lying forgotten on the kitchen table while they stood out on the balcony, leaning over to look down the street and stare at the endless Hadar Sea.

"And cheers to the Magi Kingdom," said Mrs. Cutter.

"And to the Hokmet," said Marit, "and their change of heart!"

"Cheers to that, indeed," chuckled Mandana. "I'm sure it had nothing to do with a whole world of powerful Thauma suddenly appearing on their doorstep, asking just what had happened to their cousins."

"Did you hear?" asked Mr. Cutter. "Gabriela found her twin already—a Magi guard called Alamar. She was posted to the portal and they met the very first day."

"Amazing," said a young man with very dark eyes and thick eyebrows who had turned out to be Aleksander. "Hey! Luca, not so fast!" he added, as the boy charged the length of the Cutters' lounge, his Thauma metal leg pumping.

"Oh, Kadir, turn up the radio," Mrs. Cutter called from the kitchen. "I love this song!"

Marcus's brother leaned over and turned a knob on the squat wooden machine, and a cheery jazz number rang through the apartment above the sound of the happy chatter.

Halan and Nalah sat together in the midst of the chaos, watching it all with identical grins on their faces.

"I still can't believe it," said Karin Cutter, sinking down in her own armchair and leaning over to peer at Halan and Nalah. "A queen, staying in my house. I sincerely had no idea you weren't Nalah—I hope you'll forgive me if I was rude, Your Majesty."

Halan laughed. "No, not at all. On the contrary, I appreciate all your support."

"Oh, it was nothing," said Karin, flushing slightly. "And it's so kind of you to be here, to celebrate with us."

"So . . . Nalah. The real Nalah," said Marit, leaning over to grab a cherry from a bowl on the table. "Does this mean you're royalty too?"

"Well, the Queen's Sword isn't exactly royalty, but . . . ," Nalah began. She exchanged an awkward smile with Halan. "You know what, let's just say yes. Pretty much a princess."

"Well!" said Karin, fanning herself. "And you growing up with your poor father in that little house, scraping by all these years. I'm so pleased for you, Nalah." She leaned in conspiratorially and her eyes glinted with mischief. "Well, my grandson certainly knows how to pick his friends, don't you, Marcus?"

"What?" Marcus said, unable to hear over the din.

But Karin didn't seem to mind. "Just know, Nalah, when you get older . . . the Cutters are a very respectable family to marry into. Not royalty, per se, but close!"

Halan and Nalah choked on their coffee in perfect sync.

The party was obviously going to go on all day, and maybe all night, and Nalah wished they could stay a lot longer. But eventually Halan nudged her and glanced meaningfully at the clock, and Nalah nodded and got up.

"We have to go back," she said, to general groans from the assembled Thauma. The royal guards standing at the door quickly put down their coffees and stood at attention. "You should all count yourselves lucky the queen stayed this long," Nalah added with a grin.

The Thauma crowded around to say good-bye to Halan, some of them bowing or curtseying, others shaking her hand.

"Excuse me, coming through!" Marcus said, elbowing his way to the front of the line. He stopped beside Nalah and folded his arms. "This is so weird," he said.

"I know," said Nalah.

"You're going back to the other world. But I can just . . . pop over and visit you whenever!" He grinned.

"Whenever you're done with your chores, young man," said Mrs. Cutter, leaning over to kiss Nalah and then Halan on their cheeks. "No sneaking off to another dimension to avoid trimming your seams."

"I know, Mom," said Marcus. He turned back to Nalah and grabbed her into a big hug. "I'll see you soon."

Nalah blushed as she saw Mrs. Cutter watching with a wink. "Yeah, you really will!" Nalah said, giving him a squeeze in return. They waved good-bye at the door, and then as they were walking down the stairs, flanked by the two guards, Halan turned to Nalah.

"I'd like us to stop at your old house, if that's all right," she said.

Nalah's stomach twisted uneasily. "Okay . . . but why?" There were so many painful memories caught up in that house. She immediately regretted agreeing to it. But then Halan took her hand and squeezed, and Nalah decided to trust her. She must have her reasons.

Cobalt flew down to rest on Nalah's shoulder as they turned the corner onto Paakesh Street, and Nalah was glad of the warm and heavy feeling of him. Her heart was about ready to burst. She hadn't been back to this place since her father had died. She tried to prepare herself—what would the house be like without him? Would she be able to cope with seeing it just as it was, but knowing he would never be coming back?

Perhaps they were coming to pack up her belongings,

what little she and her papa had owned, before the place was sold or maybe even knocked down. She couldn't bear the thought, but she had to keep it together, for Halan's sake. She steeled herself and followed Halan through the workshop door and into the back of the house.

There it was.

The furnace, cold and silent for the first time since her mother died. The cooling cupboard, the old armchair with its fraying upholstery, soft silk threads she used to pick at while she sat and watched her father work. The air was stale, the comforting scent of home already beginning to fade.

Nalah sighed and wrapped her arms around herself. This place would always be home, even if the roof leaked and the taps didn't work, even if the walls were still stained in some corners from the smoke, even if her father would never sit in the armchair or read from *Tales of the Magi* or make another beautiful glass charm again.

Cobalt flew over to the cooling cupboard and peered in curiously. Nalah felt her spirits lift slightly.

"That's right," she told him. "That's where you were born!"

Halan reached into the pocket of her gown and pulled out two items Nalah hadn't seen in a long time: the old leather gloves that her papa had made for her, and the framed photograph of her mother. "I wanted to make sure you got these," Halan said, handing them over. "I know they must be important to you."

Nalah took them and hugged them to her body. It made her feel close to her parents, being in this house and having these things. "Thank you," she whispered, her voice trembling with emotion.

"There's more," Halan said.

"More?" Nalah asked.

Halan pulled her from the workshop and into the rest of the house, and Nalah's heart gave a little jolt. Rani and Omar were sitting at the kitchen table side by side, facing away from them.

They looked so much like Nalah's own parents would have looked. Apart from the clothes and the jewels in Rani's hair, Nalah could have been staring into the past.

"Can you imagine?" Omar sighed. "A normal life together, with our daughter, in this place?"

"No, not really," said Rani.

Omar's hand slipped into hers. "Me neither. Nothing about us is normal. And I like it that way."

They turned to smile at each other, and Rani realized that Nalah and Halan had come in. She got up from her chair and turned to Nalah, a soft smile crossing her lips.

"I hope this is all right, for us to be here," she said. "I just wanted to tell you that I've made arrangements with the new leaders of the Hokmet. This house is to be yours, for as long as you want it. Nobody will touch a thing, unless you say it's all right. You can live here, if you want, when you're old enough, or you can give it away, or whatever you wish. It's yours to decide."

Nalah stared at them for a moment, tears running down her face.

"Oh—oh, Nalah, I'm sorry, are you . . . ?" Rani began, but Nalah flailed a hand to make her stop and turned a watery grin and shining eyes on both of them.

"Thank you," she whispered.

Rani hesitated for a split second and then hurried over to Nalah and took her in her arms.

"We still have so much to catch up on," she said. "But when I thought I might lose you, I . . . I just love you both so much." She held her arms out to Halan and she joined in the hug too. "I hope we can be a family," Rani said. "A real family."

Nalah looked up and felt her face crease up with tears again as she nodded.

Cobalt landed on her shoulder once again, and he nuzzled against her cheek. Nalah felt the warmth of him more strongly now. In fact, it was just like it had been when her father was alive. She felt Papa's love flowing through him, and she knew that if he could see them now, he would be happy.

The journey back to Maktum was a lot easier than the first time. It was amazing, Halan thought, how quickly a road through a forest could be built when the trade and politics of two whole worlds were at stake. Especially when there were hundreds of wood Thauma coming through from the Magi Kingdom to help cut back the trees. The royal family passed a crew of them on the way, and Halan saw one of them just staring up at the thick canopy, her hands on her hips, marveling at the greenness of the new world.

Maktum was quickly becoming a sort of Magi Kingdom embassy, full of enterprising Hadaris and Magi Kingdom citizens who were already right on top of working out how to trade water for magic and wood for sand. There was a steady stream of Thauma from New Hadar who'd had enough of the Hokmet, despite their new leadership and their new promises, and were striking out to make a new life in the desert kingdom. As they walked through the portal, they could wave at the poor workers from the Magi City who were going the other way, having barely paused to grab their few belongings before setting off for the land of abundance and technology.

There were going to be a lot of problems, but Halan smiled to herself whenever she thought about them. *Nalah's destiny found her in my kingdom,* Halan thought. *And it looks like I found mine here.*

She was still smiling when she sank down onto the golden cushions on the dais of the great hall, pulling Nalah down to sit next to her. They had only been back in the kingdom for an hour, but she'd wanted to throw open the doors to let her people in—and the people of New Hadar, if they wanted to make the trip—to answer their questions as best she could. To show them she was here for them.

To *rule*.

Halan was delighted to see that the very first person in the line was Soren Ferro. He swept a deep bow and then ran up to the dais and pulled both sisters into a hug. Halan suspected that the shocked gasps and gossipy chatter from the crowd pleased him immensely. He pulled back and grinned.

"I'm off to join the Shadows tomorrow," he said. Halan nodded and frowned. Nalah had told her all about the invisible desert people, but she really struggled to imagine it. "I've learned so much from them already, and I intend to explore as much of our world as I can, and then, perhaps, the other world as well," he added, and winked at Nalah. "Perhaps there are other kingdoms out there, hungry to fight for their freedom. I think the two of you have things just about wrapped up around here, so I'm going to go where I'm most needed."

"I'm sure Scorpion needs you too," Nalah said with a wink.

Soren bit his lip, his handsome face reddening. "Yes," he said. "And I need her."

"I'll miss you so much," Nalah said, pulling him into a hug. "But I know you're going to be amazing." She flushed very slightly and lowered her voice. "I know your father would be proud."

Soren sighed. "Thank you. And so would yours—Savior of the World," he added with a wry smile. "Not bad for a lowly market girl. Speaking of which, I'm going to have to borrow Forge one day if that's all right. Scorpion wanted a closer look, and well, what kind of a gentleman would I be if I refused a lady's request?"

Nalah rolled her eyes. "Never change, Soren."

"Never," Soren said, waggling his eyebrows. "But I don't want to hold things up. There're a lot of people here who have a lot to say . . . and most of them are here for you, Nalah. All those packages? *Presents.*" Nalah stared at the line of people clutching wrapped objects in various shapes and sizes, her eyes goggling. "Now that they don't fear you anymore, you're going to have get used to all the attention."

He stepped back and bowed again, and then he was off in a sweep of gray silk, every bit his old dramatic self.

Halan looked out at the line of people and got to her feet.

"Citizens, subjects. Friends and honored guests. We were once one world, with one shared history. Now I hope we will share a future. With my coronation, we entered a new era—but today we enter a new *age.* An age of peace, friendship, and good fortune. With our sister-world by our side, there is nothing we cannot do!"

The applause rang through the great hall, thunderous.

***

Nalah leaned on the windowsill at the top of the East Tower, the breeze stirring her hair. She gazed out over the city, the desert, the Sand Sea, and up to the Talons. Was that a faint glint of light she could see flashing back at her from the peak?

Beside her elbow, Cobalt hopped from foot to foot impatiently and preened the dust from the tiny glass feathers at his neck.

"One day," Nalah said, "you and I are going to go flying. But that's a project for another time."

She sat down at the worktable beside the window and ran her hand over the first blank page of the empty book that lay in front of her. She could feel a slight pulse from it, the faint echo of sap rising, the life it had lived, the endless potential of the blank page.

She knew the story she wanted to write.

Propped up beside the inkwell, the shard of Transcendent Glass gleamed with a thousand shifting colors. Halan had pressed it into her hand back in the great hall, and of all the gifts she had received that day, it was her favorite.

She stared into it for a moment, catching her own reflection at an unusual angle. Suddenly she saw her mother's face, and her father's, and Halan's, all reflected in her own. There was some of Marcus's sense of humor in her eyes, and even a little of Soren's swagger in the curve of her smile. She wondered if it was the magic of the mirror that made her see these things, or just the way she was looking.

Then, with a smile and a sigh, Nalah picked up the quill and began to write.

Sisters of Glass.

It was a story she hoped to be writing for a very long time.